COMA

Coma

K.D. KULPA

Pete's Press

To my boys,
for reminding me to dream again.

Chapter 1

- Stan -

It wasn't supposed to end like this.

Stan and his wife Liz walked along the sidewalk toward their home. It was their routine: their time to be alone while the nanny, Jules, got their three young boys ready for bed. The sun was setting in the distance over the park as they climbed the last hill, nearly reaching the final curve that would take them to their street. Although they did this every weeknight, he huffed a little from the exertion.

Holding hands, they discussed the upcoming hockey season for their oldest son, Alex.

"Do you think he's old enough to go into the dressing room alone?" Liz asked. "He can tie his own shoes. I feel like he should be able to tie his own skates now."

"What, you don't want to enjoy the aroma of sweaty hockey funk for another year?" Stan laughed. "Won't you miss it?"

Liz pushed into him with her shoulder, a smile growing across her face. "Fine … you go in and help him if you enjoy it so much."

Before Stan could reply with sarcasm, the screeching tires of a truck interrupted them, rounding the nearby corner too fast.

At first, it didn't feel significant to him. The bright lights approaching him made him momentarily think of a big, steel UFO. He still felt no indication of any danger. Then the truck jumped the curb in front of them. In his peripheral vision, Stan saw Liz freeze like an animal caught in the headlights. It all happened so fast. His only thought in that split second was, *'Liz needs to move!'*

Breaking where their hands held, he turned and pushed her, hard, just as the lights reached them. Her surprised face fell outside the beams cast by the bright light, her hands reaching out toward him, and then everything went black.

At first, the blackness was quiet. Peaceful.

Then came the noise. An awful noise.

Someone screamed nearby at first, but it quickly changed. Morphing into a more hollow, animalistic sound. The type you expect to hear in horror movies when banshees are running through the forest. It made his skin crawl. He couldn't open his eyes. Maybe it was for the best. He wasn't sure he wanted to see the source of that wail.

Then, just as suddenly, it stopped.

New sensations passed over his body as he lay still in the blackness. A burning slowly spread across his body, as though his insides had been lit on fire. The flames were trying to burst out to reach the oxygen around him, licking his skin from the inside. Stan couldn't remember seeing any fire, only the bright lights.

So why am I burning?

Flashes of scenes went by in spotty fragments. They didn't make sense. The order of them felt choppy and out of place from where he remembered being before the lights came.

First, he was on a long, hard board, unable to move. Bright red and blue lights flashed around him. Muffled voices passed by him as if he were underwater.

Then the world went black.

He couldn't keep his eyes open. When he finally convinced his eyelids to slit open, he saw a white roof above where he lay. Still strapped to the hard board, figures on either side of him were pulling him from the back of what looked like a big, white storage vehicle. The flashing lights were gone. Something hard covered his nose and mouth, making it difficult to see the white roof change to a dark sky contrasted by bright, white lights.

Then the lights faded as the world went black again.

Until something forced open one of his eyes. A man in a white jacket looked down at him. A bright light passed back and forth in front of Stan's eyes, but he couldn't blink. The lab coat man's fingers kept his eyelids pried open. Stan tried to raise a hand to swat the man away, but his body wouldn't cooperate. The man kept saying his name through the cold water. "Stan ... Stan ... Can you hear me?"

Stan had no control of his arms. He wished the rough fingertips would let his eyelids go. The burning under his skin intensified. Stan wanted to scream at the lab coat man, but the man had backed away and the world went black again as Stan's eyelids closed against his will. The darkness swallowed him back down.

Is she safe? Is she okay?

Although the thought was in his mind, in this darkness, it didn't feel like his own.

Who is she?

A woman's surprised face returned to his thoughts. Her brown eyes wide as she fell away from him. He remembered her. She was important, but why? She was falling away into the darkness, her arms reaching for him as it swallowed her whole.

Wait! Don't leave! Who are you?

A small, sharp object pierced the skin of his right arm. From it, something cold slowly flowed into him, first moving up his bicep and then spreading across his chest. As the cold liquid crept through his veins, the embers that burned beneath his skin began to fade and cool, like water splashing over a fire. The cool water brought silence to the darkness. In the silence, the walls of the world fell away, leaving Stan without gravity.

He was falling.

A thick, black expanse enveloped him as he fell, so dense even his screams would never pierce through to those around him. The void swallowed him whole.

Chapter 2

- Liz -

As they walked through the hospital entrance, Liz was sure the smell would haunt her for the rest of her life. She covered her nose, trying to block out the reek of death, blood, and bleach. The bright, white lights above her were a stark contrast to the dark world outside, making her squint at first. The nurses tried to push her away from the doors leading out of the first waiting area, but she wasn't leaving Stan to sit in some waiting room. She stepped back far enough to let them continue forward, then followed a few feet behind the flurry of activity around her husband's still body. She wasn't letting Stan out of her sight. As she hurried to keep up, she noticed the fear on one of the nurse's faces.

"He stopped breathing!" the nurse called out.

Liz hadn't thought the flurry of activity could grow any more panicked, but she had been wrong. They paused the gurney briefly to place a bag over Stan's face. As soon as it was secure, the same nurse began pumping the large plastic balloon as the rest of the group returned to wheeling down the hall.

The team of doctors and nurses led Stan into a small room on the right. Liz tried to follow, but a hand raised in front of her as she neared the threshold. Her feet skidded to a stop as she glared into the doctor's face that blocked her way.

"I'm sorry, Mrs. Stevens. You can't come any further. It's already crowded in there, and you'll just be in our way. Let us do what we can for Stan. Please ... stay out here."

She opened her mouth to argue, but the concern in his eyes stopped her.

He doesn't think he can save Stan.

She knew she needed to stay out of the way and give them their best shot at keeping her husband alive. As she stepped back, the doctor smiled tightly, without the smile reaching his eyes, before shutting the doors in her face. Turning, she looked up and down the hall. A few people had stopped at the end to watch the scene unfold. One of them was wearing a hospital gown.

A patient.

Stan's a patient.

The thought ripped at her insides. She gripped her hair in her hands as new tears began falling over the dried ones on her cheek from the ambulance ride.

This can't be happening. Please tell me this isn't really happening.

"Mrs. Stevens?" a calm voice came from behind her, startling her.

She turned around to see a nurse with a thin frame.

"Can we please step into a room so I can take a look at you? You're bleeding," he said, reaching his hand out to gently touch her back.

"No." She pulled away from him. "I'm staying here. I'm not leaving Stan."

The nurse pursed his lips in frustration momentarily. Liz glared at him. She was okay with being in the hall, but there was no way she would leave the door. She crossed her arms over her chest, wincing slightly as pain shot in her mid-back.

The memory of landing on a curb after Stan pushed her out of the way flashed in her mind. She wondered if she had cracked a rib.

"Fine ..." the nurse sighed. "Let me find a chair and my kit. I'll check you over right here. Don't move."

Liz watched the nurse hurry back down the hall. He stepped out of view into a room a few doors down. Her gaze returned to the door that blocked her from Stan. Although she could hear the muffled sounds of the activity inside, her imagination filled with the possibilities of what could be happening beyond that door.

Stan, please, don't die. Don't leave me. Not like this.

***

Six hours later, Liz found herself still sitting in the hall. She caught glimpses of Stan now and then as the doctors moved him to get X-rays and scans. Snippets of their conversations told her of broken bones and injured organs. She insisted on following close to them as they wheeled Stan around, but always ended up back at this chair. Waiting. Even though she hadn't slept yet, the adrenaline from the accident and constant worry kept her vibrating. Sleep was the furthest thing from her mind.

Instead, her mind drifted, thinking about everything she would have to do tomorrow, once they knew what Stan's condition was. She had called Jules from the ambulance, so she didn't have to worry about the boys tonight. After the nurse finally left her alone in the hall, she called Stan's parents, Ed and Karen. They booked the earliest flight out of Winnipeg. Her mom, Tammy, would drive from Kelowna first thing in the morning. Liz wasn't looking forward to her house being full of people by the end of the day, but she wouldn't be there anyway. Her place was at the hospital, with Stan.

At least the boys are safe. They'll be taken care of.

The door opened in front of her, snapping her mind back into the present. One of the main doctors that had stayed with Stan throughout the night walked out. His white coat and stethoscope hung around his neck, and droplets of blood spattered down the white fabric.

Stan's blood, she realized as a cold wave of dread passed over her body.

Although the doctor's face was sombre, she sensed relief in his features. Something about Stan's condition must have improved. She quickly rose from the chair to close the short distance between them. He towered over her by at least a foot, making her crane her neck to look into his eyes.

"Mrs. Stevens, I'm Dr. Martin."

"How is Stan? Is he okay?"

"He's in a coma. We're not certain of the extent of the brain damage yet. Only time will tell at this point. We have more tests to run, but I can tell you that he has multiple broken ribs and a broken leg. We're concerned about the bleeding around his brain as well, but we're doing our best to keep the pressure from building up in his skull. It's a miracle he's alive."

"Is he in pain?"

Liz couldn't manage to ask for more details. Although she tried to remain hopeful, thoughts about Stan not surviving kept creeping into the edges of her mind. She couldn't think about funeral arrangements. Not yet. Worry ate at her gut while she thought about their boys, about their potential loss of a father.

How will I explain to them what happened? What if they never talk to him again?

Her mind fought to grasp any string of hope, desperately clinging to the life she knew so well. The life that she had been part of less than 24 hours ago.

"We've given him something to help with the pain," Dr. Martin explained.

She could feel kindness and patience emanating from him. She knew he was trying to keep her calm and remain positive. She also knew he needed to get back to his other patients. There was nothing more he could do for Stan. All they could do was wait. Yet the thought of the doctor leaving made her uneasy. She gnawed on a fingernail as her gaze shifted to the closed doors behind Dr. Martin.

"Why don't you go home and get some rest?" he said, pulling her back from her thoughts. "Stan is as comfortable as we can make him, and now it's a waiting game. If we learn anything new while you're away, I assure you, we'll call as soon as we can."

"No, I can't leave. Not yet."

"Of course. You're welcome to stay as long as you like."

Dr. Martin placed a hand on Liz's shoulder. A new set of tears welled up in her eyes, so she averted her gaze, focusing on her feet. Taking a deep breath, she wiped away a stray tear as it fell on her cheek.

"Thanks for everything, Dr. Martin," she breathed, her eyes finally meeting his.

"Of course, Mrs. Stevens. If you need anything else, just ask the nurse to page me. Someone will check on Stan regularly to keep track of his progress. Please try to get some rest soon."

Dr. Martin squeezed her upper arm again before he turned to walk down the hallway toward the front of the main ER. She watched him as he neared the nursing desk, his clipboard swaying back and forth at his side. The rhythmic beeping of Stan's heart monitor broke her trance. It was barely audible through the closed door. She turned to face it, anxious to finally be at Stans' side, to hold his hand again. She reached to push the door open, only to have it swing towards her. Two nurses nearly collided with her as they stepped into the hall.

Jumping back, she dropped her gaze to avoid their eyes. Even without seeing their faces, she could feel their pity radiating toward her. Once they passed by, she stepped into the room before the door closed again.

She gasped, raising her hand to cover her mouth as she took in the scene. Tubes and wires were coming off Stan's body in every direction. She knew, whatever their purpose, they were the reason Stan was alive. Listening to the beeping of the heart monitor and the rhythmic sounds of the ventilator, she contemplated what her next move should be.

Looking up at the clock on the wall behind her, she saw it was nearing three-thirty in the morning. She walked over to a chair against the wall, pulling her phone from her jacket pocket. A notification told her she had missed several text messages from Jules.

-I hope everything is okay.

-I don't want to bother you, but I have that test in the morning.

-Should I see if my prof will let me postpone it?

-I can stay with the boys if you need. I'm sure my prof will understand.

-Hugs to you and Mr. Stevens.

Liz dropped into the chair. She had completely forgotten about the exam Jules had today. It gave her less than four hours until she had to be home. Her gaze shifted to Stan. His chest rose and fell to the rhythm of the ventilator. Who else could watch the boys so she could stay at the hospital? She opened her contact list and scrolled to Sarah, her best friend. She tapped the 'call' button and lifted the phone to her ear. Sarah's voicemail message instantly clicked on.

"Damn it. Why is your phone off?"

Liz hung up and ran through the list of other people they knew in Vancouver.

Who else could there be?

Most of Liz's other acquaintances she knew only through work. She didn't want to bother any of them until she was ready to tell her boss about Stan. There was no way she would be going back to work at the newspaper anytime soon. Stan only had one friend outside of his law office – Eric. He was a single bachelor in downtown Vancouver. There was a chance he would even be awake at this time, but she didn't want to call him. He didn't seem like a responsible babysitter to her. She tapped her fingernail against the side of her phone, debating whether to ask Jules to postpone her exam.

The clock ticked loudly above her head, as if a countdown had started, reminding her that time was slowly slipping away. With a heavy heart, she rose from her chair to approach Stan, carefully interlacing her fingers through his, avoiding the heart monitor attached to his finger. She didn't want to leave, but the responsibility of the boys tugged at her. Although she wanted to remain at Stan's side, her kids needed her, too.

"Stan, I don't want to leave, but I should be there when the boys wake up. They'll be scared and want to know what happened. I don't know what I'm going to say to them, but whatever it is, it should come from me."

She watched the rise and fall of Stan's chest as he breathed in the oxygen from the ventilator. He needed time to heal, all she could do was wait. Yet all she could think of was how much she craved to see his eyes gazing into hers. She squeezed his hand lightly before reluctantly loosening her grasp and turning away.

Her steps felt heavy as she returned to the chair by the door. She took a deep breath as she dropped into it and looked back down to her phone. Her reflection on the black screen looked back at her. The sporadic sobbing episodes she had experienced through the night had left streaks of mascara on her cheeks. Absent-mindedly, she rolled the bottom of her sleeve into her fingers and wiped the mascara off the best she could before putting her phone down. Leaning onto her knees, her attention returned to Stan. Conflicting emotions swirled inside her, forcing her to close her eyes and listen to the sounds in the room. She tried to focus on her breath, an old meditation exercise that used to calm her anxiety. After a few minutes, her nerves no longer felt as high-strung, her heartbeat slower.

Liz stood up and walked back to the side of Stan's bed, dragging the chair with her. She ignored the screeching sound the chair made along the linoleum floor. Plopping down, she grasped his arm with both her hands, careful not to disturb the heart monitor or the intravenous drip. She leaned over to rest her forehead on her forearms while she closed her eyes. The rhythm of the ventilator and beeps of the heart monitor offered a sense of comfort as she prayed internally for Stan to get better. She longed for him to grip her hand back or move his fingers. She longed to hear his voice.

"Stan, can hear me?" Her words were barely a whisper. "I need you to be okay. I hope you aren't in too much pain wherever you are in there. Please ... come back to me."

***

Liz still sat at Stan's bedside shortly after five in the morning. Glancing at the clock, she realized it was time to leave. She couldn't put it off any longer. Their house was at least a thirty-minute drive, especially if Jules needed time to prepare for her exam. Pulling her phone out of her jacket pocket, Liz ignored the red, low battery warning and redialed Sarah's number. Closing her eyes, she silently prayed for Sarah to pick up this time.

Please, please, please... answer the phone.

After a single ring, the phone beeped in her ear.

Voicemail.

Fuck.

"Sarah, it's Liz. I need you to call me as soon as you wake up. Stan was hit by a truck. I've been at the hospital all night. I'm heading home now, but please call me the instant you get this. I'm hoping you can watch the boys until my mom gets into the city. Call me back ... please."

She hung up before leaning over Stan. She carefully placed her hand through the wires and tubes to run her fingers through Stan's hair that lay flat on his forehead.

"I'll come right back. I promise. I love you."

She carefully placed her lips on his forehead as tears rolled down her cheeks. His skin felt cool and clammy against her dry, chapped lips. She closed her eyes, praying he could feel her. As she backed away, she wiped the tears from her face. One of her tears glistened on his cheek. She gently wiped it away, caressing his skin with her fingers for a moment. Her chest felt heavy, and her heart ached at the thought of leaving his side. Finally, she forced herself to turn her back to him and walked out of the room.

***

"We're here, ma'am," the PykUp driver said.

Liz jerked her eyes open. She had fallen asleep in the back of a stranger's car. The stress of the night, and the adrenaline wearing off, had exhausted her enough that she had passed out. She would have scolded herself for it if she had the energy or desire to care.

"Thanks."

Liz opened the car door and climbed out. Her entire body ached. She took the first few steps on the sidewalk leading up to her house before pausing. The house ahead was dark with only the porch light on. She assumed Jules was asleep in the spare bedroom in the basement, where she sometimes spent the night when Stan and Liz were going to be late. Suddenly aware that the car hadn't pulled away from the curb behind her yet, she forced her feet to continue shuffling towards the front door. She held her keychain still as she opened the lock to prevent the other keys on the ring from making any noise. She slowly moved into the house, trying not to let the door creak.

I hope no one hears me.

She needed some time alone to fall apart before she had to put herself back together for the boys. The house was dark and quiet. As she closed the door, she leaned her forehead to rest on it, closing her eyes while she turned the deadbolt. Her chest felt tight and burned as she tried to breathe. She couldn't seem to fill her lungs completely. The scent of Chinese take-out from the previous night still lingered in the air. Her mind returned to how it had felt sitting around the table with Stan, the boys, and Jules, eating and laughing. She had been happy and carefree then. If only she could go back to that moment.

I should have said no to the walk ...

She knew it was a pointless thought, but a new set of tears fell down her face. She forced herself to back away from the door, removing her sneakers one by one. As she placed them in their customary spot on the shoe rack by the door, her eyes lingered on the space that would usually hold Stan's shoes.

When will his shoes be there again?

The wall she had built up in her mind to contain the despair and grief over Stan's accident cracked. Her hands shook as she quietly made her way down the hallway to her bedroom, her keys still clasped tightly in her hand to prevent them from jingling. The pain from the metal digging into her palm helped her bite back the tears for the precious seconds needed to get into her room. Once through the threshold, she slowly closed the bedroom door behind her and collapsed onto the floor.

The wall in her mind crumbled completely and her chest felt like it was going to explode.

What am I going to do?

Chapter 3

- Stan -

Where am I?

Stan could feel something hard under him, but it was too dark to see.

Am I blind?

He felt around the ground on either side of his body. It was hard, flat, and had no texture. Could it be glass? Hopefully, it wouldn't break. He didn't want to fall again. He had thought the falling was never going to end. He couldn't remember landing. At some point, he must have lost consciousness, as he couldn't remember how he ended up here. It was too dark to even know where "here" was. Silence surrounded him.

The void must eat sound.

He couldn't even hear his own breathing.

Or am I deaf?

He needed to get up, to figure out where he was. Rolling to his side, he pressed a hand on the ground, pushing himself onto his feet. Dizziness surged through him, causing nausea to punch his stomach. He quickly dropped to his knees, bracing himself with his hands as he leaned over. He took a deep breath, fighting the urge to vomit. Gradually, the spinning of the world slowed, his stomach settled.

Okay, let's try again, but slowly this time.

He lifted one knee, placing his foot steadily on the ground. Pausing, he waited for the spinning to return. The world remained still around him, so he slowly brought his other foot up to place on the ground beside the first. Now both feet were under him, but he was still crouching low.

Slowly.

He began to straighten his legs, moving as slowly as his body would let him. He leaned slightly on his hands as he moved until his fingers barely touched the ground.

So far, so good.

A yoga instructor's voice from a suppressed memory came into his thoughts, telling him to uncurl his spine slowly, one vertebra at a time. He followed the instruction, even though the sudden memory puzzled him.

Finally, his back nearly straight, he lifted his head the last few inches.

Shit, too fast.

The world spun around him as if he were a spinning top. His body went limp as he collapsed again. Falling and spinning into the darkness.

I hope the glass doesn't break.

Chapter 4

- Liz -

Liz heard a light tapping from somewhere in the room. Her back ached and something rough pressed against her cheek. She peeked through slitted eyelids to see she had fallen asleep on her bedroom floor. The edge of the bed frame was only a few feet in front of her face. Dust bunnies littered the floor under the bed. Her mouth felt full of cotton balls. She tried to lick her lips and winced. Her cheeks were tight, as if on the verge of cracking. The dried tears from sobbing the night before formed a wax-like layer over her skin.

The tapping came again behind her, this time more forceful.

"Mrs. Stevens? Are you there?" Jules whispered on the other side of the door.

Liz sat up quickly, looking around the room.

I actually fell asleep like this?

The time after she collapsed to the floor in a heap was a blur. She remembered sobbing and shaking. Her body, finally drained of the adrenaline, had succumbed to the after-effects of the shock. She hadn't thought sleep would ever come. Every time she tried, Stan's shocked face lit by the oncoming truck's headlights flashed behind her eyelids.

The sun wasn't up yet, leaving the room covered in a black blanket that was only just beginning to lift.

"Mrs. Stevens?" Jules whispered a little louder. "If you're back, I need to get going so I'm not late."

Ignoring the pain throbbing in her lower back, Liz pushed herself to her knees.

"Yes, sorry Jules," Liz whispered back. "I'm here. Sorry I didn't reply to your text last night. I've got the boys handled. Good luck on your exam."

"Is everything okay? I didn't know what to tell the boys last night. They were really scared, so they stayed up later than usual. I hope that's okay."

"That's fine, Jules. Thanks for staying with them. Now get going. You don't want to be late."

"Okay, let me know if there's anything I can do. I can always come back."

"Thanks, Jules. I'll keep you posted."

"Okay, bye Mrs. Stevens."

The clock on the nightstand said six forty-five. Liz looked longingly at her bed from the floor. The clean, white, pillowed duvet looked warm and welcoming.

But he's not there.

She closed her eyes, sliding back to sit against the wall nearest her. Letting her head fall back, she took a deep breath. The muscles in her back throbbed, but the ache in her chest was worse. The ache for Stan. She had done the single-parent thing before when Stan had to travel for legal cases in other cities, but this was different. This was worse. She didn't know if he was coming back.

Thank God for Jules.

Liz never felt more grateful for their nanny. Jules had come into their lives less than three years earlier, when their youngest, Jack, started elementary school. Liz wanted to return to her career as a journalist. That meant they needed a nanny.

Jules had been seventeen when she showed up at their front door for the interview. Her resume said she had just finished high school. She wanted a job helping a family while she took classes at the community college nearby. Unfortunately, it was now her last year of the program, and she was dropping hints about leaving the suburbs of North Vancouver to see the world. Liz dreaded searching for a new nanny.

Liz sighed and looked towards the open bathroom door on the other side of the room. She pushed her hands into the wall behind her and slowly stood. Her phone was on the carpet nearby, under the edge of the bed.

I must have accidentally kicked it in my sleep.

She picked it up and turned it over. The screen was black. Pushing the power button didn't help. It was dead. She moved over to her nightstand and plugged it into its charge cord before turning to the bathroom. The grime and stench of the hospital stuck to her clothes and hair.

Maybe a quick, hot shower will help.

Hopefully, the scalding hot water could even wash away some of the memories from last night. She turned the shower on as hot as she could stand it before slowly undressing. She glanced briefly at her reflection in the mirror. Her eyes were red and puffy, and her skin dull and gray. Large purple bruises stretched along the back of her ribs on one side. She ran her fingers lightly over them, wincing at the sharp pain.

How did I get away with just a few bruises?

The memory of Stan's body flooded her mind. His broken form. Catching her gaze in the mirror, her anguish stared back at her. There was no time for self-pity.

Enough of that. The boys will be up soon. I can't break down now. They need me.

Stepping into the shower, she tilted her head under the steady stream, letting the rushing water drown out everything else. She closed her eyes and slowly breathed in the moist, hot air. The heat beat down on her tense shoulders, but the muscles refused to release. Her chest remained heavy, making her breaths come in short bursts. She tried to inhale deeply to calm her nerves, but even the shower couldn't wash away the tar-like blanket of anguish wrapped around her heart. The image of Stan's crumpled body being tossed into the air by the truck kept replaying in her mind, as if on some masochistic replay.

Realizing the shower was not going to have the healing power she needed, she sighed and turned off the water. Ignoring the drips coming from the shower head, she grabbed her towel off the rack outside the sliding glass. After drying off, she hung the towel and made her way through the bedroom toward the closet. The clothes lining the walls seemed to stare back at her.

What do you wear to the hospital to spend the day beside your comatose husband? Does it really matter?

She snatched baggy jeans and a white tank top. Before leaving the small space, she paused, craving something of Stan's wrapped around her. She reached into Stan's side of the closet, pulling out one of his flannel shirts. Even clean, she could still faintly smell his musky scent. She wrapped it around her shoulders and hugged it against her skin.

Walking back into the bedroom, she threw her hair up into a messy bun and unplugged her cell phone. The battery was over thirty percent charged.

Good enough.

As she walked into the hallway, the aroma of coffee hit her like a wall.

Jules made coffee.

Liz thought she couldn't be more grateful for Jules. She had always thought of Jules as the kind and thoughtful type. Now she was also Liz's hero. With a little more urgency, Liz nearly ran toward the scent. As soon as she entered the kitchen, she skidded to a stop. The small kitchen was spotless. The last time she had been in it, there were take-out containers everywhere. She couldn't believe Jules had taken the time to clean. Everything was back in place. Even the stainless-steel sink under the window that looked into the attached sunroom was empty and wiped clean.

That girl needs a raise.

Liz walked around the kitchen island to the coffee pot sitting on the gray granite counter against the wall. She put her phone face down on the counter before reaching up to open the cupboard. Her fingers gripped her usual, large pink 'Mama Bear' mug. The bright red numbers of the stove's clock caught her attention. Seven minutes after seven. Her phone vibrated, nearly making her drop the mug. She quickly placed the mug down and grabbed the phone. Her heartbeat sped up as she checked the caller ID. A mixture of relief and disappointment washed over her when she saw Sarah's name on the screen. Taking a breath to calm her nerves, she tapped the 'answer' button.

"Sarah?"

"Oh my God, Liz! I'm so sorry! I just got your message. What happened? Are you and Stan okay?"

"Stan's in a coma," her voice quavered, as fresh tears welled in her eyes. "The doctors don't know the extent of the damage yet. We don't even know if he'll ever wake up. I need to get back to the hospital to see if anything changed in the last few hours, but I can't leave the boys alone."

"I can't even imagine how you must be feeling right now. As soon as Lexi is ready, we're there. I can hang with the boys while you head back to the hospital."

"I owe you one. My mom will be here later this morning, but I don't know exactly when. I want to get back to Stan to see how he's doing, what the doctors are doing. I can't stand being gone this long."

"Lexi and I will be there before you know it. Do you need me to grab anything on my way over?"

"No, just you being here is enough."

"Okay, talk soon."

As Liz hung up the phone, she heard a creaking of a door come from down the hall. She put the phone down and walked around the island, preparing the words in her mind.

"Mom?"

It was their youngest, Jack. Liz walked into the hallway to find him standing in his doorway, sadness covering his face. As tears threatened to fall on her cheeks, she swallowed. Jack moved closer, so she kneeled to embrace him, as if he was still a toddler instead of an eight-year-old.

"Is Dad okay?"

Liz slowly brushed the hair back on Jack's head, a tear escaping onto her cheek. She brushed it away with the back of her hand before pulling back slightly to look at his face. His eyes were wide and glistening.

"Dad is at the hospital," she said, softly. "The doctors are taking really good care of him."

Another door creaked open, and Alex peeked his head out of the room he shared with his ten-year-old brother, Carson. Liz raised her hand to him while still kneeling in the middle of the hallway, preparing herself for their questions and emotions. It was going to be a long morning.

***

Forty-five minutes later, Sarah knocked at the front door, interrupting Liz curled up with all three boys on the couch, assuring them that they would see their father soon. With a quick hug to everyone, including Sarah, she left the house and drove back to the hospital. The morning traffic entering Vancouver made the trip longer than usual, so she used the opportunity to call her assistant, Jane, and Stan's friend, Eric, to let them know about the situation. She was grateful to have the excuse of driving to keep the calls short. She didn't want to break down crying in the middle of traffic.

Once at the hospital, a nurse at the front desk informed her that Stan had been moved from the ER into the intensive care unit. With directions in hand, she slowly made her way to Stan's new door. Taking a deep breath, she pushed into the room. Stan was lying on his back on the bed against the opposite wall. The ventilator covered most of his face, the familiar beeping and whooshing sounds filling Liz's ears as the door closed behind her. He looked deflated. His body already a distorted version of his former self.

Dropping her jacket into a chair against the far wall, she grabbed a second chair and dragged it to his bedside. As she sat, she grabbed onto his hand, careful again of the heart-rate monitor attached to his finger. She noticed how cold his hand felt, making her immediately wish that she had brought extra blankets or gloves to put over his icy, still fingers. Then she watched, hoping for any sign that he could feel her. A sign that he would wake up.

Chapter 5

- Stan -

Something changed.

What is that?

Before Stan opened his eyes, he could hear it. A sound coming from somewhere in the void. It was rhythmic, ebbing and flowing. A memory of a vast blue ocean under a colourful sunset burst through his mind.

The ocean?

He opened his eyes. He was lying on the ground, still in the dark. There was no ocean here. The ground was dry and flat, like glass. The sound grew louder and then, just as quickly, softened.

Could it be moving away?

He sat up slowly, curling his legs into his chest and wrapping his arms around his knees. He waited for the dizziness to return, but the world remained still this time. The distant waves continued their rhythmic pace. They were calming, even while enveloped in the dark.

The floor felt hard and cold. He wiggled his toes, the movement making him think of a sandy beach. He could faintly remember the feeling of the small, gritty particles stuck between each toe. Rubbing his eyes, he gazed in front of him, but he still couldn't see. He waved a hand in front of his face, but the movement remained unseen in the void.

Where am I?

The back of his head itched. It felt like something stabbed into the base of his skull. He rubbed at it with his fingers, imagining insects burrowing into his skin, looking for blood. Nothing was there. The itching grew intensified, as if something were crawling under his skin, over the hard bone of his skull. He rubbed harder feeling only smooth skin and strands of hair under his fingernails. No scabs or bumps. Scratching didn't seem to help.

Why is it so itchy?

Trying to ignore the itching, he returned his attention to the waves in the distance. They sounded further away now. Perhaps the tide was going out? Even though it was quieter, the presence of the sound, any sound, was a relief. His hearing still worked.

I wonder if I'll ever see again.

With that thought, and the memory of the ocean, a resolve grew inside of him – an unwavering will to survive, an eagerness to live. He made a silent vow to himself: he would find that ocean. Feeling his way through the darkness, he would do anything to find the source of that sound, no matter what he faced along the way.

Chapter 6

- Liz -

It was cold. Liz hugged herself, rubbing her arms through her thick sweater. She silently scolded herself for not wearing a jacket. If she was honest with herself, going for a walk was the last thing she felt like doing, but she needed to get out of the house. She needed to escape the constant presence of Karen and Ed. Although they were helpful, almost two weeks had passed since Stan's accident. Her mom had gone home after the first week, likely because of the crowded bungalow. Perhaps the walk would clear her head. She avoided the usual path she and Stan would take. She couldn't bear going any-where near that park again.

The chill in the air permeated her body, making her bones ache. With her head down, she walked as if facing a strong wind, even though it was calm and quiet around her. Watching her feet, not paying attention to where she was going, the side-walk suddenly looked familiar. She looked up. She was near the spot where the accident happened. The spot where her life had shattered.

How did I get here?

Pausing, she looked around. The streetlights above flickered, causing shadows along the sides of the street to appear to be reaching for her. A chill swept through her, so she turned to walk faster up the hill. Whispering voices crept from the field beside her, forcing her to look toward the brush where Stan had been thrown by the vehicle. A vast black void covered the nearby park making it impossible to see if anyone was there. Her gaze drifted to where she had found Stan's still, bloody body that day.

"*Liz ...*" a voice groaned from the blackness.

It was Stan's voice.

Could I imagine something like that?

He wasn't here. He was in the hospital. She shook her head, dropping her gaze from the spot.

I can't be here.

She took a step to speed the rest of the way up the hill, needing to get far away from that spot. As soon as her foot came down on the spot where Stan had been tossed like a ragdoll, she slipped. Flailing her arms out to her sides, she managed to stop herself from falling to the cold concrete. Looking down, she saw a shiny patch of ice on the sidewalk at her feet.

Where did this ice come from? There hasn't been any ice all night.

Suddenly, the sound of screeching tires pierced the air. Panic pumped through her body and her skin crawled. She spun in place, searching up and down the street, but it was too dark. The streetlights on the top of the hill turned off, an impenetrable black wall ended the street ahead of her. Without thinking, she took a step back in the opposite direction of the sound, only to slip again. Pain shot up through her thigh as her knee made impact with the ice. She braced herself with her hands to stand, the feeling of a thousand needles penetrated her palms. The screeching of tires came again.

They sounded closer.

Liz looked back up the hill towards the street where the truck had come screeching around the last time. Another streetlight turned off on the corner, the black wall inching closer.

Why are the lights going out?

She couldn't see the houses lining the sidewalk on the opposite side of the road. Another streetlight a few feet in front of her flickered, then turned off.

What the hell is going on?

She tried to stand up but couldn't get a grip on the ice. On her hands and knees, she debated what she should do. Her knees were raw and cold. Panic itched at the edges of her mind.

Screw this.

Crawling, she moved toward the grass beside her. She placed one foot under her, testing the traction of the grass. The grass was wet, but it didn't feel slippery.

Finally.

She quickly stood. A deafening horn blared behind her. Whipping around, she looked up the street again. Only one streetlight remained, the one closest to her. She couldn't see anything past the six-foot circle of illuminated ground at her feet.

Two small lights flickered on in the distance, like two small glowing yellow eyes, growing as they moved towards her.

No, not again.

As the truck roared closer, time seemed to slow to a crawl. She turned to run, but her legs felt like lead, frozen in place. When she finally managed to take a step, her feet flew out from under her. She landed on her back hard. The wet grass soaked through her pants, the cold permeating her skin even more. Goosebumps spread across her legs and arms. She quickly rolled onto her hands and knees, determined to escape. As she looked over her shoulder, however, the lights had grown significantly. They were moving closer, fast.

No, it can't be.

Panic ripped through her. The truck's lights emitted a yellow glow as they quickly closed the distance to her. She tried to stand, but her legs lost their feeling, making her crash back down into the grass on her stomach. This time, the pain shot through her chin as she fell face first. She quickly rolled onto her back, searching for the lights. They were only a few feet away now, the sound of an engine roared.

"No, Stan!" she screamed.

The instant the truck hit, Liz jolted up, covering her face with her arms to shield herself. Nothing happened. Everything was silent, the screeching tires gone. She carefully looked through her arms, confused. She wasn't in the middle of a pitch-black street. Four light gray walls surrounded her instead. A white, fluffy duvet covered her legs, not cold, wet jeans. She was in her warm bed in the comfort of her home.

It was just a dream.

She fell back onto her pillows, pulling the blankets over her head. The soft lavender detergent on her pillowcase filled her senses. An orange glow seeped in through the windows. The sun was rising.

I wonder what time it is.

She should start getting up early again to get some semblance of routine back, but she couldn't bring herself to get out of bed yet. Worry over Stan weighed heavy on her chest, and leftover panic from her dream waited behind her eyelids. She wondered when Stan would wake again. The hours she had spent at his bedside each day had been long and draining.

A soft bang in the kitchen pulled her out of her thoughts. She wasn't the only one awake in the house. She assumed it was Karen in the kitchen, again. Karen was always in the kitchen when she wasn't at the hospital with Stan. Liz squeezed her eyes shut as tight as she could, willing herself to fall back to sleep. She didn't want to face anyone yet. She knew Karen and Ed meant well, but she felt like they were always tiptoeing around her. As if she was as fragile as glass. She was keeping herself together, considering the circumstances. Stan was only alive because of a ventilator and a dozen tubes.

How could anyone be okay with that?

Another bang from the kitchen. Liz rolled onto her back and flipped down the blankets. The sun outside her window made her squint. Taking a deep breath, she slowly peeled herself out from under the warm blankets, placing her feet on the soft, cold carpet floor.

Here we go again.

***

"I understand this is a tough time, Mrs. Stevens," the officer's annoyance was obvious through the phone, "but we need you to make an official statement."

Liz rolled her eyes. She was tired of talking about the accident. She didn't want to relive it again.

"I don't know what more I could tell you. You know what happened. There were other witnesses."

"Yes, we've talked to them. What I need now is to talk to you."

"I can tell you right now there's no way I'm coming down to the station. I don't want to be anywhere near that man."

The officer sighed. She could hear talking in the background. Could they be talking about her?

"Ma'am, it is protocol. You are the victim's wife, and we really need your statement. The driver isn't here. You can come down whenever your schedule allows."

Her heart dropped into her stomach.

"What do you mean, he's not there? Where is he?"

"He was released, ma'am. Let's concentrate on your –"

"Are you fucking kidding me? The man was obviously drunk. I could smell liquor radiating from him when he stopped to yell at us. Yell at *us* because he thought *we* had been the reason he hit the sidewalk. And you're telling me that a drunk driver, who put my husband in a coma, is walking the fucking streets right now? Free as a bird?"

"Ma'am, please calm down."

"Don't you dare tell me to be calm. Why is that asshole not locked up?"

"Listen, it was his first offence. He's very sorry for what he did. He didn't realize that he had as many as he did, or he never would have driven that night. He has a court date. The judge will decide his fate, not us. Now, can you please calm down and come to the station?"

Liz ended the call and slammed her phone down on the table by Stan's bed. The anger coursing through her made her hands shake. She looked over at Stan. The bruises on his face were slowly changing from purple to green around the edges.

How can they let him off so easy, Stan? After all that he's done to us.

Chapter 7

- Stan -

The rhythm of ocean waves in the distance seemed to call to Stan. How far could that ocean be? The empty blackness extended in all directions. There was no light to guide him, only the sound of the waves. The world felt heavy, like gravity was stronger here, wherever *here* was. His knees ached from the weight of his body. His shoulders were heavy, as if someone was pushing down on them, trying to make him curl back up on the ground. The pressure urged him to rest, sleep, surrender. His shoulders sagged, and his steps slowed, as his body ached to give in.

I need to find the ocean.

Stan stood tall, refusing to succumb to the pressure. Something, someone, was waiting for him. Who it was, he didn't know, but he couldn't stop. With each determined step, the weight seemed to come off slightly, the push on his shoulders less intense.

I can do this. Now, which way?

He turned slowly in place, listening to the waves. When he turned his head one way, the sound became muffled. When he turned back, it became clearer.

This must be it.

It felt good to move. Every step a little easier. His muscles loosening, waking up. He wondered how long he had been lying in the darkness. How long had he been away?

Away from what? What am I missing?

He was sure there was something. It itched at the edge of his memory. Something he couldn't see. The ocean waves were important. He continued trudging toward them. As he walked, the hairs on the back of his neck prickled. Someone was watching him.

He paused, turning in a circle, but all was black.

"Hello?"

Nothing responded, but he could sense something. A presence. Something he hadn't noticed before. Turning, he quickened his pace toward the ocean, hoping whatever hid in the darkness would stay behind.

As time ticked by, as he continued to place each foot in front of the other, his urgency to reach the ocean grew. He needed to get there faster. Before whatever lay in the darkness, watching, came closer.

I need to get to the ocean. I need to get to the ocean.

Hopefully, once he got there, he would understand where he was, who he was, or what might be following him.

Chapter 8

- Liz -

Walking through the large sliding doors of the hospital, Liz was amazed at how quiet the main entryway was. She looked around at the few people sitting in the chairs placed sporadically around the room. Her thoughts briefly shifted to curiosity about why each of them was waiting.

Were they visiting loved ones, like her?

Were they here for themselves, trying to overcome some illness or attending surgery? The one thing they had in common, she realized, was that none of them smiled.

What is there to be happy about in a place like this?

She couldn't believe she had been visiting this hospital every day for two weeks now. Shaking her head, she tried to focus on her excitement to see Stan. The thought of him helped the negative thoughts melt away. Following the white walls and harsh overhead lighting, she reached the older-looking elevators. They were skinny with brown sliding doors. She pushed the 'up' button on the wall between the elevators. Within seconds, the third set of elevator doors against the far wall in the small alcove opened. Immediately moving into the small, dark elevator, she pushed the third-floor button.

"Hold the elevator!" called a voice from out of view.

Without thinking, Liz threw her arm up into the closing elevator doors to stop them. As the doors bounced off her hand, a man squeezed in beside her. She took in his black fedora, long dark gray jacket, and dark green, knitted scarf wrapped up to his nose before turning her gaze down at the floor. She wasn't in the mood for small talk and hoped he wasn't either.

"Thanks for that," he said, in an unfamiliar accent. "I'm already running late. I don't think my patients will take kindly to my preference for the stairs this morning."

Liz smiled, briefly looking up at the man. He was a few inches taller than her. His bright blue eyes beamed at her from above the scarf, so she shifted her eyes to the elevator buttons to avoid further interaction.

"I can't believe how cold it is this morning. I'm from Arizona, so I'm not used to Canadian winters. How do you stand it?"

She briefly looked up to smile at the man again. He unwrapped his scarf, uncovering a mahogany brown, five o'clock shadow on his olive skin. She shrugged lightly and returned to facing the elevator doors, hoping it would reach her floor soon.

"I don't think I'll ever get used to it."

The elevator dinged.

Finally.

As soon as the doors opened wide enough, she squeezed into the hallway, relieved to put distance between her and the happy, chatty stranger. She started slightly as he entered the hall directly behind her. She looked over her shoulder.

"Well, have a good morning, miss. Thanks again."

She moved to the side of the long hallway as she turned towards the intensive care unit, unsure of which way the man was going. When he didn't pass by her, she paused to look back. He walked away in the opposite direction while removing his scarf and jacket. She sighed before hurrying to the end of the hall to push through the double doors of the intensive care unit. The nurse behind the front desk looked up at her briefly, before returning his eyes to something he was reading. She walked up to the desk and looked down at him.

"Good morning. I'm here to see Stanley Stevens. Is the doctor in yet?"

"I'm sorry, miss," the nurse yawned, his eyes never leaving the papers on his desk. "The doctor isn't here yet. You'll have to wait until he arrives."

"Okay. I'll be waiting in my husband's room."

The nurse briefly lifted his eyes at Liz then returned to his papers. She couldn't get a read on him. Was he seriously busy or being rude?

Whatever.

Stan's room was three doors down on the right of the bright white, sanitized hallway. She swung open the door and looked around. It looked the same as it did yesterday. Stan lay on his back, the bed raised slightly, giving the illusion that he had simply fallen asleep while watching television. Cords and tubes still hung from him, but the tube meant to keep his brain from swelling with fluid was gone. One of his legs was propped up in a cast, his toes sticking out at the end. The familiar rhythmic sounds of the machines connected to Stan filled the room.

The rest of the room was the typical white, sanitized hospital surroundings. There were no windows or curtains, just white walls enclosing the room. A white dry eraser board hung on the wall on her right behind the door. It was wiped clean – no names or information written on it today. She shrugged her shoulders, taking her jacket off to drop it and her purse into one of the two chairs lined up under the whiteboard. They had skinny metal arms with thin, beige, plastic-covered cushions on the seat and backrest. Liz found them extremely uncomfortable to sit in for long periods.

"Good morning, Stan. I hope you don't mind me popping in early today."

Liz used her foot to shove the small, gray plastic door stop under the door to keep it propped open. She wanted to hear when the doctor arrived. She smiled back at Stan. He looked the same today; the hope of some positive change drained from her body. She reached under his cast to carefully pull the blue, linen hospital blanket up and over his foot, covering his bare toes. It helped her feel less powerless in the situation by helping him, even if he wasn't aware of it.

She pulled on the arm of the second chair and brought it to his bedside. She reached out and wrapped her fingers gently under his hand. His hands felt warm against her skin, her fingers still cold from the damp, frigid air outside. While watching his chest rise and fall, her thoughts drifted to memories of him before the accident. His hopes to become a partner at the law firm he had spent the last ten years working at. The constant planning of the big family vacation to Ireland he wanted to do. It was going to be their chance to celebrate his success. Stan wanted to show their boys the world. These dreams and plans now felt impossible to her. Too far out of reach, given his current condition.

"Hey Adam," a cheerful voice from the hall snapped Liz out of her memories.

She turned to look down the hallway from her chair, not letting go of Stan's hand, but the angle made it impossible to see the nursing station.

"Sorry, I'm late. Traffic was horrendous today."

Liz carefully pulled her fingers out from Stan's hand and jumped up. The chair screeched loudly against the waxed linoleum as she pushed it back into the wall. As she hurried towards the doorway, her toe caught one of the metal legs of the chair, making her lose her balance. She awkwardly regained her footing without losing momentum. She needed to talk to the doctor before he left. As she grabbed the edge of the doorway to propel herself out of the room on steadier feet, she crashed into a wall of lean muscle.

"Whoa, sorry miss."

Liz looked up from the arms that had reached out to grab her. The blue eyes and scruffy face from the elevator looked down at her. Without the fedora on, his dark hair was loose around his face. She looked down at the white coat he was wearing with a stethoscope around his neck.

"Let me get out of your way. You seem to be in a rush!" he laughed, moving to her side. "Oh, it's you from the elevator! Are you the Mrs. Stevens that Adam says is waiting for me?"

With her feet stable under her, she pulled her arms gently out of the doctor's hands. She crossed her arms across her chest and looked up at him.

"I'm sorry. I heard talking out here and I didn't want to miss you. I'm Elizabeth Stevens, Stan's wife."

The doctor smiled and brushed a loose strand of hair covering his right eye back behind his ear.

"No problem, Mrs. Stevens. I'm Dr. Danton, but you can call me Sam. How about we step into your husband's room and go through his record together? I've been away for the past few weeks, so I need to catch up."

Sam raised his right arm, motioning her into the room, while gently placing his other hand on her back to guide her. She moved back to the chair by Stan's bed, sensing Sam following. He moved to stand at the foot of the bed and raised a clipboard. She scratched at her arm nervously and shifted her weight back and forth between her feet, trying to remain patient.

Please have some good news.

"Okay, Mrs. Stevens," Sam started, without lifting his eyes from the clipboard. "It looks like we have some promising news to share with you today. There was some fluttering in Stan's heart rate last night. They checked him over and couldn't find a medical reason for it, so it's possible he was reacting to something in his surroundings. We can't say for sure what yet, maybe a loud noise startled him, but the fact that he reacted at all is promising."

Liz nearly fainted. Reaching behind her, she gripped onto the arm of the chair to steady herself. A smile spread across her face. Sam looked up at her. She didn't notice the concern written on his face.

"Now, I don't want to get your hopes up too much yet."

Too late.

"Stan has suffered serious injuries. He still has a long journey ahead of him. This isn't over yet."

"Right ... yes ... I understand," she stammered. "But can we call this a win? Or at least ... a move in the right direction."

"It would seem so. We'll keep monitoring him and run a few tests just to be sure his heart is healthy. Now, I need to get back to my rounds. I'm glad I could give you some hopeful news this morning," Sam said, moving towards the door. "I'll be back in a little while to do my checks on Stan more thoroughly."

"Thank you so much, Dr. Danton. I really appreciate you coming and talking to me so quickly."

Liz smiled down at Stan, no longer paying attention to Sam as he left the room. Grabbing onto Stan's right hand, she leaned over and kissed him on the cheek before placing her other hand on his forehead.

"No matter what the doctor says, I know this means you're coming back to me. You gave me a sign that you're still in there. I love you so much."

She stayed standing, brushing his hair off his forehead, for as long as her legs would let her. She ignored the ringing of her phone in her jacket pocket from where it lay on the other chair. She was too happy to leave his side just yet. She couldn't bear to take her attention from his face in case he gave her another sign.

The door clicked closed behind her, making her shift her body to see if Sam had returned. She was alone in the room. She shrugged her shoulders, assuming Sam had removed the doorstop when he left and turned back to monitor Stan's face. A chill ran down her spine as the room seemed to drop in temperature. The air grew heavy, and an uneasy silence settled over the room.

"Brrr, Stan, I sure hope they turn the heat up soon.

Chapter 9

- Stan -

Stan felt like he had been walking forever. Somehow his body never tired, so he didn't feel the need to stop. The ocean waves continued calling to him. The calm ebb and flow of the waves promised answers. They gave him hope he would learn where he was. Maybe even *who* he was. If only he reached the waves.

As he walked, the atmosphere around him gradually lightened. He didn't notice at first. Slowly, the shift was enough that he could make out his arms swinging at his sides. He raised his hand to his face. He could faintly see his fingers passing by.

I'm not blind! I can see!

Growing excitement made him feel jittery. His need to get to the ocean intensified. Faster, he needed to move faster. Running didn't tire him either, so he kept running until he could see a horizon forming in the distance.

There it is! Almost there.

Pink, blue, and orange streaks spread across the distant sky. He paused to take in the view. Its beauty was not lost on him. He looked back behind him. In the distance, a black wall of shadow blocked his view. It was the darkness. The darkness that he had emerged from.

I'm never going back.

Turning back to face the brightening horizon, an itch in his mind made him still. Something about the horizon was familiar. The ebb and flow of the waves brought up the memory of the sunset over the ocean again. It was important.

What am I missing?

He closed his eyes, willing the memory to strengthen. A feeling of sand between his toes rushed in. He had been on a sandy beach when he saw the sunset. His feet were bare on the cold, grainy sand. There had been a cool breeze on his face, moist from the salty water spread out before him. Something moved beside him and touched his fingertips. His hand gripped something. He looked over and saw another arm stretched out, their hands together.

Stan opened his eyes, surprised. He wasn't alone in the memory. He looked around the void he was stuck in now. There was no ocean, no sand. The arm that had been in the memory vanished the moment he opened his eyes.

Who are you?

Desperation came over him. He searched the never-ending space around him for the cause, but he was still alone. He put a hand to his chest. His heartbeat pounded hard and fast. It grew harder to breathe.

Something was in his throat.

It was hard and painful. He couldn't take a full breath. Reaching his hands up, he felt around his neck but couldn't find a cause for the choking. He dropped to his knees, trying to pull in a full breath. His chest burned from the panic overtaking him. He braced himself with a hand on the hard ground while trying to pound on his chest with the other. His eyes bulged and tears rolled down his cheeks as he tried to cough up the obstruction in his throat. It wouldn't budge. He stuck his fingers into his mouth, searching for the object lodged there, but he couldn't feel anything. His fingers scraped at the back of his bare throat.

Whatever was lodged there, he couldn't remove it himself.

Stan lay on his side, curling his knees into his chest, tears streaming down his face as he continued to cough. He looked around the darkness surrounding him, hoping for someone to help him. No one was there. For the first time, he realized how alone he felt. Terror crept into his body; he began to shake from the exertion of the coughing and panic.

The obstruction in his throat began to shift. An invisible weight pushed down on his arms as the obstruction ripped from his throat. His throat burned, as though something was pulling his throat out through his mouth. He rolled back onto all fours, dry heaving. His chest was on fire, but he could finally take in a full breath. The air around him was dry, as if he was stranded in an arid desert. All the moisture left his tongue and lips. He searched for water, for the first time remembering the sensation of thirst.

He crawled towards the brightening horizon ahead of him, hoping he would eventually find water if he followed the waves. His energy was depleted. Each inch he gained felt harder than the last. He collapsed onto his side, slowly rolling onto his back to look up at the navy sky above him. The urgency he had felt at the onset of the ocean memory returned. He closed his eyes, trying to bring back the vision. This time, the same arm reached out to him. Except not on a beach. This time it was reaching out from the darkness, a bright light beside him creating a heavy shadow, hiding the view of the arm's body. A fragment from another memory.

Why can't I remember who you are?

He brought one hand to touch his face and felt around his neck, but still couldn't find a cause for the pain. The phantom feeling of the obstruction made his insides ache. Stan laid his hand back beside him, feeling the hard, flat surface under him.

Am I dead?

He rolled onto his side, curling his knees up into a fetal position. Curling his head down, he covered it with his hands, trying to make sense of the new information flooding his mind. He needed to get out of here, that he was now certain of, but how?

Chapter 10

- Liz -

"It's just another Monday. Stan is stable and not going any-where. Going back to work... getting back into routine... it will do us all good."

Liz stared at her reflection in the bathroom mirror. With her hair pulled back into a low bun at the nape of her neck, she applied the last touches of make-up – something she hadn't done since Stan's accident almost three weeks ago. It was time to go back to work. There was nothing more she could do for Stan. She and the boys needed to get some semblance of their normal lives back. They needed her income to stay steady. Although the approval for Stan's disability payments reduced the weight of finances slightly, she liked her job and didn't want to lose it. She couldn't stay on leave forever.

"Stan will be there whether I'm at work or not. I can't spend every hour of every day at his bedside. He will heal, and I have responsibilities."

The pep talk helped. A little.

Liz sighed and stood up, straightening her white blouse and tucking it under the waist of her black pencil skirt. She picked up her favourite gold necklace. Stan had given it to her for their last anniversary. As she connected the clasp behind her neck, the small, single diamond pendant sparkled in the bright beams of the white bathroom bulb lights above the mirror. The edges of the mirror were still steamy from Liz's shower earlier that morning.

After one more look, satisfied that she was presentable for work, she opened the bathroom door. Walking to her night-stand, she glanced at the screen of her phone where it lay charging since the night before. It was already a few minutes after seven-thirty.

Damn it, I better get moving.

Noticing her unmade bed, she quickly grabbed the corner of the white duvet cover and tossed it over her pillows. After unplugging her phone, she walked into the hall. The smell of coffee mixed with cooked eggs and bacon made her stomach growl as she rounded the corner into the kitchen. Karen stood at the stovetop scrambling eggs on a large non-stick pan. The toaster sat on the counter nearby with two slices of bread popped up.

"Good morning, Liz," Karen greeted cheerfully. "I'm cooking up eggs for the boys, and there's bacon in the oven. Eat something before you go."

Liz went straight to the cupboard where the full coffee-pot sat.

"No thanks." Liz smiled, putting her phone down on the cupboard as she pulled her stainless-steel travel mug from the cupboard to fill. "I want to get to work a little early to catch up on emails. I'm not sure what I've missed these past few weeks. Are you okay with getting the boys to school without me?"

"Sure, no problem. Are you sure you don't want anything?"

Liz's phone vibrated on the island, making her pause. She turned, her travel mug in one hand and the coffee pot in the other to look at the phone. It was facedown, hiding the caller ID. Placing her travel mug on the counter, she flipped her phone over to read the caller ID.

"It's the hospital," she said, sliding the coffee pot back.

Karen dropped the spatula. Bits of egg flew onto the stovetop and floor. Liz stepped back from her and tapped the 'answer' button before frantically placing the phone to her ear.

"Hello? You've reached Elizabeth Stevens," Liz stammered, her gaze meeting Karen's wide eyes watching her.

"Good morning, Mrs. Stevens. My name is Allison. I'm a nurse at the Vancouver General Hospital. The doctor would like to see you today if that's possible. She would like to discuss Stan's transfer to another unit with you."

"Wait, he was transferred? He's not in the I.C.U.?"

Absent-mindedly, Liz bent down and picked up the spatula at her feet, handing it back to Karen. Karen took it from her but didn't move, leaving the egg-covered utensil hanging between them.

"Yes, ma'am. The doctor or nurse tending to Stan will let you know the details. When you come, please go straight to the long-term care unit."

Although Liz couldn't sense urgency in the nurse's voice, her heart raced. What happened for Stan to move out of the intensive care unit? Work would have to wait.

She covered her mouthpiece with her fingers. "Stan was moved last night," she whispered.

"But I thought he needed to be in the I.C.U. in case his vitals change?"

Liz waved her hand at Karen, signalling her return to the nurse on the phone.

"Okay, of course. I'm a little confused though. The doctor told me Stan had to remain in the I.C.U. in case his vitals became unstable."

"I'm sorry, ma'am. I can't go into details over the phone. He's stable. That's part of the reason they transferred him."

"Oh, okay. I'll be there as soon as I can."

"That would be great! Have a good morning, ma'am."

The nurse hung up the phone before Liz could say another word. She stood with the phone still pressed to her ear for a few seconds before finally setting it back down.

"Well? What did they say?" Karen implored, waving the spatula in the air.

Liz picked egg from her skirt before responding, "The nurse didn't tell me much. They transferred Stan out of the I.C.U. into the long-term care unit. I need to go to the hospital to find out the details."

"I wish they would just tell us over the phone. Stupid doctors' policies. I guess call me when you know more."

Karen turned to the sink to wash the spatula before returning to the eggs.

"Of course. I'll send you an update once I know more."

Liz finished filling her travel mug with coffee, watching the steam rise as the hot liquid hit the cold metal interior. Karen stirred the eggs before bending down to clean up the stray egg bits on the floor. Liz looked down at the top of her head, realizing she might miss her mother-in-law when she left. Karen would return to Winnipeg at some point. Ed had returned earlier in the week for work. Karen retired the year before, so she stayed, offering to help with the boys for a bit longer. Liz knew that it was also to be close to Stan in hopes that he would wake up before she left. Guilt passed over Liz. Her attitude towards Karen had not always been grateful throughout the entire experience with Stan's accident. Although they didn't always get along, Karen was doing a lot for her and her family.

"Look, Karen, I'm sorry if I have been a bit of a bitch these past few weeks. I realize this hasn't exactly been easy for you either. Stan being in the hospital, I mean. It means a lot to me that you've stayed with us to help as much as you have."

Karen paused in her clean up, slowly raising her head to look up at Liz. She stood up as tears welled up in her eyes.

Karen raised her still wet hand from the sink and squeezed Liz's wrist.

"Don't mention it. Of course, I'll be here to help until you're able to get back on your feet. This is hard on all of us."

Liz bit her lip, refusing to let her eyes fill with tears. She wanted to get to the hospital. She gently released her wrist from Karen's hand, acting as though her travel mug lid needed tightening and backed out of the cramped kitchen space.

"Okay, I better be off. I'll keep you posted on what I find out about Stan. Thanks for getting the boys fed and off to school. Tell them I love them."

She quickly turned her back on Karen before another word could be said. She closed her eyes and sighed as she walked to the entryway. With her coffee in one hand, she picked up her laptop bag that she had prepped the night before. While leaning to keep the heavy bag on her shoulder, she went to grab her purse and realized she had left her phone in the kitchen.

"Shit," she muttered, as she turned to go back into the kitchen. "Sorry, I forgot my—"

She nearly slammed into Karen coming from the kitchen into the hallway.

"Sorry, I figured you'd need this," Karen said, holding the phone out in front of her.

Liz smiled tightly before taking the phone. She noticed a steamy thumbprint on the otherwise clean, black screen.

"Yeah, thanks. Bye, Karen."

Liz discreetly wiped the screen against her pencil skirt before throwing her phone into her purse. Her back began to ache from the odd angle she was leaning to balance the weight of the laptop bag. She added the weight of her purse to her shoulder and grabbed her keys. She nearly tripped as she practically ran out the door. She could feel the weight returning to her chest and her eyes burned as tears threatened to fall. She needed to get on the road to distract herself. A fine mist covered her red Toyota RAV4, so the handle was cold and wet to the touch as she opened it. That was when she realized she had forgotten her jacket.

Fuck it, I'm not going back now.

She pulled open the SUV door and climbed in, carefully placing the laptop bag on the passenger seat before pulling it and her purse from her shoulder. She shifted the travel mug from her left hand to place it in the cup holder on the console and started the SUV. She paused, gripping both hands onto the steering wheel as she closed her eyes to take a deep breath, trying to calm down before she got onto the busy TransCanada highway into downtown Vancouver. She knew that going through Stanley Park would be faster, but she and Stan had been married there. The memories that flooded her whenever she passed through it were too much to bear with Stan unconscious in the hospital. Their future was still very uncertain. Her emotions were already unsteady this morning, she didn't need to risk it. Throwing her SUV into reverse, she backed out of the driveway, anxious to get to the hospital to see Stan. She would call her assistant, Jane, along the way to warn her she would be late for work.

***

Liz wandered the hospital for thirty minutes, searching for Stan's new room. A woman from the front desk had given her the number when she asked for directions. All the hospital halls looked identical, making her feel like she was lost in a labyrinth. Periodically, coloured stripes painted on the walls broke the white monotony. She supposed these distinct colours were supposed to signify something, but she couldn't decipher their code. Her heart raced in her chest, and her breath became shallower as panic took over.

Will I ever find him again?

She breathed a sigh of relief as she turned a corner and saw a sign for the long-term care wing above two large metal doors at the end of the hall. She hurried through the propped-open doors and scanned the room numbers on either side for 136. The hall was empty and silent except for her footsteps. Then the numbers 1-3-6 stood out on the right only a few feet away. She picked up her pace a little, excited to finally see Stan.

"Miss! Excuse me, miss!" a woman yelled from behind Liz, making her stop short. "I'm sorry, you can't just walk into any room you like!" The woman's accent had a thick southern drawl, reminding Liz of New Orleans-based television shows.

Liz turned to see a heavy-set woman rushing towards her. She was wearing red nurse scrubs with a white ID tag dangling from the shirt pocket on her chest. The red was bright against her deep brown skin. Her black hair was pulled tight in small braids wrapped in a thick bun on the top of her head. As the nurse caught up, Liz thought she looked winded from running down the hallway. Liz wondered how long the nurse had been chasing her, as she hadn't seen a nurse's desk on the way in.

"Miss, who are you looking for?" the nurse said in between breaths. "I need to see some identification. I can't just let anyone wander into whatever room they please. My patients deserve their privacy."

"I'm sorry, I didn't realize I needed to check-in. The doors were open, and I didn't see a desk. I'm Liz Stevens. I'm here to see my husband, Stan, in *that* room," Liz pointed to the door a few feet away. "His name is Stanley Stevens. So, I'm not some random person walking in."

"Yes, ma'am. I know who Mr. Stevens is. Please come with me. I have some paperwork for you to fill out. I'd also appreci- ate seeing your I.D. if you don't mind."

The nurse turned back down the hallway. Liz hesitated at first, looking back at Stan's door, before turning to follow her.

She had a feeling Stan would be in this room for a while. She didn't want to make an enemy on the first day.

"I just came to quickly see my husband. I received a call from another nurse this morning asking me to come in. Why was he transferred to this new room?"

"Once I verify you are who you say you are, I'll be happy to get into the details. It's my job, you know."

The nurse huffed as she squeezed through a small opening in the wall. The opening in the wall turned out to be a small entry to a desk.

No wonder I didn't see her. How the hell was I supposed to know this was here?

One of the windows Liz had assumed was for another hospital room was a sliding glass window. As she walked up to it, she could see the nurse sitting at a small desk behind it. The little alcove was darker than the hallway, the yellow lighting dim above the nurse. Liz squinted to see into it. From the angle that she stood, the nurse seemed to fill the small space. It was cramped with a computer, piles of paperwork, and three filing cabinets along the back wall. The nurse leaned over to grab a clipboard from a shelf against a side wall. As she reached, Liz noticed a tiny tattoo of an eye on the underside of the woman's wrist. It wrinkled a little with the woman's age but made Liz think of fortune tellers at carnivals and fairs. It was heavily faded, making Liz think it was from the nurse's younger years.

"Here's the paperwork I need you to fill out."

Liz shifted her gaze to the woman's face. The nurse's large brown eyes gave Liz chills, as if the nurse could read her mind. Liz shifted her gaze to the clipboard. Gripping onto it, she searched her purse for a pen.

"I need your driver's license or other form of photo I.D. as well," the nurse continued, holding a pen up in the open window. "My name is Ms. Bodette, but you can call me Serafine."

Liz took the pen from Serafine and placed the clipboard under her left arm to free her hands so she could pull her wallet out of her purse. Once Serafine had possession of her driver's license, Liz switched her attention to the paperwork, filling it in as quickly as possible. As soon as she finished, she handed it back to Serafine and took her card back. She then watched Serafine enter the information into the computer. As the clicking of the keyboard filled the small room, Liz looked around the disaster of papers, clipboards, and pens that filled every space on the desktop.

"Don't mind the mess," Serafine said, her eyes never leaving the computer screen. "I don't tend to sit here very often. It's rather crowded, as I'm sure you've noticed. I prefer to be out walking the halls and checking on my patients. After all, their care is what's important, not the tidiness of this desk."

Serafine shifted her eyes slightly to look up at Liz with a grin.

"Oh, I didn't even notice," Liz lied, her skin crawling slightly.

"Everything's settled here. You're welcome to go on in and visit your husband. I helped get him comfortable when they moved him over this morning, so I hope that everything suits you fine."

"Actually, you haven't said yet ... why was he moved in the first place?"

Serafine shifted, leaning back in her chair to look up at Liz.

"Oh, that's right. Well, the doctor will give you the exact details, but I can tell you that he's off the ventilator. Apparently, the nurse over in the I.C.U. got quite the shock when his heart rate tripped the alarm in the middle of the night. When she ran into the room to check on him, his hands were flexing, and he was choking against the mouthpiece. He was breathing on his own."

A smile spread wide across Liz's face. Her cheeks felt like they could crack from the strain.

"What does that mean? Is he awake?" Liz asked excitedly, taking a step toward Stan's room.

"Sorry, no. The movement was his body reacting to the ventilator. With him breathing on his own, his body fought the machinery. Unfortunately, he's still in a coma."

"Oh," Liz deflated, the hope draining from her body.

"However, it's a good sign. He's breathing on his own now, which means he's healing. His vitals have been stable since he gave the nurse that scare, so the doctor this morning decided that he could be moved. They need the beds in the I.C.U., you see. For the more critical patients."

"So, he's not considered a critical patient anymore?" Liz could feel hope coming back, although not as strong.

"He still has a long journey ahead of him. And he may never get back to being like he was before the accident. But if he's breathing on his own, that's a good jump on the way back."

"Okay. Thanks for letting me know."

"You're welcome, Miss. Have a good rest of your morning."

Liz gave a small wave and then turned from the window. She walked back towards room 136, anxious to finally see Stan. As she reached for the doorknob to enter the room, the image of the eye tattoo came back to mind. She wondered what it could mean and why Stan's nurse had it. She turned her head to look down the hall toward the nurse's desk and was shocked that, from this angle, the desk seemed to disappear. Chills ran down her back. The optical illusion of the disappearing desk made her second guess her interaction with Serafine ever happened. She startled as Serafine emerged from the wall, shuffling her way out of the tight opening. Liz laughed at herself and took a deep breath.

Just breathe, Liz. You don't need to add an anxiety attack to your plate right now.

Liz turned the knob and walked into Stan's room. The overhead lights were off and an eerie, orange glow from a rectangular lamp on the wall above Stan's head dimly lit the room. The tubes between Stan and the machines along the wall made her feel like she had entered a mad scientist's laboratory. Shadows crowded the edges of the room, causing goosebumps to creep along her skin as she tried to identify the hidden, dark shapes. Long, dark fingers crawled up the sides of the bed onto Stan's legs. It looked like a shadow creature with long tendrils was trying to drag his body down behind the other side of the bed. Her heartbeat quickened, so she turned away from the creepy scene to search along the wall for the light switch. As soon as the overhead fluorescents flickered on, the glaring beam forced all shadows to disappear. When Liz turned back to Stan, the medical equipment was its normal white hue. The creepy fingers had simply been shadows cast by folds in the blanket covering Stan's legs. The room was the plain hospital room she had expected to find when she first opened the door.

What's wrong with me today?

Liz shook her head, trying to force out the remaining fear lingering in her mind. She wasn't usually this jumpy. As the door closed behind her, she rubbed at her arms, forcing the goosebumps to recede. She startled at the loud click of the latch sliding into place.

"Stan, you'd make fun of me if you saw how I'm behaving this morning. Hell, *I'd* make fun of me. My imagination is on steroids today."

She walked over to the two chairs against the wall. The room had a layout like the old one. This one, however, had thin wallpaper with pink and blue polka dots bordering the top of the walls.

That ugly decor isn't fooling anyone. We still know we're in a hospital.

The cold, sanitized atmosphere seeped from the walls around her. She dropped her purse on the chair closest to her and moved to Stan's bedside. The heart monitor beeped a monotonous pattern. He looked peaceful, as though he was just sleeping soundly. The ventilator missing from his face allowed her to see his thin, pink lips. A beard had formed during the weeks he'd been in the hospital, although it was thin and patchy from the rubbing of the mouthpiece. She could see flecks of white amongst the beard, which made her smile. She reached up and rubbed her fingers gently in the rough, scratchy whiskers, flicking at one of the white hairs.

"I am so glad to see your face again, Stan. We miss you so much. The house feels so large and empty without you in it."

Liz leaned over Stan's body to kiss him lightly on his forehead. He smelled like soap, making Liz wonder if they had washed his hair and face after they removed the ventilator. She inhaled once more the clean scent then straightened. Her hand trailed behind her and traced circles on his chest.

"I can't wait until you come home."

Something creaked behind her, making her whip her head in the direction of the noise. A locker-sized cabinet and sink were directly behind her. The hair on the back of her neck rose as if alerting her to danger. The room was empty except for her and Stan, but something felt off. Just to be sure, she moved to the cupboard and pulled on the handle with her fingertips. The door creaked as she slowly opened it, peeking into it as soon as it was wide enough. She braced herself for something to jump out at her.

The cupboard was empty.

Inside, there were small white towels folded on the top shelf. Empty hangers dangled on a thin, silver rod below. She laughed at herself, closing the cupboard, and turned back to Stan.

"Well Stan, I guess I should get to the office. I'm too jumpy here today."

She reached down and squeezed his unbroken leg just above his ankle. She hoped to see him flinch in response, but nothing happened. She did her best to ignore her stomach sinking as her hope dwindled.

"Please keep fighting, my love," she whispered. "I'll come back later to check on you again."

She gripped his hand as she leaned over and kissed his cheek. Pulling her head back slightly, she looked at his face only inches away. A tear threatened to fall down her cheek. She bit her lip and closed her eyes, wishing it away. She gave Stan a light kiss on his lips, breathing in his soapy scent one more time, then stood up. She grabbed her purse from the chair as she moved to the door.

"Bye, Stan."

Chapter 11

- Serafine -

Serafine sat at the small, crowded desk in the make-shift room turned nurse's station. She drank herbal tea from a blue mug while sifting through notes left by the previous night nurse. She liked to read through them in case anything was missed during their quick chat at the beginning of her shift. She tapped at the sides of the mug, her long, red fingernails clicking against the ceramic until she heard movement in the hallway. Just as she let go of her mug to stand, Liz passed by the open window. Liz was looking down, digging in her purse with her hand. Serafine looked over at the stack of papers against the wall on her right, where the paperwork Liz had filled out was still on top. She felt pity for the poor woman. No one deserved to have their husband suddenly taken away, especially with kids at home to take care of. It reminded Serafine of the troubles she went through as a young mom before becoming a full-time nurse almost fifteen years ago.

She had met her husband at a café in New Orleans just shy of her twenty-fifth birthday. They had fallen in love and were married within a year of that fateful day. Within four years after getting married, they were blessed with their boys. First, Michael and then James came into the world less than two years later. They were happy, or so she thought. Until one day, shortly after she turned thirty, her husband didn't come home after work. Her two boys were at Serafine's mother's house on the outskirts of New Orleans that day. He hadn't left a note or a phone number. He was just gone, along with most of the money in their joint bank account.

Serafine moved her and her two young boys into her mother's house as soon as they could sell their small home in Lakeview. She needed help raising her two young children if she was going to keep her job. Her mother was happy to welcome them into her home, but Serafine was hesitant. Her mother had called herself a Voodoo priestess for as long as Serafine could remember. At the time that Serafine and the boys had to move in, her mother was still entertaining tourists with her Voodoo hexes and healing spells. Her mother had always claimed that Serafine had the talent to follow in the family business, but Serafine had no interest. She wanted to help people as a nurse. She didn't understand what her mother claimed was "beyond the veil." She wanted to keep her feet flat on the ground in this world instead, especially for her growing boys.

Shortly after Serafine turned thirty-three, her mother died suddenly. It shook Serafine more than her husband leaving and made New Orleans no longer feel like home. It had become a fountain of bad luck and dark memories. She went to a nearby tattoo parlour after her mother's funeral and asked for a specific eye design. It was the same eye on her mother's shop sign that would sit out in front of the house to attract paying customers. With a sore wrist, she then returned home to think over where their lives needed to go next.

Thankfully, she was able to continue working during the day to keep her income. Michael was six years old and in grade school, while James could attend the local preschool at nearly five. Serafine's dream of becoming a nurse and helping people kept tugging at her. She applied to various schools far from New Orleans that allowed part-time studies so she could continue to work while attending classes. She received a few acceptance letters back, but the one that spoke to her the most came from Canada. She spent weeks researching suburbs, schools, scholarships, and potential job opportunities until she found a plan that sounded perfect. Perfect and far away from New Orleans. As soon as the boys finished the school year, she sold her mother's home with most of their belongings. They packed up the few things they had left into a small Ford SUV and were off to their new lives in Prince George, British Columbia.

Nursing school was hard to get through, particularly while raising two young children with no partner to help, but she did it. The money from selling her mother's home and belongings helped in the early years. In her early forties, she accepted a nursing position in Vancouver. She and her boys, then thirteen and eleven years old, moved to a small apartment in a good neighbourhood. Over the following years, her boys grew into fine, young men, and moved out on their own. Michael moved out first to pursue his studies in Vancouver as soon as he turned eighteen. Then James moved out to Seattle when he turned twenty, leaving her alone in their small, three-bedroom apartment. Shortly after celebrating her fiftieth birthday, Serafine moved into a one-bedroom condo apartment closer to the hospital where she worked.

Serafine shook her head, bringing her mind back into the present. She stood to look down the hallway through the sliding glass window. Liz was no longer in sight. Serafine wondered how long she had been sitting there, reminiscing about her past. No one was around and the hallway was quiet. She decided to check on Stan one more time this morning. She had already completed her rounds with the other patients.

She shuffled sideways through the thin opening in the wall and walked to Stan's door. As she neared it, the air shifted, as if she was moving through a dense, electric forcefield the closer she came to the room. She hesitantly lifted her hand to touch the door handle. As soon as her hand touched the cold metal, all her senses told her to turn and run. She shrugged the feeling off and pushed down on the handle. The door clicked open.

"Serafine, get a grip on yourself," she mumbled as she entered the room. "Your mama believed in that mumbo jumbo, but you don't. Stop acting like there's anything to be scared of and get to caring for your patient."

The overhead fluorescents bathed the room in their bright, white light. Although she wouldn't admit to it, relief washed over her that the lights were on. She might have lost her nerve if it had been off.

"Hello, Mr. Stevens. In case you don't remember, my name is Serafine. I helped you settle in this morning. Hopefully, you can hear me today. If not, that's alright. I'll talk to you anyways, and you can just give me a sign when you're ready."

Serafine grabbed his chart and noted his heartbeat rhythms and breathing patterns. Pulling out a blood pressure machine from under the heart monitor, she wrapped the arm piece around his right arm. She pushed the button on the machine and returned to her notes. Everything looked normal considering he was a coma patient. It wasn't often she had one in her wing, especially so soon after removing the ventilator. She was a little annoyed with the intensive care unit shipping their patient over so quickly, but she knew they had been busier than usual the last week. They always needed more beds.

"Now, Mr. Stevens," she continued while packing away the blood pressure machine. "I met your wife, Miss Elizabeth. That must have been nice to have her visit. She sure is a pretty woman. You are one lucky man, you know. She mentioned you two have children. That means you need to get yourself feeling better so you can go home to your family. Don't you dilly-dally in that head of yours."

She looked down at the unconscious man beside her. The temperature of the room dropped suddenly. A tingling sensation crawled up her arms and into her body. As if against her will, she leaned down to whisper in his ear.

"Now don't you bring any demons around, you hear me? You fight them off. Whatever darkness is hovering over you, you need to fight. Do you understand? Don't let them win."

A chill passed over her as the sensation passed. She stood up with a jolt, lifting her hand to rest on her chest. The pen she was holding brushed her skin, leaving a thin, blue mark near the neckline of her scrubs. She couldn't shake the feeling that she wasn't alone in the room. Her head felt foggy.

"I'm sorry, Mr. Stevens. I don't know what just came over me. That sounded like something my mama would say, God rest her soul."

Serafine backed away from the bed, her eyes watching Stan's face. She still felt in shock, uneasy about what had come out of her mouth. She quickly returned Stan's chart to its place and backed towards the doorway. It felt like someone was watching her from the corner of the room. She startled when she bumped into the door, the handle hitting her in the back. She spun around and grabbed it, happy to leave the room. Once in the hallway, she watched Stan's face until the door slowly blocked her view, clicking into place. Relief washed over her. Her heart raced in her chest while she contemplated the door for a few seconds, thinking over what had just happened.

What has gotten into me? This is complete and utter nonsense.

She waved her hand in the air, sure there was a logical explanation for everything. She looked up and down the hallway to make sure no one was watching. She was alone. Turning, she walked back towards her desk. Before shuffling her body in through the small crevice, she couldn't help but glance over her shoulder, back toward Room 136. A chill ran down her spine as she thought she saw a shadow slither under the door.

Just a trick of the light.

She looked away, moving into the office, not realizing that the light beam shining under the bottom of Stan's door had flickered off.

Chapter 12

- Stan -

Stan sat on the cold, hard ground with his gaze turned up to the sky as waves of blue, pink, orange, and green danced above him. He didn't know how long he had been walking but had decided to take a break from the monotonous motion. This world seemed to go on forever. Although the sky brightened and the colours became more vibrant, nothing else changed. The ground was still hard and black, a stark contrast against the atmosphere above. There was no water nor breeze. The temperature remained cool, but he never shivered nor felt cold. Even the rhythmic waves of the invisible ocean had stopped, leaving him in a quiet world. He only had the bright horizon to guide him.

Bringing his knees to his chest, he wrapped his arms around his legs. His pants wrinkled as he rested his chin on his knees and closed his eyes. He hadn't only noticed the clothing recently. When the sky was bright enough for him to see himself for the first time in this world, he looked down to take stock of himself. He wore long, khaki pants with a plain white t-shirt. He didn't need to see to know his feet were bare, but that didn't bother him. There was nothing sharp or rough on the ground.

He took a deep breath and let it out. The silence wrapped around him like a blanket. A strange vibration gently pulsed into his feet from the ground. He opened his eyes and placed a hand on the ground beside him. It was faint, but it made his skin quiver. He looked around the horizon, but nothing else had changed. There was no source to the vibration as far as he could see. It was as if the ground beneath him was alive, subtly trembling with a hidden energy that both intrigued and unsettled him. It was so faint, though, that he wondered if he was imagining it.

"Don't let them win," a voice boomed overhead.

Stan quickly turned to scan around him in a wide circle, searching the bright sky above him.

"Hello?" he hollered.

He stood up, searching the horizon for the person who spoke, but no one was there. He was still alone, the horizon empty. He ran towards it, hoping it was the direction the voice had come from.

Don't let who win?

After a few minutes, the bright sky began to flicker. He stopped abruptly and looked up. The colours of the sky were fading. A click in the distance reverberated around him. Immediately, the sky turned a dark, dull gray. Shadows covered the edges of the horizon all around him. He spun around, uncertain of which direction the bright horizon he had been following could be. All around had the same dull grey sky with shadows moving like bubbling water around him in the distance.

What's going on? Why did the sky change?

A stronger vibration pulsed into his body from the ground. He knelt to touch the ground with his hand again. It felt electric, as if a shock was passing into his body through the contact. The bubbling shadows were quickly closing in around him, encircling him completely. They boiled and gurgled closer like an eruption of black lava. There was no opening for him to run. A breeze picked up and swirled around him, whipping his loose clothing against his skin. He knelt closer to the ground, watching the shadows stop a few feet away. The wind grew stronger, carrying with it a hair-raising sound. A scream travelled on it, sending chills down his spine.

The scream sounded familiar. It tugged at a memory at the back of his mind, but it refused to surface. The scream grew louder, morphing into something more sinister. He covered his ears. It seemed to vibrate against his skull, as if trying to crack into his brain and penetrate his thoughts. His head throbbed and his heart raced. His heart beat harder and faster until Stan thought it was going to break out of his chest. He wanted the bright colourful sky to come back, with its silence and calm.

He lay down on the ground, curling into himself as tightly as he could while covering his head and keeping his ears plugged. He started humming, trying to drown out the terrifying wail as it grew around him. He didn't know where the tune he hummed came from, but it was familiar and comforting. He hoped it would keep him safe from the shadows surrounding him.

What did that voice want? Why did it bring these shadows to me?

Stan curled into himself tighter, wishing he had never heard that voice from above. The hairs on his neck rose. It felt like hundreds of eyes focused on him, inching closer. If a booming voice overhead attracted these shadows, he desperately hoped he would never hear it again. All he wanted was to return to his quiet, safe world. Covering his head with his arms, he squeezed his eyes tight, humming louder to drown out the wailing circling him.

Chapter 13

- Liz -

Liz was pulling out of the parking lot of the café with a box of a dozen donuts on her passenger seat, humming. She merged into the lane that would eventually take her to the office, the morning traffic lighter as the time ticked near ten o'clock. The song she hummed was familiar, making her pause. It was her and Stan's wedding song.

Wow, where did that come from?

She couldn't remember the last time she heard it. It wasn't a common song playing on the radio unless you switched to one of the oldies stations. The stations that she frequently listened to preferred to play the current hits, or at least the hits from the last five years. The reminder of the song sent Liz's thoughts to the many anniversaries that Stan would play the song and they would dance in the kitchen, half-full wine glasses nearby. Liz felt a tear forming in the corner of her eye, so she quickly swiped it away.

"Come on, Liz," she said to her reflection in the rearview mirror. "Focus on the road right now, and the workday ahead. Get a hold of yourself."

She turned the radio to the local Top Forty channel and cranked up the volume, hoping it would help distract her from spiralling.

I can't walk into the office with puffy eyes.

Once she got there, she could switch to autopilot and get through her day without reminders of the mess her home life had become. The improvements in Stan's condition today helped lift her mood slightly, even with the worry of a steady income and bills still in the back of her mind.

Liz lost herself in the music until she turned into the parking lot of the newspaper's office space. Relief washed over her to finally be back in familiar territory. She pulled into her usual parking spot and turned off the engine. She looked up at the front office door and apprehension washed over her. Facing the real world suddenly felt overwhelming. Liz gripped the wheel and closed her eyes, taking a deep breath. A familiar '*ding*' from her phone rang out, indicating that she had received a text.

Liz reached into her purse, her fingers quickly finding the familiar shape of her phone amongst the mess. It was a new message from Sarah:

-Hey Lizzy! How's the first day back going? Just checking in. Work is dull. Text if you want to meet up later. Lex and I can bring pizza. XOXO

Liz smiled. She was so grateful for her best friend. She couldn't imagine how she would get through this mess with Stan if Sarah hadn't been sending her texts and stopping by the house unannounced to help.

Liz texted back:

-Just getting to the office now. Hospital called, so I went there first.

-He's in a new room! Will explain tonight. I'll supply the
beer.

Liz ended the message with a kissing emoji and clicked out
of the list of messages. She turned the screen off and switched
her phone ringer to vibrate before throwing it back in her
purse. Picking up the donuts for the office and her laptop bag,
she pulled the keys out of the ignition and got out of the SUV.
Glancing at her reflection in the driver's side window, she realized that the threatening tears from earlier had still managed
to smudge her mascara slightly, making the bags under her
eyes look even worse. She shifted the weight of her purse and
the donuts into her left arm, trying to clean her eyes with her
right hand. Doing her best to look less like the hot mess she
felt like, she took another deep breath.

"Okay," she said to her reflection. "I can do this. I love this
job. I'm great at this job. Just get in there and get to work."

She fixed her blouse and shifted the weight of her purse
and donuts back to her right side. Locking the doors of the
SUV, she turned and faced the office, walking back into the
real world again. The world she had to face alone, without
Stan, for as long as he needed to heal.

***

The day at the office ended later than Liz planned. The work
had piled up while she was away. It was nice to see they were
struggling without her, clearly indicating they needed to keep
her, but she didn't appreciate the long days starting already. As
she pulled into the driveway at the house that evening, Sarah's
blue Volkswagen Beetle was already there. The sun was setting
behind overcast clouds, making her headlights bring the colour
of the house back to life briefly against the dark, greying world.

She had hoped to make it home early enough to shower and get out of her work clothes before Sarah showed up.

"Oh well, here we go," she sighed, turning off the ignition.

She grabbed her purse and the pile of manilla envelopes holding drafts she wanted to work on later that evening from the passenger seat. Climbing out of the warm SUV, she shivered without a coat in the cool, moist air. As soon as she walked through the front door of the house, her nostrils filled with the scent of deep-fried foods and baked cheese. Laughter came from the kitchen. Carefully placing her things on the entryway table, she removed her shoes, absent-mindedly glancing at Stan's empty spot on the shoe rack as she put hers away. She moved to pick up the papers but paused. With her eyes closed, she listened to the happy sounds flooding the house. Sounds she hadn't heard since Stan's accident.

"Lizzy! You finally dragged yourself away from that office."

She opened her eyes to Sarah standing a few feet away, smiling and holding a half-empty beer bottle.

"Hey, I told you I'd pick up the beer," Liz complained, although she had forgotten. She grabbed the envelopes and walked towards her best friend.

"Come on ... do you forget how well I know you? I could tell by your texts this afternoon you were in work mode. Once you hit that, everything else goes out the window."

As soon as Liz was within arm's reach, Sarah pulled her into a hug. Liz hated to admit it, but she needed the embrace, even if the papers wrinkled between them.

"Unfortunately for you, I forgot how much your boys eat compared to Lex and me. You'll be lucky if they leave a single slice for you. Hurry up and change before they eat it all."

Sarah let her arms drop and leaned back, smiling over her shoulder toward the kitchen. Liz looked past her and saw everyone standing around the kitchen island, hovering over a pile of pizza boxes. Only Karen sat at the dining table with a plate, knife, and fork.

"Sorry, I lost track of time. I'm swamped catching up on correspondence and reading through drafts. There was some disagreement on the lead cover stories, too."

"No worries. Go get changed and put that stuff down. I'll fight your kids off at least two pieces of pizza. I got your favourite: vegetarian with Italian sausage instead of pineapple."

Liz smiled, "Well, pineapple just doesn't belong on a pizza."

Sarah stuck her tongue out at Liz before turning back to the kitchen.

"Did you hear me, boys? Save two pieces for your Mom. In fact, why don't you go into the living room? I'll make some popcorn for you. Karen, can you be referee so a fight doesn't break out over the remote?"

"Sure," Karen replied, standing up from the table with her empty plate. "Come on kids. What do we feel like watching tonight?"

Karen's voice faded as she moved into the living room through the doorway on the other side of the kitchen. Liz smiled watching her family leave together. It almost felt normal again, which made her heart ache for Stan. She turned down the hall to her bedroom, pausing in front of her door to consider the pile of envelopes in her hands. She spun around into the office, dropping the envelopes on the desk. Stan's desk. She usually used the kitchen table to work, but without Stan here, she might as well use the desk. He wouldn't mind. It was collecting dust. She looked around the office at all the books and pictures he had placed around the room. The room even smelled like him – clean and crisp, yet a faint, delicious muskiness. She wrapped her arms around herself, closing her eyes to inhale.

The sound of someone washing dishes snapped her back to reality. She was not alone in the house. Karen would likely comment on her poor hostess skills if she didn't get out of Stan's office and back to the kitchen. Liz quickly moved across the hall to the bedroom, closing the door behind her. Hurrying into the closet, she pulled her work clothes off, pondering the many garments hanging in front of her.

A bang from behind made her jump. She turned to look at Stan's side of the closet. The clothes swayed slightly.

Did I hit those when I came in?

The thought didn't stop the chills running down her neck. Returning her attention to her side of the closet, she quickly changed into gray sweatpants, a sports bra, and a tank top. Gazing over her shoulder to the other side of the closet, she used her hands to shift her hair up into a loose ponytail on top of her head. She moved out of the closet and leaned to turn the light off. As the closet went dark, she watched the shadows on Stan's side of the closet, but her eyes weren't adjusting. The sound of heavy breathing seemed to come from his clothing. The hairs on the back of her neck lifted in response.

There's nothing in the closet. It's just my imagination.

Not taking her eyes off Stan's clothing, she slid the closet door closed.

"Okay, my day is officially too long if I'm afraid of my closet now," she said with a laugh, turning to leave the bedroom.

As she entered the kitchen, Sarah stood over the sink with her back to Liz, wiping down the surrounding counters.

"Hey, what are you doing? Don't worry about the dishes. You're doing too much as it is!"

Sarah smiled over her shoulder and draped the dishcloth over the faucet before turning to face Liz.

"Oh, it's nothing, really. I threw most of them in the dishwasher. How was your day?"

Sarah leaned over the island to hand Liz a nearby beer. The bottle was cold and wet with condensation.

"Oh, you know, surviving. It felt good to go to work today. It helped take my mind off everything and concentrate on other people's lives for a while."

She sat down on one of the bar stools at the island, while Sarah leaned over the counter on the other side, taking a sip from her own nearly empty beer.

"Well, that's good. Getting back into a routine will help."

Liz looked down at the cold beer in her hands, leaning her arms on the counter in front of her.

"I saw Stan today. He looks better, he really does. It still doesn't look like him, though. He's a lot thinner. Only a portion of the man I married. It makes me wonder where the rest of him went."

"Don't worry, he's strong," Sarah said, extending her hand out to rest briefly on Liz's wrist. "He'll wake up in his own time. What did the doctor say while you were there?"

"I didn't get to see a doctor, but the nurse on duty told me about the I.C.U. moving Stan because he's breathing on his own again. He doesn't need the ventilator anymore."

"That sounds like great news!"

"Yeah, he's in a long-term care unit now. His vitals have been stable, and they think he's starting to react to his surroundings."

"That's great!"

"Yeah, it's a change in the right direction. We still don't know what state he'll be in when he wakes up."

"He's going to pull through. I'm sure of it."

Liz gave Sarah a small smile and squeezed her hand before taking her own back. She took a swig of her beer and put the bottle aside. She looked over at the last two pieces of pizza in the box on the counter near her, but her stomach turned.

"I don't think I'm hungry enough for pizza yet. I've been snacking on donuts, coffee, and almonds all day."

She stood up to put the pizza in the fridge. She needed to keep moving. Sitting allowed her dark thoughts to stir.

"As long as you promise to eat something before you go to bed. It doesn't have to be pizza. Hell, it can be a pint of ice cream for all I care. Just eat something, please," Sarah implored.

Liz forced a smile before responding, "Of course I will. You don't need to mother me. I'll take care of myself, I promise."

They both moved around the kitchen together, cleaning up in silence. The silence didn't last long, however, as Karen walked in.

"Well, those kids are all absorbed by the television show they turned on. I think I'll start the boys' lunch for tomorrow if you two ladies don't mind an extra set of hands in the kitchen."

"Of course. We need to be getting home anyway. Lexi has homework due for one of her classes tomorrow. Then she has swim practice tomorrow night. I might not be seeing you for a few days. Don't hesitate to call if something comes up, though. I can always move my schedule around or get that ex of mine to help."

Liz walked over to Sarah, embracing her. She quietly whispered into Sarah's hair, "Thanks for everything. I don't know what I'd do without you."

They stood holding each other for a few seconds. Karen slammed cupboards a few feet away, forcing them to step back from each other.

"Hey, no problem. What are best friends for, right?"

They smiled at each other briefly, only a foot of space between them, when Sarah turned and walked into the living room. Liz followed closely behind, avoiding making eye contact with Karen.

Chapter 14

- Stan -

Stan curled into a ball on the ground, shivering from the constant bombardment of screams and growls around him. It felt like hours had passed by. Maybe it had been days; he wasn't sure. Periodically, the growling changed, its tone rising and falling. Almost like the deep, menacing voice was forming words. The sound it made, however, was a guttural rattle Stan couldn't understand.

Then silence finally returned.

He lay still, wondering if he had gone deaf.

What if it's a trick? They might pounce as soon as I move ...

He squinted, peering carefully through his fingers. The sky above was bright with streaks of colour flying like clouds overhead. He sat up and looked around his body. The shadows were gone. For as far as he could see in every direction, there was only the black ground against the bright, colourful horizon. He was alone.

Oh, thank God. They're gone.

A noise came from the sky that Stan didn't recognize. It reminded him of muffled talking through a wall. Something you might hear when sitting in the small back room of a doctor's office, but the doctor is seeing the patient next door. A second muffled voice said something in response.

Someone else is here!

Stan quickly stood, searching the horizon for any sign of where the voices were coming from. Nothing had changed; he was still alone, so how could he hear voices? Realization washed over him.

They're coming from above.

The voices were coming from somewhere beyond what he could see. Something brushed along the hairs on his arm, like feathers dancing over his skin, making it itch. Placing his hand against his skin, he spun around to look behind him.

Could those creatures be playing tricks on me?

But he didn't think it was them. The energy was different. The buzzing electricity that came with their presence was gone. Everything was calm and quiet. Peaceful.

The murmuring continued above his head, louder now. Whoever was talking was apparently moving closer.

How can I hear them? Where are they? Where am I?

The people above him continued talking. Stan closed his eyes to concentrate on the words. After a few moments, he realized his body felt lighter, as if he were floating. He opened his eyes.

Holy shit. I am floating!

He was floating a foot off the ground. The surprise made him break his concentration on the voices. He dropped back to the ground suddenly, nearly falling forward onto his knees.

How is that possible? I can't float. Gravity would never let that happen.

Another realization hit him.

Unless this isn't the real world. Unless this is something else.

Maybe he wasn't standing in the middle of nowhere in a weird, black desert, searching for a sign of civilization. Maybe this was a completely different world.

So then how can I hear them?

He looked back up to the sky. The voices were quiet, but the sky was still bright and colourful. A deep itch settled into his leg. Absent-mindedly, he scratched at it. It wouldn't stop. It felt otherworldly, as if coming from within him.

Wait. If this isn't the real world, then is this not my real body?

He looked down at his hands and waved them in front of his eyes. They appeared solid and real. Could he have detached from his physical body? Would that explain everything that had happened to him?

How long have I been here? Days? Weeks? Please ... not years ...

He looked up again, wondering what the people on the other side of the sky looked like. Perhaps he was hearing someone near his physical body. As he searched the colourful clouds for meaning, a loud click echoed across his world. The sky instantly turned dark and gray.

Shit.

Stan looked down at his feet. The black surface below him was already bubbling. He dropped to his knees, feeling the surface with his hands. It was still solid and cold where he knelt, but the bubbling continued to rise five feet away.

They're back.

Shadowy creatures seeped out of the black floor, passing through it as if it were water. Large masses of tar-like substance bubbled up from the deep, black, endless expanse. Panicked, Stan turned to run, but the creatures were emerging all around him, encircling him again.

They only come when the sky is gray.

Stan searched the horizon for hills or mountains. There had to be higher ground somewhere. He needed to get closer to the sky. He needed to get away from these creatures. They grew taller, blocking any path from where he stood. There was nowhere to run. Their menacing voices whined again, getting louder and more persistent, making the air heavy. An invisible weight pressed down on his shoulders. He covered his head and lowered his body to the ground.

There was no escape.

Chapter 15

- Liz -

The following Thursday, Liz woke early, eager to get into the office and have a productive day. Unfortunately, it wasn't going to be the good day she hoped for. When she had walked into the kitchen to fill a travel mug with coffee before leaving for the office, Karen had announced she had booked a flight back to Winnipeg for the next day. Although Liz was tired of having her mother-in-law judging her every move, it was nice to have someone taking care of the boys. They were only just starting to get into the swing of things. She thought she would have more time before she would be alone, the only parent in the house. Typically, she would have called Jules back to take care of the boys, but Jules was gone. After so many days without needing to fulfill her nanny duties, Jules started preparing for her life after graduation. Liz knew she needed to find a replacement, but she hadn't put the time or effort into it yet.

She left the house flustered but was determined it wasn't going to slow her down. She would figure everything out. It would be fine. While driving to the office, however, she became distracted while weighing her options. She hadn't noticed that a traffic light had turned red until the last second, making her slam on the brakes. Her travel mug flew out of her hand, coffee spilling all over her suit and blouse. She had left her jacket unzipped.

"Shit!"

She was sure she had screwed the lid completely closed before leaving the house, but maybe she had been too distracted by the conversation with Karen.

"I guess this is why I have a spare outfit in my office."

Liz pulled into her parking spot and sighed gratefully when she saw no other cars were there. The office lights were off. She quickly grabbed her things from the passenger seat and ran inside, walking straight into her office to put her purse and laptop bag on her desk chair. She hung her jacket up on the coat rack by her office door and looked at herself in the mirror behind it.

"Good morning, hot mess."

Coffee stains had spread across her white blouse. She shook her head and walked over to the closet in the back corner of her small office space to pull out her spare suit. She carried it out to the bathroom near the common area. As she walked into the shadowy bathroom, she flicked on the light switch. Nothing happened.

"Oh, come on."

She flicked the switch up and down repeatedly. Nothing happened.

I guess I'm changing in the dark.

She shrugged her shoulders and walked over to the counter. Someone had left a nightlight plugged into the wall above the bathroom sink, casting a faint yellow glow. There was no way she was changing in the toilet stall; it would be pitch black. She quickly removed her stained clothing, carefully folding them and placing them on the counter before picking up her other suit. As she looked at her reflection, she realized even her white bra had coffee splashed across the front. She brushed at it.

"Great," she muttered.

As she pulled her new, blue blouse over her shoulders, the toilet flushed in the stall behind her. She spun around. The door was open a few inches, but she couldn't see the toilet itself.

"Is someone there?"

Pulling her blouse closed over her chest, she reached out and slowly opened the bathroom stall door. Her heart pounded in her chest, making her blood drum in her ears. The room felt freezing. Goosebumps spread over her skin, and the hair on the back of her neck rose.

As the stall door opened more, it squealed in complaint. She could barely see the white toilet glowing in the small space. Dark, black shadows covered the back wall and floor behind the toilet, but no one was there.

Okay, the toilet is just acting up. That's all.

She turned back to her clothes on the counter by the sink. Liz threw her legs into the pants before buttoning her shirt. She didn't want to be in this room alone anymore. As she began buttoning up her blouse, the nightlight flickered, dimming slightly. She thought she saw movement behind her in the mirror's reflection. She wouldn't admit it to herself, but a light breeze seemed to pass over the back of her neck.

"Nope, I'm out of here," she muttered, grabbing her clothes under her arm, and rushing to the door.

She felt better the instant she moved into the bright common room. The lights, although glaring, were welcoming. Even the temperature of the space was warmer. She threw her dirty clothes onto a chair nearby and finished changing before heading back to her office. After placing her coffee-soaked outfit in the closet, she made a mental note to ask Jane to have it drycleaned later that morning.

Now, coffee.

Walking back to the kitchen, she pulled the plastic brew basket from the machine. After filling it with coffee grounds, she slid it back into place and hit the red button to start the coffee. Almost immediately after the water started percolating, hot water spewed in every direction. She swore as she frantically tried to turn the machine off without getting sprayed, but the power button wouldn't stop the water. Finally, she pulled the plug out of the wall. Liz looked around at the water all over the kitchen and her clean clothes in disbelief.

"You've got to be kidding me. What is up with today?"

After searching through the various cupboards in the kitchen, Liz found some paper towels and began wiping up the water. She threw the attempted coffee grinds into the compost under the sink. Giving up on coffee altogether, she grabbed a diet cola from the fridge. She didn't like soda first thing in the morning, but at least it had caffeine.

Once back in her office, she assessed herself in the mirror again.

"Well, at least it's only water this time. Now pull yourself together." She scowled at her reflection. "Great ... now I'm talking to myself."

Shaking her head, she turned to sit down at her desk. She turned her laptop on and took a deep breath while she punched in her login credentials, then took a swig of diet cola and got to work.

*＊＊

Liz had forty-five minutes before her focus was interrupted. Bob, her boss, was the first one to walk through the door. Liz's office had a clear view of the entrance, so he immediately noticed her and came to stand in her doorway, still wearing his long, brown coat and carrying his black leather briefcase.

"Liz!" he exclaimed. "Are you the only one here so far? I feel like these young people we hire are coming in later and later each day. I guess coming in before office hours isn't a concept they teach anymore."

Liz smiled, not giving a clear indication of agreeing or not, as he made himself comfortable in the chair across her desk. Liz noticed he was avoiding direct eye contact.

Here we go.

She did her best not to roll her eyes.

"Actually, it's probably a good thing I got to see you before the office is busy. I wanted to talk to you about your request for a raise. I went over the books, and I just don't think we can swing it right now."

Bob pretended to be picking at lint on his jacket. Liz glared at him over the laptop on her desk. She had a good idea of what 'the books' said. She was certain that there was more than enough room to give her a more appropriate salary, unless they had other plans for that money that she didn't know about.

Without looking up from his important lint hunting, Bob added, "I realize you're in a particularly difficult situation right now, so I want to help in any way we can. What if we shortened your hours in the short term so that you don't have to work so late? We won't reduce your pay."

At this offer, Bob looked up at Liz, clearly satisfied with himself. She looked down at her hands still hovering over her keyboard. Her fingers shook in anger, so she curled them into fists and pulled them under the desk. Bob seemed to recognize that his offer wasn't going over as well as he had planned. His gaze dropped to his own hands in his lap, and he squirmed in the chair.

"If that doesn't sound reasonable to you, I can give you your typical annual raise early. When it comes time for the annual review, we can consider whether we can afford to give you a second increase."

Liz bent her head down slightly, trying to avoid Bob seeing the sneer that spread across her face. One percent was the going rate for annual raises at the office if she was lucky. She reminded herself that Bob didn't have to do anything, so she sighed.

I suppose I should be grateful he's doing anything ...

With Stan in his current situation, she didn't have much choice. She couldn't quit her job and look for a new one. Liz looked up at Bob, making sure to keep a grateful expression on her face, "I appreciate that you've been thinking about this, Bob, I really am. I'm wondering if we can meet in the middle. I would greatly appreciate the annual raise starting now, with the promise that we will review it again in four months. I also feel that perhaps I should spend less time physically in the office. I can use Stan's office at home to work remotely on a part-time basis. That way, you won't be paying me more for fewer hours, but I will be able to be home when the boys need me."

Bob contemplated her counter-offer, looking at Liz while chewing on his bottom lip, his hands wringing in his lap. Both were signs that Liz knew meant he was considering saying yes.

After a few seconds that felt like hours to Liz, Bob finally responded, "Okay. I think that sounds like a fair deal. I'll get Betty to draw up the paperwork for us to look over and sign on Monday."

Liz felt some of the tension release from her jaw.

"That sounds wonderful, Bob. Thank you for taking the time to talk it over with me this morning. I really appreciate it."

"Right, of course."

Bob gathered his things and stood. He paused for a moment, looking down at Liz while she smiled calmly up at him.

"It's great having you back in the office, Liz. You had us all worried. It was a terrible thing to happen to you, Stan, and the kids. You've all been in our minds during your absence. I still wonder if it's too soon for you to be back."

"Thanks, Bob," Liz said, straining to continue smiling. "I'm happy to be back. I was going stir crazy sitting at home and the boys need their routine to return, too. Even if it isn't quite the same as it was before. Stan will be home when he's ready. I appreciate everyone's concern, but honestly, we will be fine."

Liz dropped her gaze back down to her laptop. She was finished with this conversation and hoped Bob would take the hint. Standing over her in the awkward silence that followed, Bob seemed unsure if he should press further.

"Okay, I'll get out of your hair. I'll see you in the morning meeting to chat layouts."

Without waiting for Liz to respond, Bob turned and walked out of her office. Sitting perfectly still, she waited for the familiar click on his office door indicating he had shut his door. As soon as she heard it, she quickly moved to shut her office door, letting out a sigh of relief as the door clicked shut. Her eyes were stinging as tears threatened. She didn't want anyone to see the nervous wreck she was becoming.

Why couldn't it be at least 5 percent?

Was one percent going to cover any unknown costs for Stan? What if his insurance coverage ran out or never came through? What would Christmas look like if she couldn't afford their monthly expenses? She hated the situation that a drunk man had put her in. She missed Stan.

I can do this, she reminded herself, pulling her shoulders back. *I have to.*

Chapter 16

- Stan -

Stan curled into himself, trying to block out the noises of the creatures swirling around him. They encircled a few feet around him, never getting closer, but never stopping their incessant wailing. They were loud; their vibration pounding against his skull relentlessly.

Maybe this is my life now.

The thought of living out the rest of his days surrounded by this torment was too much to bear. Slowly, he sat up, staring into the sea of swirling black shadows. They moved so quickly they blurred together, making it impossible to find any details of their bodies or faces. Among the mass, a small yellow slit glowed, like a shooting star passing across a black night.

Is that an eye?

A shiver ran through him. The mass seemed to shift in response, swelling as more yellow slits appeared, all in pairs, spinning around him.

They know I can see them.

He looked down at the ground near his feet, trying to push away the horrifying thoughts of what the rest of the creatures' faces might look like. Glowing yellow eyes, long and sharp.

What could their mouths look like?

The mass swelled again. Stan realized that with each swell, the black mass inched closer to his feet. Concentrating on them allowed them to move closer.

Shit. Think about something else.

He closed his eyes, trying to think of anything else. The beach that he used to think was nearby. Water splashing against small grains of sand, and the smell of saltwater in the air.

But what if this is it? What if I can never leave? Is this really a way to live?

Returning his gaze to the black mass inching closer, Stan wondered if he should just walk into it. He didn't know what would happen, but could it be any worse than sitting curled up in a ball, waiting for an inevitable end?

What if those voices never come back? I can't go on like this.

Suddenly, a familiar voice rang overhead as the sky brightened, as if the sun suddenly rose. The creatures squealed as they shrank back into the ground around his feet. The voice above mumbled. He recognized the lilt and tone.

It's her! The woman from the beach. She's here!

He opened his eyes excitedly, searching the sky for her face. The light was almost blinding, as if her presence brought the sun. Squeezing his eyes shut, he strained to reach out to her mentally, focusing on her voice. He immediately felt the pull like before, but stronger this time and within reach. Something about her voice was easier to grasp than the others. His feet slowly broke free from the gravity holding him to the black surface.

"Stan, I love you."

His eyes flew open in surprise, almost causing him to lose his grip on her voice.

Stan! My name is Stan!

The memory of his name flooded in. This woman was someone he loved very dearly. His heart opened to that love now.

Maybe she is the key.

Maybe she could pull him out of this world, back to the world where his physical body was. He closed his eyes tightly and focused on her presence, feeling himself slowly breaking free. She was an anchor to the real world. She could free him from this awful place. Free from the shadow voices and their insistence to keep him glued to this lonely world.

A different voice boomed, making him jump.

"Excuse me, but what are you doing here?"

It was another woman's voice. The one that had come with a warning last time. He couldn't understand them as their voices became muffled. Both voices grew softer and harder to hear. They were moving away, out of his reach.

"No! Don't leave!" he yelled at the sky.

No longer tethered to her, Stan felt a heavy weight take over, dragging him back down. Back into his binds that kept him from escaping. As he crashed onto the vast, black surface of this world, he felt himself sink into what felt like quicksand. He had gotten so close. He had almost escaped, but the love of his life left too soon. He tried to stir more memories about her. Sitting on the ground, waiting for her return, he tried to force the image of her face to the surface.

What's her name?

He could almost see her. She had long brown hair. When she left it down, it would drape across her eyes. Brown eyes. He closed his eyes, trying to focus on the image in his mind. Those big brown eyes used to look up at him lovingly.

Right, you're shorter than me.

Stan quickly stood back up, opening his eyes to scream at the sky, "Why can't I remember? Please, come back! I need you! I can't escape this hell without you."

Silence. He sighed in defeat, returning to his curled form on the ground as the sky shifted to darkness, as if the sun had been blown out like a candle. The creatures were returning. He closed his eyes and focused on the woman's face, or at least the parts he could remember. Those brown eyes would have to keep him sane until she could return to save him.

If only he could remember her name.

Chapter 17

- Liz -

"Ms. Bodette ... Serafine ... I'm sorry I'm here so late. I just needed to see my husband. I had ... a hard day."

It was after visiting hours, but Liz came to the hospital anyway. She was hopeful the nurse on duty would understand. She hadn't expected Serafine.

"I realize that Mrs. Stevens. I let you have ten minutes even though I shouldn't have. Heck, even I'm not supposed to be here right now. The night shift started over an hour ago, but my shift change hasn't bothered to show up yet. Apparently, none of us are going to get what we want tonight."

"Fine. Thanks for the brief ten minutes, I guess. Have a good night."

Liz stormed towards the end of the corridor to leave the hospital. She couldn't believe she had driven all the way here for only ten minutes. The entire day had felt like a day from hell. She wanted the comfort of her husband's hand in hers.

"It's not like I'm disturbing anyone sitting quietly in his room," Liz muttered to herself as she neared the corner at the end of the hall.

"Mrs. Stevens, wait!"

She turned in surprise. Serafine was jogging towards her.

"Come back, Mrs. Stevens!" Serafine whisper-shouted, flailing her hands in front of her.

"What?" Liz asked, confused.

Serafine paused in the middle of the hallway, gasping for breath. She motioned for Liz to come closer. Lis walked quickly back, trying to keep her expression neutral. The confusion, mixed with amusement at the spectacle, was probably clear across her face.

"It's Stan. He must have felt you nearby. I want to try something before you leave."

Liz's mouth dropped open. She stuttered, "What do you mean? He did something? He moved?"

"Shhhhh," Serafine looked around and waved her hands at Liz again, this time motioning for her to keep quiet. "Patients are trying to sleep. And you aren't even supposed to be here."

She turned and motioned for Liz to follow her. They walked in silence back to Stan's door, where Serafine paused, checking that the hallway was clear before opening it. The light in the room was still on, flooding the room with the bright, white, fluorescent light. Stan was still where Liz had last seen him, the blanket slightly mussed where she had been sitting a few moments before. She wasn't sure what Serafine was talking about until her gaze shifted to Stan's face.

"His eyes!" she exclaimed, forgetting she was supposed to be quiet.

Stan's eyes were wide, staring blankly up at the ceiling. She ran to the bed and placed her hands on his chest, leaning over him to look down into his face.

"Yes," Serafine said, walking around to the other side of the bed to stand across from her. "This sometimes happens with coma patients. Their eyes open involuntarily. However, given you were just in here, I thought it might be worth testing to see if he responds to you. Your voice is familiar to him, so maybe it will spark something. It's worth a try."

"Oh, Stan. I'm here. Can you hear me?" Liz pleaded. "Please give us a sign if you can hear me."

She held her breath, waiting for a response. Anything to indicate he could hear her, feel her. Even the air in the room felt still. As they watched, his eyes remained open, unmoving. She placed her hands on either side of his face, hoping it would help, but he continued to stare straight up at the ceiling. The way he stared was eerie. His eyes seemed to look right through her, staring at some unseen horror. Chills passed through her body. He looked frozen in terror. Even though she was happy his eyes were open, worry over what was happening in his mind crept into her thoughts. Serafine seemed to know what she was thinking.

"Now, don't worry about his staring off like that. It was probably involuntary after all ... he probably doesn't even know they're open."

Liz couldn't bring herself to move. Looking down into his eyes, she couldn't stop fear from crawling under her skin. His expression was unsettling.

"Right, okay," she muttered, slowly straightening back to standing. "So, you don't think he meant to open his eyes?"

"We may never know, Mrs. Stevens," Serafine responded, reaching over to put her hand on Liz's where it still rested on Stan's chest.

Liz looked up at her, smiling slightly. Serafine squeezed her hand a little.

"I have to admit, I don't see a lot of coma patients. I'll let the doctor know, though. They can run some tests tomorrow to see if it means anything more. I'm sorry if I got your hopes up."

Serafine gave a final squeeze to Liz's hand, along with a small smile, before letting go. The angry air that was shared between them only moments before dissipated completely. Liz smiled back at her and then shifted her gaze back to Stan's face.

"Okay, I'll come back tomorrow to see him again. Maybe if I keep coming back, he'll give us a clearer sign."

"That's a great idea. But, please, make it a little earlier next time. The night nurse is not as understanding as I am."

Liz couldn't help but let out a snort of laughter. The thought of Serafine as the lenient one surprised her. Serafine shuffled sideways along the side of Stan's bed, indicating it was time for them to leave. Liz leaned down and kissed Stan's cheek.

"Goodnight, Stan. I'll be back tomorrow. I love you."

She turned to search for her purse, which she had dropped on the floor when she had first seen his eyes. Neither of them had realized her purse had fallen in front of the door, causing it to remain propped open. With her purse in hand, she felt Serafine touch her gently on the lower back, giving her a small push through the doorway. Liz smiled to herself again while swinging her purse over her right shoulder, grateful Serafine was the one she got to be with tonight after all. Rifling through her purse, she searched for her phone and keys as they moved into the hallway. Serafine closed the door behind them.

"Thanks for letting me see his response. Even if it turns out to be involuntary. Seeing a change in Stan still puts a better ending to my day than I ever could have asked for. I know you didn't have to call me back."

"No problem, Mrs. Stevens. Let's just keep the exact time of your little visit between us," Serafine said, smiling sideways at Liz.

"It will be our little secret," Liz replied, feeling a warmth growing between her and the nurse. Maybe she had been wrong about Serafine. "Have a great night, Serafine. And please, call me Liz from now on. I have a feeling we'll be seeing a lot of each other."

"Sure. Goodnight, Liz."

They walked down the hallway side by side, until they reached the nurse's station hidden in the wall. Smiling once more at each other, they split up. Serafine moved to the small nurse's desk while Liz continued walking.

On the drive home, Liz found herself humming their wedding song. She was glad she decided to go to the hospital tonight. She still didn't know what she was going to do about a nanny, or about Karen flying back to Winnipeg the next day. At this point, all that mattered was that Stan had opened his eyes.

He must *have heard me. He was showing me that he's still in there, that he's coming back to me.*

Surely this meant he was going to be okay. They were going to be okay. She couldn't think of another reason for his eyes to open like that.

Chapter 18

- Serafine -

Stan's eyes continued to stare up at the ceiling. The whites around his pupils shone as if frozen in terror. A sense of foreboding gripped Serafine. His face brought up memories of her mother teaching her about the signs of possession. Serafine reluctantly reached out, placing her hand over his eyes. His skin was cold and clammy against her warm fingers. At first, his eyelids refused to budge, but she wasn't giving up. Gripping her fingertips onto his eyelids, she pulled them down. She took a step back and dropped her hand to her side, sighing with relief. With his eyes closed, he looked like he was sleeping peacefully. Serafine made a final note on the clipboard and placed it back in its placeholder before leaving the room.

He's not possessed. He's in a coma.

Once the door clicked shut behind her, she walked toward the nurse's station. The hallway was eerily quiet, but it was getting late, so she wasn't overly surprised. She sat down at the desk and pulled her romance novel from the drawer to read. The lights overhead flickered before turning off. The hall lights continued to shine through the small window above the desk.

Well, that's odd.

She stood back up to move into the hall. As she passed over the threshold of the small office, the lights began flickering in the hall. They changed from a bright, white glare to a murky gray.

What's going on with these lights?

It was faint, but she could hear humming from somewhere down the hall. Walking towards the sound, she paused at each door she passed, pressing her ear against them to find the source of the hum. As she approached room 136, the humming grew louder.

Of course, it's his *room.*

Reaching out, she placed her hand on the cold metal of the door handle. It vibrated ominously against her skin. She took a deep breath and opened the door, stepping into the room. The hospital room was gone. Instead, a dull gray sky was overhead. The walls were replaced by tall, dark shadows dancing around the hospital bed where Stan lay. In a panic, she turned back to the hall, but more shadows hovered behind her, only inches away. The hall was gone. The doorframe seemed to stand on its own with no walls to hold its weight. She backed away from the shadows as they bubbled and churned around her.

The humming was right behind her now, so she turned. The hospital bed was gone, along with Stan's body. Instead, a man huddled in a ball on the black floor at her feet, his arms covering his face. His body was blurred around the edges, making him look like a wet painting that hadn't quite dried yet. The man was the source of the humming, curled over his knees, fingers plugging his ears. Serafine reached her out to touch his shoulder.

Does he know where we are?

As soon as her fingers made contact, the man startled, looking up into her face. Immediately she recognized the wide, scared eyes staring up at her. It was Stan. Something was wrong with his face, though. It was longer and skinnier than she remembered, the skin seeming to hang off the bone.

Stan opened his mouth as if to scream, but his chin kept getting longer, his mouth opening unnaturally into a long, oval shape. His human teeth transformed, melting and lengthening, as if made of clay. Long, sharp fangs protruded at angles all over his enlarged mouth. The back of his throat was black, like a giant hole. She tried to step back, but an invisible force pulled her body toward him. His mouth had a force of gravity as it continued to spread wider. His head tilted back wide like a giant snake, and she was pulled headfirst into it. His throat constricted around her and became tighter and darker as she was dragged in further and further. She tried to open her mouth to scream or cover her face with her hands, but the hole was too tight. Her arms were trapped at her sides, unable to move. Her lungs felt like they were being squeezed flat, making it difficult to breathe.

Serafine closed her eyes, hoping the end of this torture would come soon. Enveloped in darkness, gravelly, deep voices began to speak all around her. She couldn't understand their language, but they were angry. They were growing louder. Whoever they belonged to was getting closer, trying to catch up to her. A small opening with a red glow appeared ahead of her in the tight tunnel. As it grew, she saw a black, shadowy creature emerge from it. It crawled towards her. Its eyes glowed yellow and a lime green luminescence dripped from its horrible mouth full of jagged teeth. Teeth that looked an awful lot like what had grown from Stan's deforming mouth at the start of the tunnel.

The creature was skinnier than she was, its claws able to reach out towards her, dragging its body along. She tried to move, to wriggle herself back down the tunnel, but she was stuck. The creature kept pulling itself closer to her. She opened her mouth to scream again, bracing herself, as the creature's claws rose to slash at her face. The scream was muffled as it came out of her throat, but the tunnel eased slightly around her. She pulled her arms away from her side as hard as she could, finally feeling the constriction lifting. Yanking at the material surrounding her, she opened her eyes and saw that the creature was gone. She kept pulling at the sides until her head finally broke free.

It was her bedroom. Her blankets wrapped tightly around her.

It was all a dream.

Sweat dripped off her eyebrows into her eyes. Her night-shirt stuck to her skin under the blankets. She slowly worked to unravel her arms from them and sat up in the bed, looking at the shadows that enveloped her room. The clock on her nightstand said it was exactly three o'clock in the morning.

'*The witching hour,*' Serafine's mother's voice warned in her head. '*The time the supernatural are at their strongest. Sera, baby, you need to protect yourself. That man's in trouble. They all are.*'

Serafine squeezed her eyes shut, willing her mother's voice away. She didn't need this. She hadn't asked for any of this.

No. I left that world behind in New Orleans. It's not following me here.

She sat in her bed, her eyes still closed tight, debating what to do next. She hadn't heard her mother's voice in her head since the boys were young. She had thought maybe it was a figment of her imagination, her mind craving the sound of her mother's voice. Her mother couldn't really be talking to her.

If I was smart, I would roll over and mind my own business.

'*Serafine Ophelia Bodette ...*' her mother's voice demanded. '*You don't ignore your mama. Now go and phone that poor woman and warn her. Her family is in harm's way, and we don't turn our backs on people in need.*'

Serafine flinched at the command. Even though she didn't want to believe in ghosts, she still couldn't ignore her mother's voice, whether it was her imagination or not. Slowly, she rolled out of her bed and went to the phone in her kitchen. She picked it up from the counter and moved to sit at the small kitchen table. She picked up the receiver, dialling the hospital. Adelaide, the night nurse, picked up and instantly began apologizing again for being late earlier that night, repeating the excuses she tried earlier. Serafine didn't have time for this.

"Now, I already told you, what's in the past is in the past. What's done is done. Listen, I need a favour. I forgot to tell Mrs. Stevens something earlier, and now I can't sleep because of it. Can you look up her number for me?"

She wrote down the phone number Adelaide listed over the phone and hung up without another word. She sat looking down at the number for a moment, unsure of how to explain to Liz the darkness that shrouded her unconscious husband. The creature's face was still fresh in her mind. She could feel its hot, moist breath on her face and the stench of it as it clawed closer to her. She could almost feel the sting of its claws as it reached for her face.

She couldn't ignore her mother's warning. Her gut told her something more was going on, whether she wanted to believe it or not. She needed to tell Liz something before it was too late.

Chapter 19

- Stan -

Stan couldn't believe his eyes.

While curled into a ball, plugging his ears against the noise of the creatures, he racked his brain for ideas to escape the hell he was living in. He didn't know when the voice of the woman from his memory would return, when her energy would be back to connect to, but he hoped it was soon. He would be ready. The gravity of her presence could pull him from this miserable existence. He just needed a plan.

He hadn't noticed something new creeping up behind him from the shroud of shadows swirling around him. The mix of wind and screaming that penetrated his skull made him oblivious to the movement at first.

Then the energy around him shifted.

The static in the air lessened. He was almost able to take a deep breath again, the weight on his chest lifting. That was when he felt a presence hovering over his back.

He turned, raising his arms in preparation to fight, but the thing looking down at him was different. It wasn't a black, blurry mass like the others. There were no yellow eye slits staring down at him. Instead, a shimmery, white mist hovered over him, bright against the black mass behind it. It emitted a calming, quiet energy. As it leaned down over him, warmth radiated out from it.

What are you?

He shifted to his knees to move closer to the mist, noticing the shape change as he did. Two large, brown eyes looked down at him from within the mist. A face was forming.

Could this be an angel? Here to save me from this hell at last?

Stan reached an arm out above him, lengthening his fingers to touch the warm face amongst the wispy fog. It looked human.

"Thank God," he exhaled, happy to finally see someone like him. "I've been searching for others. Do you know how to get out of this place?"

Just as his fingers were about to touch the cheek of the woman standing before him, the ground started shaking violently. A loud hum filled the air. Dropping his hand back to his side, he looked around. The shadows had stopped swirling and thousands of yellow, glowing eyes stared at them as if thousands of heads had turned to watch them. Then a long, black tentacle rose from the ground just inches from his knees.

"Shit!" Stan yelled, falling back away from the sticky, black limb.

The tentacle wrapped itself around the woman standing amongst the mist. He watched in horror as her mouth opened in shock, a silent scream forming on her lips.

Then she was gone.

The tentacle had pulled her into the ground. Down where the shadows go when the sky changed colour.

"No!" Stan screamed, pushing himself back to his knees. His hands searched the ground in front of him where the woman had stood only seconds earlier. She was gone. The ground was black, solid, and cold again. The shaking slowed, returning to the menacing vibration it had been before the woman appeared.

He looked up. The creatures standing around him continued to stare, thousands of glowing eyes focused on where he sat.

"What did you do? Why did you take her? Bring her back!"

Slowly, as if on cue, thousands of slits appeared on the faces of the creatures. At first a thin line, but it slowly spread. The corners lifted on each side as the line grew longer. Long, jagged teeth emerged as the lips parted.

They were grinning at him. Thousands of long, ghastly smiles went on for miles in every direction. Whoever she was, she was never coming back. They wouldn't let her. Of that, he felt sure.

"You bastards!" Stan yelled as he jumped to his feet, running up to the first line of creatures standing in front of him. "Let her go! Let *me* go! I don't belong here!"

The heads of the creatures fell back simultaneously, showing rows of sharp, jagged teeth shining green in the low light. A buzzing sound filled the air, rising and falling in volume. Stan spun around. The same movement was mirrored in every direction.

They're laughing at me.

Thousands of creatures were laughing at him in his misery. Anger coursed through him, giving him a boost of confidence that he hadn't felt in a long time. He walked up to the creature closest to him until he was only inches from its face.

"Fuck you!"

The creature closed its mouth and stared into Stan's eyes. It leaned forward, putting its face inches from Stan's. Its breath was vile and rotten, like something had died in the creature's mouth. Stan recoiled, taking a few steps back, and covered his nostrils, trying to block out the smell.

As the creature smiled again, obviously enjoying the reaction from Stan, all the others behind it returned to spinning, blurring behind the single creature that stood smiling at Stan. The screaming returned, forcing Stan to cover his ears. Slowly, the lone, still creature turned its body and stepped into the crowd of black mass swirling by until Stan could no longer see it.

There has to be a way out. They can't keep me here forever.

Stan spun around with his hands still covering his ears. The black mass returned to swelling and moving like it had before the white mist arrived. They had gotten rid of her. He was alone again.

They won't let me go.

They wanted to keep him in this world. But why?

"What do you want from me?" he yelled into the mass, but they ignored him. The wind picked up, whipping at his clothes and forcing him to kneel back down and cover his head.

He had to find a way out. The woman in his memory had to come back. He needed to figure out a plan to escape so that he was ready when she returned. The sky would be bright, and the creatures would hide, allowing him to focus.

It's my only chance.

Chapter 20

- Liz -

A sharp, shrill beeping startled Liz awake. A heavy material was over her head, making everything dark. She clawed at it, panic rising in her chest, until her head broke free. The surrounding room was dark, but she recognized it immediately. It was her bedroom. She was curled under her duvet cover. The annoying beeping was louder outside the heaviness of the duvet. She slammed her hand on the nightstand. As soon as she felt the cool, slim case of her phone in her hand, she looked at it through squinted eyes, the bright screen glaring, to turn the alarm off. She settled back under the covers on her back, curling the duvet blanket over her hands and tucking it under her chin. She looked around the room. Dark shadows lurked in every nook and cranny. It was six in the morning, but the sun wouldn't rise for over an hour. That was November in North Vancouver for you. Karen was leaving today, so Liz wanted to get up early to get a good start on her Friday, but the bed was warm, and scenes from the accident had filled her dreams.

Taking a deep breath, she sat up. The air in the room instantly cooled her skin. She rubbed the sleep from her eyes and peered over at Stan's side of the bed. The blankets were disturbed by her thrashing, but his pillow lay untouched. The groove from his head was long gone. She reached over to touch his pillow, feeling the sting of his absence. Closing her eyes, she rolled to the other side of the bed to turn on the lamp. Warm, amber light quickly filled the room, forcing Liz to blink against the brightness. A shadow moved by the opening in her bedroom doorway, catching her attention.

Who could that be? The boys shouldn't be up yet.

Pulling her legs out from under the warm blankets, she placed her feet on the cold, hard floor beside the bed. Standing, she moved to the bedroom door and opened it slowly until she could peek her head into the hall. It was empty. The light was on in the kitchen, casting a soft glow towards where she stood. The faint scent of coffee reached her. The familiar scent perked her up slightly, so she opened the door fully, about to step into the hall to walk to the coffee pot. The sink turned on in the kitchen, making her pause.

Karen.

She rolled her eyes. Spinning around, she walked to the master bathroom to grab her housecoat hanging on the inside of the door. After wrapping it around her, she tied the belt snugly around her waist and grabbed a hair elastic from the top bathroom drawer. While she pulled her hair up, she left the bathroom and stalked back towards the hall. As her hand touched the bedroom door handle, she took a deep breath, preparing herself for whatever mood Karen was in. Finally, she raised her head high, and repeated the phrase, *Today is the last day,* in her mind as she walked to the kitchen.

"Good morning, Liz. I'm surprised you're even home! I thought you'd be at the office already," Karen muttered.

Karen was already perched on her favourite chair at the kitchen island, wearing black pants with a large yellow knitted sweater that went up to her chin. She didn't have a coffee in front of her yet, but the newspaper was spread out, covering half the kitchen island in its black and grey print. Toast hung carelessly from her fingers as she leaned in to take a bite from it, causing crumbs to spill all over the paper. Liz forced her best fake smile and shuffled into the kitchen, quietly walking around the island towards the coffee pot.

"Hey, Karen. What time do you get up in the morning? It seems like no matter what time I wake up, you're already in here. I'm starting to wonder if you ever sleep!"

"Oh, I'm not usually up this early, but that mattress in the spare bedroom downstairs is horrid! I toss and turn all night, and then my back hurts by morning. It will be good to get back to my own bed tonight. The mattress that Ed and I bought is wonderful. You should really consider getting one for your guest room. It does a better job than that overpriced thing you have."

Liz did her best not to let her smile falter. She turned her back on Karen to focus on the coffee, grimacing as she pulled a mug from the cupboard.

"Sure, Karen. Send me the info, and I'll have a look."

Silence returned to the kitchen while Liz poured the steaming coffee into her favourite pink mug. The odd crunch of Karen biting loudly into the toast was the only sound in the room. With coffee in hand, Liz turned, avoiding eye contact with Karen, and walked out of the kitchen, hurrying back to her bedroom. She didn't realize she was also holding her breath until she finally had the door closed behind her and she let it out in a loud sigh. She leaned back into the door, carefully taking a sip from her mug. The caramelized, earthy aroma of the medium roast filled her nostrils, giving her an ounce of energy. She raised her shoulders tall, not realizing how much they had shrunk in the presence of her mother-in-law.

"Just remember, she leaves today. Just get dressed and go to work. She'll be gone by the time I get back."

With that small boost in confidence, Liz peeled herself off the door to get ready, but a light knock rattled the bedroom door behind her. Envisioning Karen on the other side, she closed her eyes, contemplating if she could get away with pretending she hadn't heard it. Sighing, she reached out and turned the doorknob, opening the door up with her fake smile back on. There was no one there. She poked her head out the door, looking up and down the hall, but it was empty.

Did I imagine it?

Shrugging, she closed the door, turning to go into the bathroom to have a shower.

***

Forty minutes later, Liz stood with her ear pressed up against the bedroom door, listening. She didn't want to run into Karen again on her way out of the house, so she waited, fully dressed, for the main floor to become quiet. As soon as it seemed Karen was back in the basement, she tiptoed to the entryway and quietly pulled her jacket from the closet. She shrugged the sleeves on but didn't bother zipping up her coat. She slipped both her laptop bag and purse onto her left shoulder and leaned down carefully to pick up her high heels, carrying them out the front door. Her feet were wet and cold the instant she stepped on the concrete outside. A thin layer of frost covered everything in a light, white blanket.

"Damn winter," she whispered, shifting the heels onto her left arm to lock the front door behind her.

On the front of her feet, she ran across the cold, icy ground to her SUV, making sure to hit the unlock button on her key fob. She jumped into the driver's seat as soon as she reached the door and dropped everything into the passenger side. She wiped her wet feet against her hands, trying to warm them, as she gazed at the windows of the house. The windows remained dark and empty. She slipped her feet into the heels, her breath forming small clouds as a shiver ran through her.

"Okay, let's get out of here."

She turned on the ignition and backed out of the driveway, avoiding a look back at the windows again. She worried that Karen may be trying to wave her down. Once the house was safely in the distance behind her, her shoulders loosened.

"I so need a massage if my shoulders are ever going to become less tense," she said, absent-mindedly reaching down to grab her coffee with her right hand.

Her fingers fell into the empty cupholder, and she felt the crumbs along the bottom from the many years of travelling with children. She looked down at it in regret.

"Damn it! I forgot my coffee."

Her empty stomach growled.

"Well, screw this, I'll just pick something up. There's no way I'm turning around to go back now."

Turning left at the main road, instead of her usual right, she drove to her favourite café nearby to pick up a large caramel macchiato with an egg and bacon breakfast sandwich. Thankfully, the extra stop only added ten minutes to her commute to work. When she finally pulled into the office parking lot, Bob's beige Lincoln SUV was already in his parking spot.

"Damn it, why's he already here?" Liz blurted.

She pulled into her parking space and turned off the engine. Balancing her coffee and sandwich, she sneaked into the office, hoping Bob wouldn't spot her. Luckily, he was nowhere in sight. Placing her things at her desk, she pulled her phone from her purse before hanging her jacket in the back closet. She returned to her office door, peeking around the edge to ensure Bob wasn't coming before she quietly closed it. Moving to sit at her desk, she pulled out the now grease-lined sandwich from the bag. After taking a large mouthful, she searched for a napkin to wipe her hands dry before picking up her phone to check the screen. She had a voicemail. Clicking on it, she turned on the speaker phone button to listen to the message while taking another bite of her sandwich.

"Good morning, Mrs. Stevens. This is Serafine Bodette. If you recall, I'm the nurse from the hospital. Now, don't you worry yourself too much. This isn't official hospital business. I feel silly for even calling, but my conscience just won't let me rest until I do. I have a bad feeling about Mr. Stevens. Now, this will sound like complete nonsense, but I couldn't sit by and not tell you what my gut is telling me. My mother, God rest her soul, believed in crazy notions of spirits and evil, so it's likely her fault I get these feelings. Anyways, I think Stan is having some difficulty coming back. His soul is stuck in some sort of limbo. You know, the world our souls can go when our bodies aren't doing so well? If you believe in that sort of thing anyway. Part of me feels like something evil is lurking in the shadows, trying to keep him from coming back without them hitching a ride. Now please don't call the hospital about this. It's just a gut feeling I sometimes get. I don't want to lose my job. You can decide what to do with this information, which may mean calling me crazy and deleting this message, never to think about it again. I won't blame you, and I won't bother you again. All I'm saying, Mrs. Stevens, is be careful. And please, visit Stan often. You may be the anchor he needs to pull him out of whatever darkness he finds himself in."

The message clicked off.

Liz was frozen in place, her hand lined with grease and hovering over the sandwich where she had dropped it onto her desk. Chills penetrated her entire body, her mouth agape as her mind processed everything she heard. She stared down at the phone. The instructions from the robotic voice of her voicemail asked her what to do next.

Gradually, the feeling came back into Liz's arms. Awareness of time passing as she stared at her phone seeped in. She looked at the last bit of the sandwich on the desk. Her stomach turned and she closed her mouth to avoid vomiting. She went over Serafine's message again and again in her mind.

Was that why his eyes stared up at the ceiling like that? Was he trying to ask for help?

Liz shook her head.

"Oh, for crying out loud, Liz. Think about this rationally for a second."

She picked up the napkin and nervously wiped the grease from her hands. Wrapping up the remainder of her breakfast in the old wrapper, she wiped up the grease from her desk where the sandwich fell and threw everything in the trash. Liz then stood up, clicking the button to hang up her phone, and walked out of her office to the women's washroom. She needed a moment away from it all to clear her head. The thought of Stan being trapped in some other dimension, his soul unable to escape the grips of some unknown evil, was terrifying. It also sounded like utter nonsense, as if she was living in some sort of horror movie. Her mind was so focused on convincing herself that she didn't believe what Serafine was saying on the phone that she didn't notice the lights in the bathroom flickering while she stood in front of the sink. Watching the soap as it lathered in her hands, goosebumps crept up her arms. The temperature in the bathroom was significantly cooler. Her gaze shifted to her reflection above the sink.

"That nurse is just worried about Stan, just like I am. I appreciate her concern, but I won't get sucked into her crazy world. She likely had a bad dream during the night and mistakenly thought it was some sort of supernatural, psychic warning. All will be fine. Stan will be fine."

The toilet flushed behind her. She spun around to look at the stall. It was open halfway but empty. The door seemed to vibrate.

"Someone really needs to fix that fucking toilet."

The lights flickered again, dimming significantly. Liz turned back to the mirror, reaching for the paper towel dispenser on the nearby wall. As she pulled the paper out, movement in the mirror caught her eye. A black, thick shadow was peaking from behind the toilet stall door behind her. Liz shrieked, turning to face it, but the stall was empty. Spinning back to the mirror, she checked the reflection again. The shadow was gone.

What the fuck is going on?

She turned, kicking the stall door with her foot. It slammed against the inner wall of the stall with a loud bang. Nothing was there.

"Who's in there? What is going on?" Bob's voice boomed from the hall. "I'm coming in!"

"Shit," Liz spun to the door, forgetting that she wasn't alone in the office.

Bob stormed in, his face red and eyes wide.

"Liz?" he said. "What are you doing in here? I heard screaming, and then a loud bang. Are you alright?"

Liz raised her still-dripping hands, the paper towel long since forgotten on the floor. "Sorry, yes, I'm fine." Her shaking fingers exposed her lie.

Bob watched her for a moment, his eyes searching her face.

He doesn't believe me.

"Maybe you should go home, Liz. You've been under a lot of stress–"

"I said, I'm fine!" she demanded, louder than she had planned. Wiping her hands on her pants, she stormed past Bob. "Sorry, I just slipped, that's all. Everything is fine."

Without looking back, she walked quickly to her office, closing the door behind her.

Great, now he likely thinks I'm crazy. What if he changes his mind about the raise or part-time hours?

She closed her eyes. The memory of the shadow figure in the reflection was behind her eyelids, waiting for her.

Maybe I am starting to lose it ...

She let out a deep sigh and moved to her desk. She hoped immersing herself in work would help her forget the dread and fear that crept into her body, but something nagged at her in the back of her mind.

What if Serafine is right?

Chapter 21

- Serafine -

Serafine woke with a start. She blinked at the bright sun shining through the big window overlooking the city. Her back ached as she shifted in her living room chair. She looked around, confused. The events from a few hours earlier, including the voicemail she left Liz, bubbled up. Her shoulders sank heavily as regret filled her.

Why did I go and do that? What if she calls the hospital? I could lose my job.

She rubbed at her lower back. A remnant from falling back to sleep seated instead of on her memory foam bed. She contemplated how she could fix it, make the voicemail go away, but nothing came. Slowly, she pushed her hands against the arms of the chair to stand and moved over to the phone. She picked it up, ready to push the numbers in for Liz's phone number, but she couldn't find the little piece of paper that she had written it on. Clicking the phone off, she leaned over, searching the floor.

Where did it go?

Walking around to the kitchen, she finally found the yellow piece of paper tucked under a closet door.

How did it get way over here?

Carefully, she leaned down to pick it up. Turning it over, she considered the phone number. Suddenly, she didn't want to talk to Liz anymore. The idea of calling to apologize or back-pedal felt pointless.

"What's done is done," she exhaled. "Might as well go about my day. At least I don't have to be at the hospital until Monday."

Crumpling the paper, she threw it into the trash in the cupboard under the sink. The phone call from the hospital to reprimand her would likely come, but she wasn't going to sit around and wait for it.

I'll go to the market today, get some shopping done. Maybe I'll swing by the library first.

She ran out of books to read a few days earlier, so she needed new ones before her next shift anyway. Romance books were her favourite. A stack of library books waited to be returned in her shoulder bag in the closet. It would be a good task to take her mind off the voicemail.

Hopefully, Liz will heed my warning.

Serafine couldn't stop the thought from entering her head. Worry for Stan's soul still pulled at her. Something was going on with him, she was sure of it. Although she couldn't say exactly what, and others may call her crazy for thinking it, something evil was making plans for him and his body.

But what can I do about it?

Chapter 22

- Liz -

Liz managed to leave work early that afternoon to pick up the boys from school. With Karen gone, she would have to switch to a hybrid working arrangement: in the office while the boys were at school, and home when they weren't. She was grateful Bob had accepted the idea – still accepted it, even after her episode in the ladies' washroom. The rest of the day, she focused solely on her work; the news of the world that day took over her thoughts. She worked through lunch, hoping to prove to Bob that her outburst wasn't a reflection of her ability to get her work done.

I can't go back on leave. I can't lose this job.

Then the joy in the boys' voices as they piled into the SUV, excitedly telling her about their day, helped her forget about the bad start to her day almost entirely. Life was good. Stan would be okay. They would all be okay. Serafine was wrong.

Once Liz pulled into the driveway, the boys piled out of the vehicle and ran into the house ahead of her. As she followed them in, she picked up their shoes and jackets scattered about the entranceway. Chattering and laughter echoed down the hallway from their bedrooms. Alex was the first to walk by towards the living room.

"Alex, I'll order pizza in a bit, but I need to get some work done first. While I head to Dad's office, can you grab a snack for you and your brothers?"

"Sure, Mom."

He turned into the kitchen out of her sight. By the time she cleaned up the floor and put away her own jacket and heels, the other two boys had passed by, already arguing about what to watch on television. Liz rolled her eyes, smiling at their resilience, as she picked up her laptop bag and turned towards the office.

As soon as she entered the small room, she paused to breathe in its scent. Stan's presence wasn't as strong as it used to be. Although the room looked the same, it felt emptier, different. Walking around to the desk chair, she pulled her laptop out of her bag and laid it gently on the black desk mat before dropping her bag onto the floor. She pulled the remote for the CD player out of the top desk drawer. Stan's favourite jazz discs lined a shelf on the right side of the room. She hit 'play' on the remote and the room filled with one of his favourite jazz albums. She closed her eyes to listen to the melody, thinking of his smile whenever they danced to this song.

I wish you were here to dance with me now.

A tear threatened at the corner of her eye, pulling her from the memory. She looked around the office and sadness washed over her. Remembering the real reason for being in the office, she pulled the chair out from under the desk and sat down, immersing herself in her work and losing track of time.

Almost two hours went by before she looked up from her laptop. She lifted her arms above her head to stretch. The muscles in her shoulders ached from the movement so she leaned back slightly in the chair, allowing the edge of the back of the chair to lightly massage her shoulders. She was amazed the boys hadn't interrupted her yet, asking when the pizza would arrive. She turned everything off and stretched one more time before standing up to walk to the kitchen. She went straight to the cupboard by the fridge to pull out a wine glass and put it in the ice bucket in the freezer. Then she pulled the pizza menu from the junk drawer on the other side of the fridge and dialled the number on the front. Chatter from the television filtered in from the adjacent room. The boys were distracted and unaware of the lack of food being delivered, but she likely didn't have long. A teenager answered the call, so she whispered their usual order before hanging up. She tiptoed down to her bedroom to change into something more comfortable.

She slid into the closet. The small space was cool, but she quickly pulled off her work clothes, searching for her favourite grey sweatpants that had UBC printed across the back. As she placed her leg in them, a shadow passed by the closet opening in her peripheral vision. She turned to face the bedroom but couldn't hear any movement. The unmistakable click of a door closing came from somewhere beyond her view from the closet. Stepping a foot into the bedroom, she looked around. The light overhead kept the room bright; only the underside of the bed cast a dark shadow.

Otherwise, the room was empty.

"Boys, are you in here?"

The bathroom door was closed. She walked to it, placing her hand on the wood door. It was icy against her palm. She slowly turned the doorknob and opened it slightly. The room was dark inside, making it hard to see through the crack in the door.

The doorbell rang, making her jump out of her skin. The bathroom ahead was dark but appeared empty.

For crying out loud. Maybe Serafine's voicemail affected me more than I'd like to admit.

She spun around to run back into the closet and pulled a white T-shirt over her head.

"Who the hell could that be? It's too soon for pizza," she contemplated out loud as she ran to the front door.

The boys hadn't moved from the living room and Liz could hear their excited chatter about something on the television.

She hollered sarcastically, "Don't worry boys! I've got the door."

She opened it only wide enough to peek her head around the edge to see who was there. Sarah and Lexi stood on the doorstep, beaming. Sarah wore dark jeans with a grey hoodie, carrying a six-pack of Coors Light in her arms. Lexi had two large white plastic bags that strained against the containers they held. A large red symbol on the bag told Liz it was Chinese food.

"Hey, Lizzie! Lexi and I thought it might be fun to bring over the awful take-out your mother-in-law refused to let in the house. Then maybe we can grab some ice cream after ... if you're up for it."

Liz backed up enough to let Sarah and Lexi enter the house. They both kicked off their shoes and pushed into the kitchen with Liz following close behind.

"We actually just ordered pizza!"

Sarah dropped the case of beer on the counter of the kitchen island before turning to Liz.

"With your boys, there's never too much food," she said with a laugh.

Lexi dropped the bags on the counter in front of Sarah, who instantly started pulling things out of the bags and opening the containers on the kitchen countertop.

"Why don't you grab plates, and we can dine on our first course of Chinese food? Pizza can be course number two. Lexi, go tell the boys we have food in here."

Lexi walked through the kitchen to enter the living room while Liz pulled down a stack of plates from the cupboard, placing them near the food. She then pulled out serving spoons and forks, following Sarah around the kitchen, placing one in each of the food containers as she went.

"Chinese! Awesome. Did you happen to grab those awesome egg rolls, Aunt Sarah?" Alex asked as he rounded the kitchen island to grab a plate.

"What about those dumplings? And where's the pizza?" Carson complained, looking through the containers.

Liz wrapped her arm around her best friend and squeezed her. They both looked at each other and laughed as the kitchen grew noisier.

Chapter 23

- Serafine -

Serafine managed to keep herself busy for the entire day. Avoiding the hospital and the phone in her apartment, she had spent most of her time in malls, the library, coffee shops, and finally the grocery store. Carrying two bags of groceries and one bag with a stack of romance novels, her shoulders ached from the weight. Although she was only a fifteen-minute walk from her apartment, the sidewalks were wet, and she didn't think her body could carry everything all the way there. It was also getting dark; her typical dinnertime had already passed.

I'll take the bus. That's what an unlimited bus pass is for anyway.

She hurried to the nearest bus stop that would take her in the direction of her home. A cold, wet breeze hit her face and sent chills down her back.

"It's sure cold tonight," she muttered.

Bundling her knee-length, purple jacket around her neck, she was grateful to see the bench at the bus stop light up before she was close enough to sit down. The bus pulled up to the curb, so she wouldn't have to wait in the damp cold. As she waddled closer, the door slid open. The bus hissed as it settled into waiting for her to board. She placed one foot up onto the step, the warm air of the bus inviting her in.

"Good evening, miss. You look like you had a good shopping day."

"Oh ... yes ... well, I was out and about, and I needed a few things," she replied, smiling up at the bus driver as she lugged her bags up the few steps.

He was wearing a navy uniform with a white label on the sweater's sleeve. White, wispy hair framed his face, and his dark brown eyes shined from behind a crowd of wrinkles as he grinned at her. Serafine swiped her card and sat down in the closest seat to the front before the door closed and the bus pulled away. Shifting her purse onto her lap and the bags onto the floor, she leaned her head onto the cold glass of the nearby window and closed her eyes. The vibrations shook her brain in her skull as the rumbling engine moved her closer to home. Her muscles relaxed as she sighed, relieved to settle into the cushioned seat.

The bus turned down a street, making her lean in her seat. She looked out the window. It was already hers.

I must have nodded off!

Reaching up, she pulled the string above the window to alert the driver that her stop was next. As the bus pulled up to the curb near her apartment building, Serafine shifted her bags onto her shoulders and arms the best she could before pulling herself up with her right hand gripping the nearby bar. The bag on her left shoulder shifted, almost falling off. Nearly losing her balance, she gripped the bar tighter to keep herself upright.

"Are you alright there, miss? Do you need help?" a voice called from behind her.

Once steady, Serafine let go and lifted the strap of the bag back into place before looking over her shoulder toward the direction of the voice. A young man was getting up from his seat in the middle of the bus. An earbud dangled over his jacket collar as he came down the aisle toward her. He wore a black hoodie under a jean jacket. The hood was up over his head and his black backpack was left abandoned on the seat beside where he had been sitting.

Serafine put up a hand to stop him, "No, no. I'm alright. Thank you."

Shuffling her feet toward the front of the bus, a cold wind whistled through the already open door. She shivered, pausing by the driver before taking the steps down toward the sidewalk, moving slowly to be sure of her footing. She could feel the eyes of both the bus driver and the young man watching her closely. When she was finally on the curb and away from the bus, she turned to see the door still open and the bus driver watching her.

"Thank you for the ride," she called back as she shuffled away, waving her hand at him to go.

"Are you sure? I can wait here a moment to make sure you make it inside."

"No, don't be silly. I'll be fine. I live right there," she said as she motioned to the nearest building.

"Alright, have a good night, Miss."

The door squealed shut, and Serafine watched as it pulled away from the curb, her gaze shifting to the young man in the middle of the bus. He was back in his seat with his earbud back in his ear. She smiled at him as he passed, his eyes never leaving hers until he was out of sight.

Nice young man, she smiled to herself.

With the bus turning out of view at the end of the street, she shuffled towards her building. The sidewalk looked shiny. A thin layer of ice covered the path between her and her door.

Damn winter. The wet sidewalks freeze too fast once that sun goes down.

She was surprised the local community hadn't already put salt out. The area she moved into was usually thoughtful and on top of things like that. It was normally well-kept and clean. Thankfully, the bus stop was only two buildings down from her front door, so she pushed her bare hands down into her jacket pockets, leaning slightly to ensure the bags on her shoulder wouldn't slide off. She shuffled her feet like a penguin to make sure she wouldn't slip. Tipping her chin down into the collar of her jacket, she tried to keep most of her skin covered from the cold wind ripping between the tall buildings. As soon as the warm air rushed over her in the foyer of her building, she sighed in relief. She felt older tonight, like the stress of Stan's predicament had aged her another ten years. She moved through the lobby, past the small, empty desk that usually had a security guard, to the elevators on the far back wall. She pushed the 'up' button and then stood watching the numbers on the digital screen above the doors slowly tick down from the tenth floor. She let her bags drop to the floor beside her feet while she waited.

A flicker of movement out of the corner of her eye surprised her. She hadn't noticed anyone else in the lobby. She turned to smile at whoever was standing nearby, but no one was there. Searching around the small area, she was still alone. Two empty black leather chairs against the far wall, with a small table in between, showed no sign of recent use. The desk on the opposite wall was still empty. While peering around the room, the reflection in the glass windows of the front doors caught her attention. Something about it looked off. She could see herself in the reflection from across the lobby, but nothing else. The reflection was dark behind her as if she were standing in front of a large, empty void.

The ding of the elevator startled her, making her spin back to face it too quickly. Dizziness washed over her, making the edges of the elevator blur even though it was only a few feet in front of her. She gripped her forehead with her hand as the doors slid open. Leaning onto the side of the opening, she picked up her bags and stepped in, letting the bags drop again as soon as she crossed the threshold. Using the handles on the walls of the elevator, she slowly turned to face the lobby, backing up until her back pushed up against the railing at the back. The doors remained open as if waiting for someone to enter. Serafine felt her stomach flip. Something felt wrong.

Oh, for goodness' sake, she scolded herself. *I forgot to push the button. That's all.*

She stepped her right foot forward, careful to hold onto the railing. She pushed the button for the eighth floor and then returned to the back wall. The doors still didn't close.

"Well let's go," she said, leaning forward a second time to jab at the close door button.

The doors finally started to slide shut. She leaned back, sighing with relief. Just as the elevator doors were only a foot apart, a woman with wild, black, curly hair ran by the opening. The doors shut before Serafine could get a good look. She shook her head as the elevator rose.

Now who the blazes was that? Someone was out there with me.

She shifted her gaze to watch the red digital numbers increasing on the right of the doors. As the elevator neared her floor, the changing numbers slowed until they paused on the number eight. Her floor. She was happy to be almost home. She couldn't wait for the safety of her apartment.

As soon as the doors opened wide enough, she picked up her bags and shimmied out into the hallway. The warm beige walls and burgundy carpet were inviting, but a chill passed down her back. She still didn't feel safe, from what she wasn't sure. Dragging some of her bags on the floor behind her, she turned to her right, shuffling quickly to the last door on the left, room 813. Her apartment. She pulled her keys from her jacket pocket and fumbled with the lock for a moment. Three knocks echoed from down the hall. Looking over her shoulder, a shadow quickly hid around the corner at the end.

Someone was watching her.

While still watching the spot where the shadowy head had disappeared, she continued to fiddle with the lock. The hairs on the back of her neck rose. She could feel eyes watching her, but the hall remained empty. The click of the lock opening prompted her to quickly turn the door handle and rush into the apartment. As soon as she was through, she pushed the door with her hip, closing it with her weight, and clicked the deadbolt back into place.

Serafine kept her hand still on the deadbolt and let go of her bags completely, letting them drop to the ground. Looking up at the sliding chain that she rarely used, she picked it up and slid it into place. Feeling better from the extra protection of the door, she removed her jacket and wet shoes and placed them in the closet on the right. The entryway was small, with the same dark wood flooring that spread throughout the entire apartment. The black carpet she had rolled out to prevent water and salt from the outside world was spotless except for the fresh wet spots from her shoes. Slowly, she leaned into the door to peer through the small peephole into the hall. It was empty. Serafine exhaled.

Okay, whatever it was, I'm safe in here. Maybe tea will calm my nerves.

She picked up her grocery bags before moving into the kitchen, leaving the bag of books by the door. She lifted the grocery bags onto the grey counter near the sink on the island before turning to flick the switch on the bottom of the water kettle against the wall. The small clear button glared red as the elements in the kettle turned on. Turning back to her bags, she pulled out each of the groceries and began putting them away.

Something banged on the wall in her living room, startling her. An apple slipped from her hand, falling to the floor, and rolled out of the kitchen under her small dining table nearby. She shifted her gaze over the island into the living room. She could see her reflection in the dark glass of the window on the other side of the apartment.

"Damn it," she muttered.

She scanned her eyes back over the living room space one more time. She could hear the muffled sounds of her neighbour's television through the wall.

Okay, it's just the neighbour. Now calm yourself.

Walking over to the table, she bent down and grabbed the apple. She turned and placed it into the fruit bowl on her kitchen counter. The click from the kettle indicated the hot water was ready, so she shifted to grab a mug from the cupboard above. Then she opened the drawer below to pull out a chamomile teabag. She ripped it open, dropping it into her red mug before grabbing the kettle and pouring hot water over it. Steam rose from the mug as the water filled it until it reached the top and threatened to overflow. As the tea steeped, Serafine turned back to look at the living room. Usually, she wasn't so jumpy, as the neighbours banged the walls regularly and it never bothered her before.

Everything going on with Stan must be making me extra sensitive. I need to relax.

Standing up straight and taking a deep breath, she moved toward her bedroom to change into something warm and comfortable. As she reached into the room to turn on the light switch, an electric current passed through her arm. All the hairs on her body stood up at attention, as if warning her to prepare for flight.

Someone was standing in the middle of the room.

Their outline was barely visible in the dark space, but she could sense them. She flicked on the light switch, prepared to turn and run, but the room was empty. She blinked her eyes again, sure of what she saw, but no one was there.

Could I be seeing things? Or did something follow me home?

'Careful dear,' her mother's voice warned in her mind.

Shaking her head, she took a deep breath and walked into the room, doing her best to brush it off. The temperature of the space was a few degrees cooler than the kitchen.

It could just be the heat on the fritz ...

Walking to her dresser against the far wall, she pulled open the top drawer to search for her warmest pyjamas.

Hot tea, warm pyjamas, and maybe some hot soup. That's what will make me feel better.

Even as she assured herself, the hairs on the back of her neck rose. She couldn't shake the feeling that she wasn't alone in the empty room. Someone, or something, was watching her.

Chapter 24

- Stan -

Stan huddled in a ball on the cold, hard ground. Tormenting roars erupted from the mass of shadows circling him. They wouldn't stop bombarding him. He covered his ears tightly with his hands, squeezing his eyes shut, trying to prevent them from penetrating his skull. Their growls and mumbles were unrecognizable, but he was certain the fear that overtook his body was exactly what they wanted. He hummed the song that had become his only comfort in this dark realm. The melody reminded him of the woman that could save him. The memory of her hair and eyes blurred around the edges over time since he last heard her voice. He was worried that soon he would forget her entirely. He assumed that his memory slipping was why he was in this place to begin with. Something must have happened in the other world for his mind to become a jumbled mess. Something that forced his soul to be trapped here.

Suddenly, the atmosphere around him shifted. The menacing voices stopped. The world didn't seem so dark, as light penetrated his eyelids. He carefully opened one eye. Bright, beautiful colours splashed across the sky above.

"Good morning, Stan."

It's her! She's here!

Stan stood up to stare into the sky. Electricity coursed through his body. The ground was still sticky like tar, but her presence made him feel lighter already. The creatures were nowhere in sight.

"Can you believe it's Saturday again already?" she continued. "Alex, Carson, and Jack are here to see you, too."

He closed his eyes as he became enveloped in the loving caress of her voice. He could feel a cord wrapped within his chest pull tight. He focused on that sensation and felt himself starting to lift, but his feet still tugged at the tar-like substance on the ground. A sensation of fingers stroked his right hand. He opened his eyes slightly to check, but nothing was there. Not in this realm.

She must be holding my hand.

That touch strengthened the connection he felt with her. He raised his right hand above his head, feeling himself being pulled up into the bright colourful sky above him. She continued talking, but he didn't concentrate on the words. Getting free of this world was too important. The longer he stayed, the more likely he may become trapped forever. As he rose, the tar-like fingers gripping his feet loosened. Finally, his feet broke free of the last snare, and his upward momentum increased.

A scream erupted below, nearly breaking his concentration on her touch, her voice. He glanced down at the ground. Four long, black tentacles emerged from the ground and were reaching for his feet.

"No!" he yelled, kicking at them while trying to keep his concentration on the connection in his chest.

He looked back up at the sky, hoping he could rise faster. The screaming below was deep, heavy – something wasn't happy about his leaving.

Don't let them sidetrack you. Stay focused, he coached himself, keeping his eyes above. Then he closed them, letting the woman's force pull him towards the sky.

Yes, please ... get me out of here.

As he moved into the clouds, the brightness of the sky dulled. He opened his eyes, careful not to lose concentration on her physical touch. The colours in the sky had faded. Now, he was moving into a dark tunnel. A tube slowly squeezed around his entire body, keeping his arm stuck reaching above. Flashes of light passed by as he continued to rise. Small, star-like flares sparkled in the distance, as though the tube was invisible and he was passing through a dimension of outer space, trying to break back into the earthly realm.

What is happening?

With his arm still stretched out above him, the tunnel squeezed snugly against his shoulders, waist, and legs. He continued to be pulled forward. The stars became lines of light streaming by. The sound of her voice was faint against a loud whooshing that surrounded him. It reminded him of a massive waterfall. The noise was almost deafening. He squirmed to reach his other hand to his ears, but it was no use. The tunnel was too tight.

A bright light suddenly broke out in front of him, at what Stan hoped would be the end of the tunnel. It was quickly growing and becoming brighter as he sped straight towards it. He squeezed his eyes shut, trying to tilt his head down away from the light as it became large and blinding. At first, he worried he was headed for the real, burning sun.

At least I'm not where the creatures are anymore. I guess this is the end.

He braced himself, but the heat never came.

Instead, he broke free of the confines of the tunnel and erupted into the brightness, like a child suddenly birthed from the confines and darkness of its mother's womb. He fell onto the floor of a cold, white space. The light was too much. His eyes burned behind his eyelids. Bringing his hands up to cover his face, he tried to stand on the new ground below his feet.

Using his hands to act like a roof over his eyes, he looked around the new space he had landed in, but he couldn't see clearly. There were massive, white lights glaring down at him from overhead, enveloping the room in the blinding glare. The floor was no longer sticky beneath his feet. He was free to move around. The whooshing sound had stopped, replaced by silence.

"Mom, can I go find a vending machine? I'm hungry."

The voice, although recognizable, boomed in Stan's ears. It was excruciatingly loud. He quickly shifted his hands from covering his eyes to covering his ears. The sound caused painful vibrations in his head. He backed away from the noise until he felt a solid wall behind him. He continued to back away along the solid barrier, now with his eyes closed and hands covering his ears until he reached a corner where the wall met a second. Curling himself down into a seated position, he covered his entire head with his hands and arms, hiding his eyes and ears from the terrifying new space that surrounded him.

What is this place? What sort of hell did I get pulled into now?

Chapter 25

- Liz -

"Alex, I swear you have a hollow leg. You're always hungry."

Liz let go of Stan's hand to reach for her purse on the floor beside her chair. She rummaged through the bottom feeling for her wallet. Pulling it out, she opened it to slide her credit card out of its slot and handed it to Alex. He immediately stood up from where he sat against the wall on the floor.

"Here. Take your brothers with you. I assume they're hungry, too."

Carson and Jack immediately looked up from the tablets they had brought to the hospital. Although she didn't like it, the boys were willing to stay for longer visits when they had something to do.

"Thanks, Mom."

The boys rushed out of the room together, leaving her alone with Stan. Dropping her purse back to the floor, she returned her attention to him, grasping his right hand in both of hers. Before the boys had interrupted, she thought she had felt a faint grip of Stan's fingers around hers. Initially, a scream of excitement bubbled up, but she stifled it back down before it made it past her lips. She wasn't sure if she imagined it, so she didn't want to excite the boys. Now, with the boys out of the room, she willed Stan to grip her hand again. She closed her eyes to focus on the sensation of his skin against hers.

"Please, Stan, do it again."

A few minutes passed, the only sound was the ticking of the clock on the wall. Finally, she sighed.

Maybe it was another involuntary thing.

Stan's hand remained limp in her grasp. She opened her eyes and looked imploringly at his face, wishing for any sign.

"Stan, we all miss you so much. We can't wait for you to come home. It's just not the same without you. Whenever you're ready to get out of here, just let me know."

Liz smiled slightly. The minutes slowly ticked by, but she remained crouched over the side of Stan's bed, her hands gripping his while watching his face. Her body ached from the curve of her back. Her mind drifted to the boys, who should be returning from the vending machines down the hall any minute. Releasing Stan's hand, she stood and pushed her hands to stretch her lower back, willing her now stiff muscles to move. The door handle shook. She turned to face the boys as they entered, but the door didn't open. The long silver handle slowly turned again, until it reached the halfway point before being released.

Maybe their hands are full.

Walking to the door, she pushed the handle down to open it fully. There was no one standing at the door. She stepped out of the room, holding the door open with her outstretched arm behind her, looking up and down the hall. It was empty. There was no sign of the boys or the nurse.

Weird.

She moved back to sit back down in her seat. The door clicked closed behind her. The handle jiggled again, this time with more force.

Okay, seriously.

As she turned to look at it, a loud bang rattled the door.

"What the fuck?" Liz jumped up angrily, thinking the boys were playing tricks on her. As she reached out for the door handle, another hard bang made the door vibrate violently in the frame, making her pull her hand back against her chest in surprise.

"What the hell are you guys doing?" she said, panic rising as uncertainty came over her.

Who else could it be?

As she reached for the door handle, her heart thudded loudly in her ears. Carson's voice broke the brief silence. He was getting closer. She opened the door to scold the boys, but they were still a few feet down the hall, Jack leading the way. She peered down the hall in the other direction, expecting to see someone walking away, but it was still empty. There was no sign of the nurse or other hospital guests anywhere. The hairs on the back of her neck rose as chills passed down her back. Then the boys were in front of her, pausing to give her a quizzical look. She turned her attention back to them, putting a smile back on her face.

"I sure hope you didn't cause any problems for the hospital staff while you were gone," she said, stepping back to let the boys enter the room.

Alex walked into the room last holding up her card. "Nah, we didn't even see anyone. Here's your C-C."

Liz smiled, putting her credit card into the back pocket of her jeans. "Thanks, Alex."

The boys settled back down on the floor against the wall, content to eat their vending machine haul and stare at their tablets. She examined the hall one more time. Still empty. Shrugging off the uneasy feeling, she turned back to her chair, this time leaning back to relax her sore muscles. She reached over to Stan's arm with her left hand, rubbing it lightly. His coarse hair was rough against her palm. She returned to watching his face while listening to the boys, hoping their familiar energy would usher a response from Stan.

This continued for thirty minutes before Jack stood up in front of Liz. He leaned against the side of Stan's bed, facing her.

"Mom, it's cold in here. And I keep feeling like something is touching my leg. It's creeping me out. Can we go?"

She looked down at her watch. "Oh wow, it's already been an hour." She let go of Stan's arm and reached for Jack's hand. "Sure, we can go. I'm sure your Dad enjoyed having us for a visit. How about we stop for lunch on the way back?".

Jack smiled and squeezed her hand back. "Yeah, lunch would be good."

"Okay, let's go."

Carson remained huddled over his tablet with Alex watching over his shoulder. They both avoided Liz's gaze, focusing on whatever game was on the screen.

"Carson, turn that off now. We're going home. Get your jackets on and say goodbye to your Dad on your way out. Just wait for me in the hallway please."

She stood up, gently guiding Jack towards their jackets piled on the floor in the corner. Carson still didn't move. Once Liz reached out for the tablet, however, Carson handed it over with an eye roll before standing up to join his brothers who were already getting ready to leave.

Alex walked to Stan's bed first, touching Stan's hand briefly while uttering a small, "Bye, Dad."

Carson mimicked his older brother, but Jack leaned over to lay across Stan in an attempted hug, saying, "See you, Dad. I hope you feel better soon."

The boys then all moved into the hallway, where they stood waiting for Liz. As the door closed slowly behind them, she could hear an argument start over where to stop for lunch. She smiled before turning back to Stan.

"They miss you, Stan. They may not show it very well, but I can tell. The hospital is still a little scary for them. They aren't used to seeing you like this, so hurry up and get better. I'll come back tomorrow. I love you."

She grasped his hand one last time, waiting for a moment, hoping for even the slightest squeeze of his fingers back. Finally, she let go and turned her back on Stan, moving out into the hallway and letting the door close behind her without looking back, unaware of Stan's eyes suddenly opening behind her and slowly turning to watch her walk out of the hospital room.

Chapter 26

- Stan -

As the door clicked shut, silence enveloped Stan. He was grateful for the end to the deafening voices. He huddled in the corner of the room, covering his ears with his hands and squeezing his eyes shut against the brightness. Although the voices were familiar, they were too loud and hard to understand. After a few minutes, another click rang across the room. Everything beyond his closed eyelids went dark. The blinding overhead lights were off. He slowly opened his eyes and dropped his hands from covering his head. His eyes slowly adjusted to the dim space. Everything was blurry, but a dim, orange glow from the opposite wall didn't bother his eyes as much, allowing him to take in his new surroundings.

He slowly stood, using the wall as leverage. It felt strange being in such a small, enclosed space after spending so much time in the vast, empty world he had awoken in. An electrical humming came from objects against the far wall. Although still blurry, a shiny square object sat on his left, approximately the height of his hip. Stan reached out to touch it, but his hand passed through it. Leaning closer, he realized the shiny material was the metal arm of a chair. He tried again to touch it. This time, his hand stopped on the cool metal. It was hard and strong against his fingers. He tried to push against it, but it didn't budge. Putting all his weight into it, he crouched over and placed both hands on the arm of the chair, pushing against it with all his strength. Nothing happened. The chair was immovable. Confused, he gave up and shifted towards the larger object in the center of the room, closer to the electronic noises.

It slowly became clearer as he approached. It was a bed with plastic rails on all sides. He looked over towards the beeping and humming sounds, his eyesight finally adjusting to this new realm. The machine beside the bed came into focus. It was a heart monitor.

This must be a hospital room.

He grasped the railing at the foot of the bed as he continued to review the room. Curtains hung on the ceiling behind him near a door. A second chair sat angled towards the bed on the left side. The floor on the right side of the bed was empty of furniture. Stan looked down at his hands where they gripped the hard plastic railing. The bed had a blue blanket wrapped tightly around the bottom of the mattress. Someone was lying in it. He was not alone in the room. He lifted his gaze towards the head of the bed, his eyes coming to rest on the person's face.

You look familiar.

He loosened his grip on the frame of the bed and walked around to the right side. As he came closer, the features of the face became clearer. He fell backwards onto the hard floor.

"That's my face!" he yelled out in shock.

From his seated position on the floor, he tried to make sense of where he was. Then, as curiosity took over, he slowly stood back up. This time, he wrapped his arms around his body before moving closer to the bedside, near the head of the body that lay in the bed. He looked down at the face, recognizing the open, brown eyes and the wavy hair as his own. His hair was longer than he remembered, and there was rough stubble on his face that was normally clean-shaven.

But it's my face.

Stan looked down at the familiar body on the bed, the chest rising and falling with each breath. He recognized the arms lying on top of the blankets. He rubbed his own as his eyes moved down towards the hands resting on the top of the blankets. When he reached the left hand on the bed with his eyes, he looked down at his own left hand, holding it only inches away from the one on the bed to compare the two. Other than the bonier look of the hand on the bed, they were identical. Both bore similar scars and moles along the back, with black, coarse hair starting at the wrist and going up the arm. He reached out to touch the hand on the bed where it lay. As soon as his finger touched the skin, a shock coursed through his body, causing him to recoil away from the edge of the bed. The body on the bed also twitched, responding to the jolt of electricity that passed between them.

This is all too bizarre. I need to get out of here.

Stan turned to walk to the door on the other side of the room. He reached out his hand, wrapping his fingers around the metal door handle. Like the chair, the cool metal felt hard in his hand, but he could not move it. Placing his right hand over his left, he pushed down harder. It didn't shift an inch. None of this made any sense. He looked back towards his body lying on the bed, shrinking away from it. He didn't want to be in this room anymore. There had to be a way out.

He raised his hands and pulled his fingers through his hair, trying to decide what to do next. Dropping his hands back to his side, he resigned to walk back to the chair near the back of the room. He gave it one more shove, but it remained still. Giving up, he dropped into it and stared at his physical body in the bed.

I guess I have to wait.

He didn't have to wait long. Within the hour, a woman in a white coat walked in. She had porcelain skin and long blonde hair pulled back into a neat, tight bun at the base of her scalp. The woman held a clipboard in her hand and a black stethoscope hung around her neck, the silver end shining in the glare of the overhead lights. Stan realized she must be his doctor. As she moved to check his body's vitals, he watched from the chair. She worked quietly, periodically humming a song he didn't recognize.

After checking the machinery hooked to his body, the doctor dropped her clipboard on the foot of the bed. She looked over at his face on the pillow, leaning her right thigh lightly on the bed's railing, as if contemplating something. Then, she slowly turned to pull the blankets up and exposed one of the body's feet to the air. She ran the bottom of the pen up the sole of the exposed foot. Stan's physical body didn't respond, but Stan, in his ethereal form, could feel a strange sensation at the bottom of his right foot as he watched.

The doctor considered this for a moment and then said, "Stan, if you can hear me, my name is Dr. Bractor. I'm going to try something different. You might feel a small pinch."

She pulled out a small and white package from her pocket. She gripped the top of it and pulled it apart, exposing a thin needle. Pulling the needle from the packaging, she briefly looked at the sharp tip before she bent and pushed it into the bottom of the body's heel.

"Son of a bitch!" Stan yelled as an electric jolt shot up his leg from his right foot.

His physical foot also jerked on the bed.

"Good, Stan!" Dr. Bractor exclaimed. "That's what I want to see!"

She smiled down at his body as she wrapped the needle back into the plastic and dropped it into a large, bright yellow container hanging on the wall near the door. She moved back to the bed and pushed his physical foot back under the blanket, ignoring the small droplet of blood that had formed on the heel. Once his foot was covered and the blankets tucked back under the mattress, she picked up her clipboard and wrote something down, smiling. Then she looked over at Stan's body, letting the clipboard drop to her side.

"Keep up the good work, Stan. I'll be back later."

With that, she turned and left the room, flipping the light switch off as she went, sending the room back into the orange glow. Stan leaned back in the chair, gripping his sore foot with both of his hands. He glanced at the bulge of his physical foot under the blue blanket.

Hopefully feeling pain is a good sign. Maybe it won't be difficult to reconnect with my body. But how?

He stood up and began pacing along the foot of the bed.

Why didn't I reconnect the instant I was back in this realm? What more do I need to do?

He didn't want to leave the room in case the woman who saved him returned. As he paced, he wondered if others like him might be wandering the hospital. If there were other spirits, or whatever he was, perhaps they could help him understand this strange, ethereal existence he was trapped in. He stopped pacing to glance at the door.

A small break from the hospital room might be worthwhile. I won't stay away long. In case she comes back.

Since he knew he wouldn't be able to open the door, he turned his thoughts to how he could get out of the room. The doctor never pulled the door closed behind her. Instead, she had let it close slowly on its own. Perhaps he could sneak out the open door during the next visit by a nurse or doctor. Walking over to the wall closest to the door, he crouched into a half-seated position, ready to jump out of the room the next time it opened.

He didn't realize just how long he would have to wait.

Chapter 27

- Serafine -

Serafine enjoyed a quiet Saturday. She was grateful the only phone calls she received were from her two sons checking on her. Neither the hospital nor Liz called.

Perhaps she is ignoring my message. Or maybe she hasn't listened to it yet.

Either way, Serafine was going to enjoy the quiet while she could. Something told her it wouldn't last long. The weather outside grew colder, so she spent most of her time in her apartment. She ventured out once in the late morning to walk to a nearby park, just to get some movement in. The cool, wet air made her body ache, so she didn't stay out long. Instead, she busied herself with laundry and cleaning the small space. As it neared six o'clock, her apartment was the cleanest it had been all week, and her laundry was washed, dried, and put away.

Maybe I'll get into my pyjamas early and watch some tele-vision while I eat a light supper.

Walking into her bedroom, she flicked on the light. The energy in the room was electric, making her hair stand on end. Her thoughts returned to the shadow figure she had thought was in the room the night before. Her gaze passed over the room, but no one was there, not even a shadow creature. She was alone, even if it didn't feel like it. Then her gaze stopped on her closet door propped open a few inches.

Did I forget to close that when I hung up my clean clothes? She contemplated, moving across the room to close it.

Something shiny in the upper corner of the shelf inside caught her attention. As she got closer, she realized it was the silver lock on a box glinting. She carefully reached up to pull the box down, shifting years of dust that had settled around it. It had been her mother's. Serafine originally placed it on that shelf almost ten years ago, when she first moved into this apartment, shortly after her youngest, Michael, had moved out of their family home. The house was too big and too empty without her boys.

The weight of the box was almost too much for her as she pulled it into her arms, just about losing her balance. It was heavier than she remembered. She carefully blew at the dust while shifting her face away from the particles forced into the air from her breath. Walking with her head tilted away from the dust, Serafine moved to the dresser against the opposite wall. She carefully placed the box down, making sure all edges of it were safely on the top shelf. She slid it sideways, so the lock was facing her.

The key. Where's the key?

She walked to open the drawer of her nightstand by her bed. Reaching in, she felt around the bottom of the drawer, her fingers searching for the feel of the small metal key. A thud came from the living room, louder than the ones from the day before, making her jump. Her arm stung instantly thanks to a long scratch left by a stray sliver of wood sticking out the top of the drawer. Her quick movement caused her to slide against the sliver. She looked down at the thin, red mark along her forearm. Tiny droplets of blood seeped from the shallow scratch.

"Now what is making all that noise?"

Rubbing at her arm with her other hand, she closed the drawer. Leaving the dusty box on the dresser, she moved back to the closet and pulled out a long, rose-pink nightgown, quickly changing out of her scrubs. Then she pulled down her thin, yellow housecoat from where it hung on the back of the bedroom door. The cloth of the long sleeves made her arm sting slightly, so she absent-mindedly rubbed at it. Walking through to the living room, she flicked on the lamp by her chair. She didn't notice a tall, dark shadow on her bedroom door frame reflected in one of the windows by her chair. Instead, she looked down at a book lying on the floor by her feet. The book she had been reading the night before had fallen to the floor.

Maybe that's the bang I heard. It must have been just far enough on the edge to finally fall off. Or something is trying to get my attention ...

Serafine bent down to pick it up, careful to bend at her knees so as not to hurt her back. As she stood up, her gaze moved to the window. Her eyes focused on the doorframe of her bedroom and the hairs on the back of her neck rose, but she wasn't sure why. Shrugging her shoulders, she dropped the book on the small table tray beside her reclining chair. She picked up the remote from the same table and turned the television on to the Women's Network. Then she turned back toward the kitchen. As she passed by the nearby bookshelf, a memory overcame her. It was another from the day she moved in. She recalled unpacking a few books that she had kept of her mother's. She had placed them along the bottom shelf of the bookcase, thinking that she likely would never read them anyway. Slowly kneeling on the floor, she looked along the spines of the books.

A deep purple notebook at the far end caught her eye. It felt familiar. Without any thought, she pulled the notebook from the shelf. Opening the front flap, the scent of lavender surrounded her. Her mother had always smelled like lavender. She closed her eyes and let the scent envelop her, warmth from the memories of her mother filling her body. Finally, she looked down at the pages and saw her mother's handwriting. It looked like one of her mother's spell books. Placing her free hand on the arm of her chair, she pulled herself back to standing. She left the book on top of the romance book she'd just picked up; it would be nice to sift through it while she ate.

Moving to the kitchen, she prepared a small tuna sandwich on a whole wheat dinner bun with a side of raw carrots and celery. She laid the meal out on a white plate before turning to make a cup of tea. While moving around the kitchen, her thoughts returned to the small box of items that belonged to her mother.

Perhaps there is something in there to bring me some peace of mind. In case these shadows turn out to be a larger bother than I realize.

Not that she wanted to believe it, but her instincts insisted that something dark had been watching her after sending Liz a warning. Wondering where she may have put the key, she hoped to return to it and review the items later that evening.

Serafine picked up her plate and mug before shuffling into the living room to place both on the tray table by the books before sitting in the reclining chair. A tingling sensation crawled down the back of her neck. It felt like someone was watching her. From her seat, she passed her gaze over the room. Nothing was out of the ordinary. As she turned to look out the window beside her, a dark mass moved in the corner of her eye making her gaze dart to the reflection of her bedroom doorway. She had thought she saw someone standing there, but the doorframe was empty now. She paused, watching the reflection silently for a moment. She didn't notice she was holding her breath.

"Oh, for heaven's sake. You're letting your mind play tricks on you! Let it go," she scolded herself loudly.

Pulling the small tray table closer to the front corner of her chair, she picked up the tea mug. Carefully sipping at the hot liquid, she settled in to watch the television. As she placed the mug back onto the tray table, her mother's notebook fell to the floor. Serafine sighed loudly, trying to shift around the tray table to see where the book landed without spilling her tea. It had fallen onto its spine, the pages spread open. A sketch of the black creature from her dream looked up from its pages. A feeling of knowing spread across her. The sketch included the long, jagged fangs and drool dripping from its chin. Although the sketch was black and white, she could see the greenish tinge in her mind's eye.

My mother has seen these things before?

She reached down and carefully picked up the book with one hand, holding it open to the current page. Forgetting about the television show, she read her mother's notes as she snacked on the food beside her.

***

After reading through quite a few pages, an ache in Serafine's lower back made her wince. She reached down in between her body and the soft, cushy back of the recliner to rub it. Looking up from the notebook to the clock hanging on the wall, she realized over an hour had passed. Pulling her hand away from her back, she picked up the remote from the tray table and hit the red button on the top. The television faded to black, and the apartment was quiet. Even the sound of the neighbour's television was gone. She usually didn't mind the quiet, but tonight the silence wasn't relaxing, it was suspicious. Especially after reading the pages in her mother's notebook about the creatures from her dream. The silent apartment no longer felt safe.

In the pages she'd read, she learned that her mother had helped people overcome these creatures before. If what her mother had written was true, the creatures from Serafine's dream weren't the ones to be afraid of. Those creatures were simply the minions of something much more dangerous and powerful. Reading through the passages, Serafine learned that the beings that controlled the lesser minions could not enter the human realm without a host body. The host body had to be weak, either through illness or the soul's tether to the body had to be in a weakened state. The creatures that Serafine saw in her dream were able to cross the dimensional boundaries, but they were weaker in the human realm, typically going unseen like a shadow in the corner of your eye. They could only influence objects, disguising themselves as poltergeists to the untrained medium. She shook her head.

Turning the page, there was a final entry in her mother's handwriting. Serafine gasped when she read the date on the top of the page. Her mother had written this note on the same day she had died.

My dearest Serafine,

I'm so sorry. I never thought it would come to this, but you need to know the truth.

If you have found this, it may already be too late, but I have to try. I fear that I am not long for this world. I've been involved in a private order for the past few years. We've been tasked with preventing the dark beings from the previous pages from entering our world. I have tried to keep you shielded from this life, as I don't want this to fall on your shoulders. It is not an easy life to live, and I fear for my grandbabies' safety. I have shrouded you all in the strongest protection spell I know. I have also dipped this notebook into a potion that will keep your protection strong. Please, keep this book somewhere close. Never get rid of it. There's too much at stake. They're closing in around me now, but they haven't found you. They can't see in our world, but once they have your scent, it's too late.

It's too late for me now.

If these creatures have found you, you must find the gris-gris. The gris-gris will hide you from their scent, allowing you to get away. I have made three for you and the boys. Once you are hidden, find someone to re-administer the protection spell. I have included a list of the names of people I trust in the back of this notebook. Call them only if necessary. They may already be compromised, but I hope one of them can help you.

Stay safe, baby girl. Don't face these creatures yourself. Get away from them as fast as you can. I'm sorry I won't be there for you anymore. Know that I am proud of you. I always have been.

I love you.

Forever, Your Mama

A tear fell down Serafine's cheek as she gently closed the notebook. Lifting it to her face, she breathed in the scent of her mother one more time.

Could this be really what's happening? Have these creatures found me?

Placing her hands on the arms of the recliner, she rocked her body forward onto her feet. She winced again as the ache in her lower back complained. Rubbing at it, she leaned back to stretch out fully. Placing the notebook down on the seat of her chair, she backed away from it slightly.

At least the boys are far from here. But what am I going to do?

Chapter 28

- Stan -

Hours passed in the hospital room. Though Stan was grateful for being back in the realm with his body, he didn't appreciate the obvious passing of time. The tick-tock of the clock in the room seemed to echo. He remained crouched by the door, listening to movement in the hallway when it came, but it always passed by. Periodically, shadows would pause in front of his door. He would suck in his breath, sure the door was finally going to open, only for the shadows to move away.

Where are the nurses? Or the doctor? She said she would come back.

Although he hadn't spent much time in this new realm yet, it seemed strange that it had been so long since anyone checked on him. Finally, he grew frustrated and bored of watching the doorknob, so he stood and returned to pacing at the end of the bed. The orange glow from the light above made shadows form in the dips and hollows of his physical body's face. He tried to avoid looking directly at his body, worried that it might move on its own if he stared too long. Instead, he concentrated on the curtains bunched up against the wall. They were white with two thin blue horizontal stripes along the bottom. They weren't long enough to touch the floor but hung to the height of his knees.

Maybe I can move a simple curtain, he thought, reaching out to grip the edge.

Although he felt the fabric between his fingers, it wouldn't shift. No matter how hard he pulled, the fabric felt like it was made of steel instead of cotton.

Why can't I move anything in this world?

He threw up his arms in frustration, running his hands through his hair. Turning, he returned to pacing, his hands on his head, wondering how he would ever be able to make anyone aware of his existence if he couldn't even move a simple curtain.

A bang from behind made him spin around.

He wasn't sure where it came from. The orange glow gave everything an eerie quality. The sink was empty with nothing but pipes underneath the countertop. To the right, there was a long skinny cabinet. The door of it was open about a foot, but Stan couldn't see inside. Carefully moving around the bed, his eyes turned to watch his physical body as moved. A chill went through him as he neared the edge of the bed to peek into the open cupboard door. Although he didn't like watching his body, having it behind him made him even more uneasy.

The cupboard in front of him was dark. The orange glow behind him didn't reach the inner compartment. He squinted his eyes to focus harder on the small space. It was too dark to see the entirety of the cupboard, the back blanketed in a dark shadow, but it appeared empty.

Another bang came from the other side of the cupboard door. This time, followed by a rattle, reminding him of metal hitting a solid object. Abandoning the search of the cupboard, he looked at the sink. The tap was off, and the sink was empty. Standing in front of it, he peered down into the drain for a source of the sound. It was black but empty. He listened intently, waiting for the banging sound to happen again. When it came, the mirror above the sink visibly shook. His gaze slowly moved up the mirror. It didn't hold his reflection, not even of the room behind him. Instead, it was as if he was looking through a window. A vast, empty horizon with a gray, dull sky extended within the mirror edges.

No, it can't be.

A shadow passed by the mirror quickly, startling him. He took a step back. The horizon in the distance was growing darker, as black masses moved towards the mirror between them. They bubbled and churned like black lava, just like they did while he was in the other realm. They moved closer, coming faster, like a tsunami of lava rushing toward him. He took another step back, but his back hit the railing of the hospital bed. He couldn't take his eyes off the mirror and the mass of shadows running towards him. Then a long, black tentacle crashed against the mirror from the other side, causing it to vibrate from the impact.

That was the banging sound he had heard, only now it was getting louder.

The slimy tentacle slowly dragged down the mirror on the other side, leaving a long, black stain. Stan hurried along the edge of the bed wanting to put distance between him and the mirror. When he reached the end of the bed, he held onto the railing as he continued to back away to the other side. Something shiny flashed in the corner of his eye, coming from the head of the bed. Not wanting to take his eyes away from the mirror for long, he quickly glanced at the head of the bed. His body's eyes were staring at him, the whites of them glistening in the yellow glare of the light above. Another bang crashed against the mirror as Stan raised his hands to his face, trying to block out the horrifying look in his body's eyes as they watched him back away further.

When his back hit the wall on the opposite side of the room, he shrunk down to a seated position, wanting to get as much space from both the mirror and his physical body on the bed as he could. He looked back to the mirror; the shadows were gone. A reflection of the ceiling tiles was all he could see from the angle that he now sat on the floor in the corner of the room. He looked over at the bed, but he couldn't see his body, only the side of the railings. A shadow of his physical arm showed through some of the holes in it.

The door handle twitched forcing his gaze to move again.

No, they can't be here. They can't follow me into this realm.

The door handle shook again.

He pressed his back into the wall harder, wishing he could pass right through it. The handle fully turned until it was vertical. The door began to open, so Stan prepared himself to run ... somewhere, anywhere ... but instead he felt frozen in place.

The instant the door opened, revealing who was standing there, her name fell from his lips.

"Lizzie," he breathed.

She was here, walking through the door. Her big, brown eyes searched the room until they settled on the bed. Her hair was pulled back tight into a ponytail with wisps of hair framing her face. Her lips turned up in a gentle smile as she reached over and clicked on the light switch. The overhead light flickered to life, chasing the shadows away from the room. She walked over to the side of the bed.

"No, Lizzie, wait," he stammered, frantically getting up to warn her.

As she pulled the chair near the bedside, he glanced over to his face on the pillow. His body's eyes were closed, and his face was peaceful.

Wait, but... he thought, *its eyes. They were open.*

"Good morning, Stan," she said, bubbly. "I hope you don't mind me coming alone today. The boys are with Sarah and Lexi."

Stan couldn't move. Liz dropped her purse to the floor, pulling off her black jacket and draping it against the back of the chair. She leaned in, grabbing onto his physical hand with both of hers. Her touch to his physical body caused small sparks in his hand while he stood at the end of the bed watching her. He glanced back at the mirror hanging over the sink. It reflected the hospital room, nothing more.

"The boys enjoyed seeing you yesterday," she continued. "At least, I think they did. You know how hard they are to read sometimes."

She let out a small laugh, making his knees weaken. He hadn't realized how much he missed that sound, how much he missed her. The memories of their lives together came rushing back. Even though he hadn't been able to remember her in the other realm, he now understood the urgency he had felt to come back was all to do with her. He walked around to the other side of the bed to stand across from her. Looking down at her in awe, he kept a careful distance from touching the skin of his physical body. His entire being yearned to wrap his arms around her and feel her body against his. Her sheer beauty dumbfounded him, so much so that he couldn't bring himself to speak. As if feeling his gaze on her, she dropped her eyes to the floor under the other side of the bed and tucked a piece of the stray hair framing her face behind an ear.

"Stan?"

Her gaze returned to the face on the bed. He wished she would look directly at him, at his ethereal form. He wished she knew how close he really was. Her eyes looked lined with worry, and they shimmered as tears shined along the edges.

"Can you hear me? God, I miss hearing your voice. I miss talking to you. There is so much I wish I could tell you."

"I'm here! I can hear you!" Stan exclaimed, bending over the bedside and trying to lean his face closer to hers. "Lizzie, you pulled me through. I'm back. You saved me."

His stomach fell as he realized she couldn't hear him. She looked down at her hands wrapped around his.

"I know the doctors say you're progressing in the right direction. I just wish you would wake up. These past three weeks have been so long. I miss you so much."

A tear broke free from Liz's left eye and fell down her cheek. Without thinking, Stan leaned over the bed to wipe it from her cheek. He froze, his finger only inches from her skin as he realized that he could see the faint outline of her lips through his hand. He brought his hand back to his face, studying it. When not near Liz, it seemed like a normal hand. When he moved it to hover over her body, he could faintly see the texture of her clothing through it.

Wait, I'm transparent? Like a ghost?

Stan looked down in surprise. He was still wearing the white t-shirt and khaki pants as before. He was able to pick up the fabric of his clothing in his hands. However, there was no texture to the clothing. The colour of it hung in the air, but not like real fabric. He lifted it over his eyes. It was transparent too.

No wonder no one can see or hear me, I can hardly even see myself!

Stan punched at the air in anger and yelled, "Fuck!"

"Stan!"

The surprise in her voice made him spin around to stare at her. Her eyes were wide, and she was leaning over his physical body, her right hand gripping its hand. Her left hand rested on top of his head.

"Did you just try to talk? Can you hear me? Oh my God, Stan! You can hear me?"

She moved both hands to cup his face and leaned in closer. Faint electricity passed over his cheeks as he watched from the end of the bed. A knock on the door interrupted the intimate moment. He looked to the door and then quickly back to Liz. She was standing up straight, turning towards it to see who was entering. One of her hands still rested on his body's chest.

"Mrs. Stevens?" came a soft voice through the door.

A woman with short, curly, brown hair poked her head into the room.

"Yes? Oh my God, you wouldn't believe what just happened!" Liz exclaimed, excitement pouring out of her. "Stan just tried to talk! At least, I think that's what he was doing. He groaned."

The nurse opened the door further to lean against the doorframe, her hand resting on the door handle. Her thin frame was hidden by loose-fitting, navy scrubs with small white stars speckled across the fabric. The nurse smiled at Liz, her eyes never looking towards Stan.

"That's great news, Mrs. Stevens!"

Stan could tell by the nurse's tone that she didn't feel the excitement that Liz did. Her mind was on something else.

"I will make a note of it for the doctor. Now, I'm in a bit of a jam here. There's a man out here that wants to talk to you. I didn't want to let him by without asking you first."

Liz's face dropped from excitement to uncertainty. Stan walked closer to the two women, confused about what was transpiring.

"What do you mean? Who is it?" Liz asked.

The nurse looked down at her hand that was gripping the door handle. After her silent pause saturated the room, she responded, "The man's name is Darrin. Darrin Polinski."

Stan stared at the nurse. The name didn't mean anything to him. He returned his gaze to Liz and saw the colour had drained from her face. She was no longer full of joy and excitement. The air around her now vibrated with anger and confusion. He looked back to the nurse in search of a clue as to why that name would cause Liz to react that way.

"What could he possibly want from me?"

Stan moved to stand closer to Liz. Her eyes were glazed over as she stared past the nurse.

"I'm sorry, Mrs. Stevens. I warned him how inappropriate this is, and you have every right to demand he leave. But he's rather insistent. I think he hopes to make amends for what happened."

Liz crossed her arms over her chest. Stan continued to inch closer to her, careful not to touch her in case the electrical current was something he would feel with everyone.

"He thinks that an apology could ever make up for what he did?" Liz muttered at first, but her voice slowly rose in volume as anger filled her words. "For what he did to our family? Look at my husband for God's sake! Would a simple apology be enough for you?"

"I understand how you feel, Mrs. Stevens. Honestly. What happened was an unbelievable accident and that's something he'll have to live with for the rest of his life. I'll tell him it's not a good time right now."

The nurse closed the door softly as she turned back into the hallway. Liz continued glaring at the door. Finally, she turned to look back toward Stan's body on the bed as a tear fell down her cheek. Stan, now only a few feet away from her, instinctively reached out to touch her shoulder, stopping only inches from her skin. He moved his hand over her shoulder and saw the hem of her shirt through it.

I can't comfort her. I can't do anything.

He dropped his arm back to his side, helplessly.

"Oh, Liz. I wish you could see that I'm here. I wish I could do something to make you smile again."

"I'm sorry, Stan," Liz said as she leaned over to grasp his hand again. "I wanted to spend time with you today but having that man outside the door is too hard. I need to get out of here. If I leave now, I might be able to sneak off before he can figure out a way to corner me on my way out."

Leaning over the railing on the bed, she kissed his cheek. One of her tears dropped on his face. She smiled grimly and wiped it away with her fingers.

"I love you, Stan. Keep getting better, my love."

She picked up her jacket and pulled her arms into it quickly. Without zipping the front, she leaned down to grab her purse off the floor before turning to the door. Opening it slightly, she peeked into the hall.

Stan realized this was his chance to get out of the room. He could follow her. He quickly moved to stand a few feet behind her, ready to run out as soon as she moved into the hall. She paused just inside the room and took a deep breath. Then she threw the door open the rest of the way to step out. Her hand propped open the door behind her, as if she somehow knew he would follow her out.

Stan quickly squeezed through the small space she made behind her. Sighing in relief, he smiled over at his wife. She had rescued him again without even knowing it. Except she was looking down the hall, frozen with her eyes wide. Stan quickly turned to see a man standing with the nurse, roughly twenty feet away. The man, who he assumed was Darrin, and the nurse had stopped talking. The man's hands were frozen in front of him, as if pleading with the nurse, and both of their faces had turned to look at Liz.

"Mrs. Stevens," the man stammered, his voice barely audible.

Liz turned and rushed towards the doors at the opposite end of the hallway before another word could be said by Darrin or the nurse. Stan took one final glance towards them, their mouths both still hanging open in shock, and then turned back to follow Liz.

"Mrs. Stevens! Elizabeth! Wait ... Please," Darrin pleaded behind them.

Liz didn't show any sign of slowing down. She jogged, nearing the corner that would take her out of view. Stan looked back briefly to see the nurse had placed a hand on Darrin's arm, preventing him from following. Darrin watched Liz leave, a look of pain and grief passing over his face. Then Liz and Stan were through the doors and around the corner, quickly moving down the next hallway to take the next turn. Stan concentrated on keeping up with Liz, not paying attention to the path they were taking. The hospital hallways were like a maze, and he was unsure of what would meet them at every turn.

Finally, they came to a small row of elevators. Liz walked towards the button in the center wall and hit the down arrow. She paced back and forth, impatiently waiting for the doors to open. Stan watched as she slowly moved to peer around the corner they just came from. He assumed she was worried about being followed by Darrin. The ding of the elevator bell made her jump slightly. Following her into it once the doors slid open, he veered to the right to keep space between them. She hit the button for P1. After a few seconds, nothing happened, so she hit the button again, peering into the elevator lobby as she did. When the doors finally closed, she let out a sigh of relief and leaned against the back of the elevator, gripping the small silver railing behind her. She leaned her head back and closed her eyes. The overhead lights were white, just like the rest of the hospital, but the walls were shiny, likely made of stainless steel. Everything in this hospital felt sterile and cold.

"That was way too close," Liz said, bringing Stan's attention back to focusing on her.

Her eyes popped open as she started to pace the small space in front of him.

"Who does he think he is? How dare he come and interrupt my quiet Sunday morning with my husband! At the hospital where he put Stan to begin with!"

The air in the elevator became electrified as Liz's anger rose. Rage radiated off her, quickly saturating the small enclosure. She paced until the elevator slowed, forcing her to reach out and brace herself as it stopped. As soon as the doors opened, Liz rushed out of the elevator into the parking garage. Stan followed her out, not wanting the doors to close between them.

Cars were parked in rows as far as he could see. Concrete posts were spaced in a pattern across the parking level, a large yellow "P1" labelled on the top of them all. The atmosphere here was different from the hospital. Although the temperature didn't bother him, he could tell that it was much colder. The air was crisper than it was in his hospital room, not humid and stuffy.

Stan turned and realized that Liz was already a long way ahead of him, starting to zigzag through the parked cars. He ran to catch up to her, careful not to run into any cars on his way. As he neared her, he immediately recognized her SUV nearby. Stan smiled as they came to stand by it until the realization that he didn't know what to do next came over him. She didn't know he was following her, so she wouldn't know to open a door for him. He watched her go to the driver's side door and get in, leaving no time for him to jump in with her.

Quickly running to the passenger side door, he peered in at Liz as she dropped her purse on the floor of the passenger seat. He didn't have long to figure out how to get in. Panic rose in his chest as his short window of time ticked by. He looked down at the empty passenger seat, his mind racing through thoughts on how he could get her to open the door. The panic made his ethereal form become electrified. He closed his eyes, wishing he was already in the seat next to her, visualizing what it would feel like to be beside her.

"Oh, Stan. Why did this ever happen to us?"

Her voice sounded close, surprising him. He opened his eyes. He was in the passenger seat, just as he had been envisioning. He looked out the passenger window to the spot he had just been standing.

"Okay, so I can move through solid objects then," he said to himself, looking around the vehicle. "I just need to figure out how the hell I did that."

Liz let out a soft whimper. He looked back towards her. She was hunched over the steering wheel, her arms crossed on the top of the wheel and her forehead resting on her forearms. He hated seeing her so distraught, especially when he couldn't talk to her or comfort her. Without thinking, he reached over and touched her shoulder, offering solace.

The moment his hand gripped her shoulder, a jolt of electricity exploded up his arm. It was a different kind of electricity than he had felt with his own body, but still surprising. Liz's head jerked up and looked down at her shoulder as Stan recoiled away from her. As he realized that she had felt it too, something pulled at his torso. An invisible force tugged at his body, and it was getting stronger.

"Liz!"

He grabbed at the car around him trying to anchor himself to it, but it was too late. A second later, he was no longer in the SUV. He looked around, recognizing the walls and bed in front of him. He was back sitting in the chair in the hospital room. His unconscious body breathing only a few feet away.

"Damn it!"

Chapter 29

- Liz -

Liz froze in the driver's seat, staring at her shoulder. She had felt something touch her. It felt like a caress but with an electric current. It was oddly familiar. After a few seconds, she shrugged.

Maybe it was just some weird static electricity.

She shifted the SUV to reverse and backed out of the hospital parking spot. During the drive back to the house, her thoughts slowly returned to Darrin's appearance at the hospital. She wondered if this was the first time that he had shown up at the hospital hoping to run into her. She had been also receiving strange phone calls for the past few days at her office. She had brushed them off as either a wrong number or scams. Whoever was on the other line always hung up when she answered. Now she wondered if it had been Darrin trying to reach out. The thought of him on the other end of the line listening before hanging up made anger course through her.

"As if I would ever want to talk to him," she muttered.

As she pulled into her driveway, she paused to ponder the house. Her boys were in there. She couldn't bring this anger inside. They didn't deserve it. She had to let it go and be the loving mom they needed. With her hands still on the wheel, she closed her eyes and tried to let the anger dissipate. She took a deep breath and thought about the boys, likely getting hungry for lunch. She thought about bundling up the experience with Darrin and letting it float away from her, as if she could send it off in a hot air balloon into the sky. After a few more deep breaths, she opened her eyes.

Don't let that man ruin your Sunday on top of everything else. Let it go and be the mom your kids need right now.

She let out one final breath and then grabbed her purse from the floor of the passenger side. Climbing out of the vehicle, Liz nearly slipped on the icy driveway. The December weather had left a thin sheet of wet frost on the roads that morning, which had turned into a thin layer of ice that the sun hadn't touched yet. She carefully shuffled to the front door and opened it. A pocket of warm air rushed out and warmed her face. The delicious aroma of food cooking in the kitchen and the laughter of her boys in the living room welcomed her. She stood for a moment in the door frame allowing the joy in the house to wash over her, the anger finally melting away completely.

Closing the door behind her, she took off her jacket and shoes without alerting anyone of her presence. She dropped her purse on the table in the entryway before moving into the kitchen to see what smelled so good. Sarah was leaning over the kitchen island with the newspaper laid out in front of her. She was wearing a black turtleneck with Liz's pink frilly apron straining to cover her best friend's chest. Liz laughed, causing Sarah to look up at her and smile.

"Hey, Lizzie! I wasn't expecting you back so soon. How was Stan?"

Liz walked closer to the island to look past Sarah at the multiple pots simmering and steaming on the stove. The smell made her mouth water. She hadn't realized how hungry she was.

"He's okay. I didn't get to see the doctor today, but I'm very excited to say that Stan tried to talk to me!"

Sarah's face beamed with joy.

"Well, at least I think he was. Really ... he groaned. I don't think it was my imagination. I wanted to stay longer to see if he would do it again, but we were rudely interrupted."

Sarah's face changed from excitement to confusion. "What do you mean you were interrupted? What happened?" She walked around the island to stand closer to Liz.

The sting of tears threatened Liz's eyes as she replied, "The nerve of some people. Guess who decided to show up at the hospital today. I can't believe the audacity to come to the hospital where Stan is unconscious thanks to him."

"No ... That drunk driver guy was at the hospital? Really?" Sarah said, wrapping her arms around Liz in a tight embrace. "I can't believe he was there! You'd think he would have the decency to call first."

Liz leaned back out of Sarah's embrace, wiping the tears from her cheek. She turned her back to Sarah to sit at the island.

"Well," Liz continued, "maybe he tried calling first. I don't know."

"What do you mean?" Sarah asked, beside her. "You've never said anything about him calling."

"Well, I don't know for sure. I never really thought about it until the drive home today. I've been getting these weird phone calls at work, but I thought they were scam phone calls or something. Whenever I picked up the phone, the line would cut out. No one ever talks on the other end."

Sarah walked back around to the stove to stir something in one of the pots. Then she turned back to lean against the counter in her original position, facing Liz.

"Didn't you try to look up the phone number on your caller ID?"

“I would have, but the number was unlisted. I honestly thought it was just a scammer.”

Liz looked down at her hands, picking at her nails with their chipping, blue nail polish. “Anyways, I don’t want to spend any more time thinking about him. I am so mentally exhausted.”

“You know, you’ll need to forgive the bastard someday. I know it won’t be easy, but it also isn’t good for you to hang onto this anger. The boys need to see you forgive him and move on.”

She looked up at Sarah, who was looking back at her with imploring eyes. This wasn’t the first time Sarah reminded her that forgiveness would have to come someday, but she wasn’t ready yet. She needed to hate him. She couldn’t forgive him until Stan was awake. She couldn’t forgive him until she knew Stan was going to come home.

“I can’t. Not yet.” Liz looked back down at her hands for a moment, her response hanging in the room. Finally, she slammed her hands down on the countertop, making Sarah jump. Liz forced a smile. “Okay, enough about that. Tell me … what is causing that delicious smell?”

Chapter 30

- Serafine -

After reading the ominous letter from her mother the night before, Serafine had expected her sleep on Saturday to be filled with nightmares. Instead, she had a peaceful sleep, waking up in a quiet apartment on Sunday morning.

Since she already had cleaned the apartment and done her laundry the day before, she spent Sunday reading other journals and books that once belonged to her mother. She hoped to learn more about what happened after the final letter in the first notebook. The journals and books, however, didn't speak of the secret society. Her mother had unusual entries, about travelling to various cities in the southern United States, but she never wrote about who she met while there.

Shaking her head at yet another entry from her mother about helping a friend in New Orleans with a 'troubled spirit,' Serafine picked up the dishes from her small dinner and carried them into the kitchen, limping stiffly. Her pace was slower than usual. She placed the dishes on the counter near the sink.

"I'll get to those tomorrow morning before I head into work."

Monday morning was coming quickly. She would have to return to the hospital and learn if anything had transpired from her voicemail over the weekend. The phone had been silent all day, so she hoped that was a sign of the Monday morning she was about to have.

Walking back through the living room, she turned off the lights and made her way to her bedroom door. She needed to sleep. Everything she had read and experienced over the last seventy-two hours was overwhelming. She felt like she had fallen into a nightmare and couldn't wake up. Perhaps if she went to bed and had another good night's sleep, she would wake up tomorrow and everything would go back to normal. It would all have been a bad dream.

She wasn't sure she could handle the truth. Fighting off invisible creatures that were chasing her from another dimension. Her gaze moved to the phone hanging on her wall. Land-lines weren't common nowadays, but she insisted on having one. She wondered if it was too late to phone Michael or James to make sure they were okay.

"Oh, don't be ridiculous, Serafine," she assured herself, hanging her head in her hands. "They're fine. There's no point in worrying them."

Then her bedroom door slammed.

"What the hell is going on in this house?" she yelled, gripping her chest with her right hand as she turned to face the door.

She gripped the counter of the kitchen island nearby, steadying herself. Watching the door, her mind drifted to the creatures in the nightmare she had about the tunnel.

"Okay, Serafine. Those creatures can't really harm you," she assured herself. "If Mom was right, and this is really happening, you need to stay strong."

Slowly, she shifted her grip on the counter until she reached the end of the kitchen island, moving towards the bedroom. The crack along the bottom of the door was dark. The light in her bedroom was off.

"Alright, whoever you are, I want you to listen to me," she called towards the door, unsure what she was talking to. "Leave my property this instant! You're not welcome here, do you hear me? And you'll never be welcome here, so get the hell out of my house!"

A thump came from behind the closed door.

My mother used to say to sprinkle salt ... something about salt to keep out evil.

She peeled her fingers from gripping onto the counter to grab a box of salt from the cupboard above her stove. With salt in hand, she walked to her bedroom door, reaching her hand out to the handle. It was cold, even though the temperature in the apartment was a balmy twenty-five degrees Celsius. Just the way she liked it.

Her heart raced in her chest; her mind still wasn't entirely sure any of this was real, but she was beginning to believe her mother's warnings. Likely a good reason not to call the police at this point. She didn't want to be hauled away to a home. Or worse, a psychiatric hospital. If what her mother said was true, she needed to get that box of her mother's items. She needed to see if she had packed the *gris-gris*. She slowly turned the handle and pushed the door open. She was prepared to turn and run in the other direction if she saw someone, or something, standing in her room.

The room was dark.

She reached in carefully, scanning the room without looking where she was reaching. Flipping the light switch, the room flooded with a bright, white light again. Serafine's eyes adjusted quickly and scanned the room for anything out of place. The box of her mother's items lay upside down in the middle of the floor near the dresser where it had been sitting since yesterday. It was still closed, as the lock didn't budge during the fall. The dust that had been caked on it had left a line of dirt along the carpet where it had rolled.

Something didn't want Serafine to have the box.

"So, here you are, trying to get into the box of goodies that my mother left me."

She stepped into the room, holding the salt out in front of her like a shield. One foot, then the next, slowly moving towards the box. Her eyes scanned around the room, checking every shadow for any sign of eyes watching her.

"I demand you leave this building this instant!" she yelled around the room, waving the salt in the air as if she could physically hit the creatures with it. Small grains of salt flew from the container and sprinkled onto her carpet from the motion. "Get out! You're not welcome here. I banish you!"

Feeling she had done the best she could, Serafine turned back to the box lying on the floor. Placing the salt container on the nearby dresser, she bent down to carefully pick up the box and place it on the foot of the bed. She walked around to the nightstand on the opposite side of the bed and pulled the drawer open. The key glimmered in the light in the middle of the drawer as if it had been waiting for her. She gripped the key, the metal cool against her skin just before the drawer slammed shut, nearly taking her hand off at the wrist. The force of the slam caused the lamp to fall on its side, but she ignored it.

"You really don't want me opening this box," she whispered. "Now, I'm *definitely* going to open it."

She turned back to stand at the foot of the bed, leaning over to push the key into the small hole of the lock. The light overhead flickered as the key turned easily and the latch clicked open, despite years of sitting on a shelf. The bedroom door slammed, making her jerk up and look at it. Her lower back ached.

"Well too bad," she yelled at the door. "My Momma left me things that can get rid of you, and I intend to use them. You're not welcome here, ya hea'?"

She quickly lifted the latch and placed her hands on either side of the box's lid. She paused for a moment to glance around the room before lifting it. Various talismans and charms lay scattered in the box. Two small, black books with runic symbols engraved in gold lettering were tucked up against the side of the box. The smell of incense and sage lifted from it, flooding Serafine with even more memories of her childhood. Taped on the inside of the lid was a faded picture. A woman with wild, curly black hair that was barely held away from her face by a thick purple scarf was smiling at the camera. Coins dangled from the purple scarf, hanging down the one side of her dark mahogany face. The woman wore a black dress with a second scarf, this one golden yellow, wrapped around her hips. Her eyes were dark brown and warm, full of love.

Mom.

Her mother's hands were resting on the shoulders of a small girl who looked no more than four years old. Bottle-like glasses accentuated the girl's big brown eyes. She had black hair like the woman in the picture, but it was pulled back into two, tight pigtails on either side of her head.

The young girl was Serafine, of course. She couldn't remember the exact date of the photograph, but she remembered those glasses. She had hated them and was so happy the day she was able to take them off, amazed that she had outgrown her far-sightedness enough to not need them anymore. She affectionately brushed the edges of the photograph with her fingers, careful not to rip it. Fond memories of her mother and the fun they had in their old kitchen back in New Orleans flooded through her, causing a tear to well up in her eye.

Don't become a blubbering mess. She wiped away the tear. *This ain't the right time for that.*

The bedroom was quiet and still. It felt like a thick haze had lifted from the small space. She looked up briefly from the box to look around again. The silence wasn't ominous anymore, it was calm. Looking back down at the items strewn about the box, she knew they were the reason the creatures were gone. They had been forced away by some sort of powerful talisman she kept from her mother.

I can't believe she was telling the truth all along. This stuff actually means something.

Unfortunately, no matter how much she touched and looked through the items, she couldn't remember what each item was meant to do, or which was the *gris-gris* that her mother had told her to find. The hours she spent listening to her mother tell her about each of their purposes were too fuzzy, buried under years of life and memories of her children and the hospital.

Then she remembered a notebook she had kept when she had packed up this exact box all those years ago. It was an inventory list that her mother had kept in her shop. Serafine had used it to highlight the items she kept versus gave away or sold. She moved the items around the box with a new fervour, searching for the notebook that would help her make sense of the box's contents. It was in the bottom of the box under bottles of various coloured liquids. She pulled it out and flipped through it, searching for the description of what the *gris-gris* looked like. She hoped one might be able to help Stan. Perhaps it was the one item that could maybe save his life and bring him home to Liz to live their "Happy Ever After". She couldn't stay and help him fight the creatures, but perhaps she could leave a *gris-gris* with him. Then she had to find one of her mother's associates in the society. Maybe they could help her get the creatures off her back.

She hoped she had enough time.

Chapter 31

- Stan -

Alone in the room again, Stan paced along the foot of the bed. The evening nurse had just left, reporting nothing new for his body as Stan watched. Within seconds of her leaving, the room went dark as the familiar *'click'* of the light switch echoed across the room. He looked around nervously, no longer feeling alone. Glancing over at the mirror above the sink, he waited for the dark scene to shift, but it kept the reflection of the hospital room in the soft orange glow. He moved into the corner of the room and put his back against the wall, taking in his surroundings. Only his eyes moved in their sockets as he looked around his peripheral vision for anything that might indicate danger.

Is it possible something could even hurt me right now?

The room was blanketed in shadows where the orange light couldn't reach. The air was still. Even the curtain against the wall didn't move. Although he didn't need to breathe in his current ethereal form, Stan realized he had been holding his breath. He breathed in deeply, the familiar motion calming him slightly. However, he couldn't shake the feeling of a nearby presence. He started to move around the room, checking under the bed and in the small space on the other side of the room.

They were both empty. Feeling a tad childish, he gave up and walked over to his chair in the corner, sitting down heavily, and put his head in his hands.

I need to get out of here.

He brushed his hands through his hair until they stopped on the top of his head. Allowing his lowered head to rest in his hands, he closed his eyes. His mind returned to Liz and the SUV.

How did I teleport myself into the vehicle?

A low hum was building in the room, too quiet to notice at first. The noise grew louder, pulling him out of his thoughts of teleportation briefly before it stopped. He waited, still curled over, listening, unsure if he had actually heard something. The low hum started again, even louder than before. He opened his eyes and lifted his gaze to the machinery hooked up to his physical body on the other side of the room. The noise continued to grow louder before pausing again, reminding Stan of an engine struggling to stay running. He kept his eyes on the machinery, but nothing on the screens indicated it was coming from them.

A loud growl reverberated behind him, like a large dog sneaking up behind his right shoulder. He jumped out of his chair and spun around to look at the wall. There was nothing there.

Of course, there's nothing there. I'm sitting up against a wall, nothing can be there, Stan reasoned. *Calm down. I need to calm down and think.*

Even while trying to reason with himself, he couldn't move his eyes away from the wall behind the chair. His body was alert, prepared to fight or flee for his life. He backed away until he felt the frame of the bed hit his back. He lifted his hands to hold onto the bar behind him, not taking his eyes from the wall. He waited, listening for the sound to start again. After a few slow seconds ticked by, Stan was unsure if he had heard anything to begin with.

I guess they can officially call me Casper the Scaredy *Ghost.*

Shaking his head, he brought his right hand up to cover his face. A light tickling of his pant leg around his left ankle made him pause, but he didn't move. It wasn't until the tickling grew tighter, becoming a painful grip, that he realized how wrong he had been to put his back to the bed. Long, black fingers gripped his ankle from under it. Before he could kick his leg away, the hand pulled. Something was trying to drag him under the bed.

Thankfully, Stan still had his left-hand gripping onto the bed frame. His arm twisted painfully as the creature tried to pull him harder, whipping him onto his back, but he didn't let go. He looked down at his feet, straining to see what was pulling him. It was hard to make out, but a black arm stretched across the floor, attached to the thin, black hand gripping him. The strong fingers wrapped tightly, their jagged, sharp claws cutting into his pant leg. Black tar oozed off the fingers, staining his pants. He strained to see what the arm belonged to but realized that there was a gaping hole along the back side of the room where the white linoleum used to be. A pulsing red light made the edges of the hole glisten like blood. The arm of the creature reached up out of it.

Stan screamed, realizing the creature was trying to pull him into the hole. With his left arm straining to keep hold of the bed frame, he raised his right arm to grip the bottom of the bed. A second black arm reached out of the hole, feeling its way toward him, searching for his other leg. He kicked the first arm that was gripping his ankle as hard as he could. Pain shot through his ankle as the kick connected, forcing the creature's grip to loosen just enough. Stan used all his strength to push back into a seated position, his left leg free from the creature's hold. He let go of the bed and quickly shuffled backwards, crab-walking towards the door. From his seated position, he could see the glowing edge of the hole growing larger behind the bed. The arms moved around the lip of the hole, feeling around as they searched for his legs.

He stood up and slammed his back against the door, reaching his left hand behind him to grip the handle, trying to convince it to open. It wouldn't budge. Scraping noises came from behind the bed, like nails scratching a chalkboard. He assumed this meant the creature was clawing its way out of the hole after him. He didn't want to wait around and see what the full creature looked like.

Focus. I need to get to the other side of the door. Just like I did with Liz and the SUV.

He turned his back on the creature and closed his eyes. Trying to focus his mind on what the hospital hallway looked like, he placed both hands on the door. The scraping sound grew louder behind him. Something large was dragging across the floor, inching closer. Stan took a deep breath and closed his eyes as tight as he could, a battle cry escaping his lips as he realized he may not escape.

Suddenly, the world shifted.

Behind his closed eyelids, the darkness lifted, and light penetrated through his eyelids. It was now bright around him; bright and quiet. He carefully squinted one eye open, unsure if he was still alive or if the creature was giving him false hope.

I did it! I'm in the hallway!

Stan spun around. His gaze scanned the hospital door down to the floor just in time to see one, long, black, tar-covered finger come out from under it. The finger curled up and gripped the bottom edge of the door before dragging its black claw, disappearing back into the room. A deep scratch was left behind, a faint black stain within its crevice. Stan's heart thumped loudly in his chest as he raised his eyes to the door handle. The doorknob twitched once, twice, and then went still.

Stan didn't move for a few minutes, watching the door handle for any indication the creature was following him. Everything was still and quiet in the room, allowing his heartbeat to slow down and his body to relax. He hoped this meant the creature had crawled back into the hole he had come from, unable to follow Stan into the hallway. He was sure it would try to strike again, but for now, he was safe. He turned to walk down the hall in the same direction he had followed Liz earlier that day, looking for hospital rooms that might be open. There had to be others like him, wandering the halls, waiting for their bodies to let them back in or die off. Maybe they could help him understand what was going on.

And what I can do about it ...

Most of the doors along the corridor were closed. It was unclear if they were empty or kept closed to protect the patient's privacy. He tried teleporting into some of them, but without knowing what the rooms looked like, it was impossible. He didn't dare assume the rooms looked identical to his in case he accidentally teleported back into his own, where the creature may be waiting. A pull around his waist tightened as he continued walking like a safety line ensuring he never strayed too far from his physical body. As he turned a corner, a shadow passed by his peripheral. He turned to face it, but the hall was empty.

"Hello? Is there anyone there?"

Silence.

He continued walking away from his ward, peering into an open door on the right near a window, but it was empty. Spinning around, he moved back into the hall, debating which direction to go.

"Code blue, code blue. East wing, room twelve," a mechanical voice boomed through a speaker above his head.

Stan looked up and down the walls, trying to decipher which part of the hospital he was in compared to the code blue. A team of nurses broke out of a side hallway behind him. He spun around in time to see them running directly at him. Pushing up against the wall, he made himself as thin as he could to avoid contact with the people running by. Their nervous energy flowed like a current.

Once they passed, he pushed off the wall to follow them. Hopefully, he wouldn't be the only one like him drawn to the commotion. The group of nurses turned down a curve a few meters away, so Stan ran to catch up to them. As he came around the corner, he stopped abruptly. The hall stretched out before him, empty.

Where did they go?

A commotion nearby made him search along the walls. A door slowly closed three rooms down on the left side of the hall. He ran to it, but it clicked shut as soon as he reached it. He leaned his ear against the door, straining to hear what was going on inside. A man was talking, his tone indicated he was either angry or in a panic. Stan sighed, stepping back. He wouldn't be able to get in no matter how hard he tried. He turned back toward the hallway he had come from but stopped suddenly as two wide, blue eyes stared up at him, inches from his face.

"What the hell?" he yelled, jumping back.

A woman stood in the hall in front of him. Her curly, red, unkempt hair shot up in every direction around her face. Her blue eyes were wide and staring as if looking right through him. Dark bags under her eyes were emphasized by her hollow, pale cheeks, which were drawn tight against her cheekbones. He could see the creases of the wall where it met the floorboards through her white dress.

She was like him.

"Miss!" Stan exclaimed. "Can you hear me? Are you okay?"

Stan searched her face, but she continued to stare past him as if looking at something behind him. He glanced over his shoulder, but the hall was empty. Turning back to speak to her again, he jumped back. She was only a foot from his face again. This time, her gaze focused on his eyes.

"Help … me … please," she whispered.

The smell of rot and decay invaded his nostrils from her breath. Wincing, he tried to put space between them, but she inched closer, bringing her hands up to touch his chest. He stepped back again, trying to remain out of her reach. Her features morphed as they moved together. Her skin pulled tighter on her face. The bags under her eyes dropped further down as her eyes bulged in their sockets, threatening to pop out. As she reached her hands out to him, her fingers grazing his chest, Stan looked down at them. They were growing thinner, her fingernails shifting on their nailbeds as they started to loosen from the skin and fall off, plopping onto the linoleum floor.

"Please, they're coming for me," she pleaded. "You have to help me!"

He continued to back away, putting his hands up, hoping to keep her off him. Quickly peering over his shoulder, he searched behind him for anyone who might be able to help. The woman let out a bloodcurdling scream, snapping his attention back to her. She hysterically grabbed at him while looking at something behind him. Her eyes grew even wider as they bulged, until one finally fell out of its socket, dangling while still attached to its optic nerve. A streak of dark blood dripped down her sunken cheek.

"Hurry, they're coming! Help me," she begged, gripping her bony fingers into his shirt, leaving blood droplets and smudged fingerprints on the white fabric.

Stan grabbed her arms. Her bones were brittle underneath the sagging, nearly translucent skin. One of her bloody, yellow fingernails dropped onto his arm. He recoiled, forcefully pushing her away from him. Her grip loosened from his shirt, and he started to run backwards down the hallway. He looked back over his shoulder to make sure his path was clear.

A shadow moved on the ceiling above him, making him freeze. A black creature was crawling on the ceiling, black tar oozing from its body, dripping a black trail behind it on the linoleum floor below it. Its head was black and faceless as it crawled closer to them.

Stan pushed himself down into a crouching position, trying to keep away from the creature as it passed over. It didn't seem to notice him as it crawled towards the woman still screaming in the hallway about ten feet away. The creature's long, black arms pulled its dragging body along the ceiling. Its body ended abruptly at the hip, leaving a legless stump. Its two black arms stretched and pulled it along, leaving a streak of tar behind on the shiny, white ceiling, like a slug leaving a trail of slime. The creature used long, black claws on its three fingers to dig into the ceiling, leaving small gouges as it dragged its weight toward the woman. Stan recognized the sound of it moving across the ceiling. It was the same sound that had been inching closer behind him in his room.

"No," he grimaced, trying to move further away from the creature.

It stopped crawling toward the woman, pausing on the ceiling. Stan froze, holding his breath, as the creature turned its head around to face him. Its neck contorted to allow its head to spin in his direction without turning its body. Small, yellow, glowing creases cracked open above its mouth. Its mouth slowly opened, revealing long, jagged teeth protruding in rows down into the throat. Green drool oozed out along its gums as it hissed at Stan, searching along the wall where he crouched.

The woman screamed again.

The creature's head whipped back to face her. She was backing away slowly now as her body disintegrated further, making it harder for her to run. The creature sped up, as if fueled by her fear. It easily caught up to her, positioning itself directly above her. The woman tried to scream again, but a strained gurgling sound came out instead. Thick, black blood poured from her mouth, spilling down her chin and onto her white dress. She crouched down on the floor, crawling toward Stan in a final attempt to escape the creature. The black head turned around to face her, its mouth opening again to reveal its teeth. The creature seemed to smile as it turned to crawl towards them. Stan remained still; his gaze unable to leave the creature's face.

It's blind. It only reacts to sounds and movement.

There was nothing he could do for the woman now. She fell onto her stomach and began dragging her body toward him. Her skin was shedding where it contacted the linoleum floor, leaving bloody streaks trailing along behind her. He debated picking her up to help her make a run for it, but he worried she would break in half wherever he grabbed her. He also didn't want the creature's attention turning back to him. He had a family to think about.

So, Stan stayed crouched down like a coward.

The creature adjusted itself to be directly above the woman before letting go of the ceiling. The woman didn't see it coming. She was staring at Stan, her one eye dangling from its socket and bouncing off her cheekbone as she crawled on her elbows toward him. She reached out a hand, desperately trying to grab for his leg, but he was still over a foot out of her reach. That's when the creature landed on her back. She let out a final, gurgling sound as the floor below her cracked below the weight of them. Slowly, the cracks grew wider, a red glow shooting up from them. As the hole grew, she fell into the opening, the creature riding on her back. Her scream grew softer and more distant. Curious what was in the hole, Stan rolled onto his hands and knees to move toward the edge of it.

A black creature popped its head up from the hole, looking in the opposite direction. Stan froze, one hand still hovering above the ground only a few feet away. The creature slowly turned to face him, its eyes looking directly at him. Stan held his breath, trying to remain perfectly still. Slowly, the creature dropped back into the hole, its eyes never leaving the area of the hall where Stan kneeled.

Once the creature was out of sight, Stan remained still. The hole shrunk until it returned to the same white linoleum that was there before. The sounds of the hospital returned to normal. Stan looked at the floor in front of him, where the bloody trail of the woman had been only moments before. The floors were back to a clean, shining white. He looked up. The white ceiling was back to normal, as if what Stan had just witnessed never happened. He looked down at his shirt. Even it was back to being white and clean again. Except a small hole was now present on his shirt, where her long, dagger-like fingernails had clawed at him for help.

Movement down the hallway made Stan look up, ready to run if the creature had returned. It was the group of nurses leaving the room that had the code blue. Their faces were full of sorrow and disappointment as they slowly moved down the hallway, back from where they had come.

Stan quickly stood up, running to the door before it closed. A nurse and a doctor stood at the foot of the hospital bed. Their backs were turned away as they spoke to each other over a clipboard that the nurse was writing notes on. Stan shifted his gaze towards the bed. Red, curly hair shot out in all directions from the pillow. As he watched, he saw the woman's eyes pop open, her face slowly falling to the side to face him. He strained to keep his eyes on her face as the door slowly closed. Her lips curled up into an evil grin before the door clicked shut between them.

Chapter 32

- Liz -

Liz worked quietly at Stan's desk until she heard a commotion coming from the entryway of the house. The boys were home.

Is it four o'clock already?

She looked up out the window to her left and saw the sun already descending. A thin layer of snow blanketed the streets. Winter was officially here. Putting her papers aside, she stretched her arms above her head, her back and neck stiff from working slouched over the desk.

Liz stood up and walked into the hallway, calling out, "Hey boys. How was your day? Did the bus ride home go okay?"

Alex was the first to come into view, walking across the hallway into the kitchen. On his way by, he briefly turned his head to acknowledge Liz, saying, "Hey Mom. Yeah, we managed okay, except Carson made us miss the first bus."

"I did not!" Carson whined from around the corner. His head popped into view as he continued, "I had to find my other mitt. It was in the Lost and Found bin."

Carson shot a look in Alex's direction as Liz came to stand beside him. She wrapped an arm around him in a half hug.

"Alex was no help. He and Jack just stood at the front doors and made me go look by myself."

"You found it, didn't you? Would you rather I held your hand while you looked?" Alex teased from the kitchen, out of Liz's view.

"Alex, be nice to your little brother."

Liz gave Carson a small squeeze as he looked up at her with a small smile before letting him go to walk in after Alex. She could hear Jack in the entryway closet. Alex was standing with the refrigerator door open, his head hidden. Liz walked to stand beside him as he searched for something to eat.

"If I am going to trust you to take care of your brothers, I need to know that you'll help them out when they need it."

Alex looked over at her, his hazel eyes almost at the same level as hers. It made Liz pause as she realized how tall her eldest was getting. How much older he looked.

"Sorry, Mom. I'll help the brat next time," he commented with a sneer as Carson walked by to the pantry.

Jack walked in within a few feet of Carson, beaming, "Hey Mom! You should have seen the traffic that the bus was stuck in. This snow is causing everyone to drive like maniacs, right?"

Liz smiled as she recognized Stan's words coming out of Jack's mouth. She walked over and ruffled Jack's hair.

"You bet, kiddo. Good thing it's supposed to warm up tomorrow. This snow won't stick around for long."

The boys each continued to load up their arms with snacks while Liz watched from the kitchen island, listening to their conversations about their day at school. As they all moved towards the living room, she stood to go back to the office.

"Boys, please don't eat too much right now. We'll be having supper in an hour or so. I need to get back to work, so I don't want to hear any fighting, okay?"

"Okay, Mom," they all said in unison as they disappeared into the other room.

She heard the food dropping into a pile on the coffee table before a muffled argument over what show to watch broke out.

"Seriously, boys, no fighting!" Liz repeated over her shoulder as she left the kitchen. "And no T.V. until homework is done."

Once sitting back down behind the desk, she opened her laptop. A new email from Jane with the subject, *'ICYMI'* had come in while she was with the boys. Liz double-clicked on it and the email popped up in a new window on her screen.

Hi Mrs. Stevens,

I want to make sure you're aware of the interview that Mr. Barcley has set up for later this week. I don't think he mentioned it in this morning's meeting, but he brought it up at an impromptu meeting shortly after you left this afternoon. The gentleman he is interviewing is currently employed as an editor at a Seattle newspaper, but he is looking to move to the Vancouver area.

Anyway, I just wanted to let you know since you missed the meeting. I hope you are surviving the snow!

See you tomorrow,

Jane

Liz stared at the email in disbelief. *Bob in interviewing someone for an editor position? What editor position?*

He had failed to mention an opening during their talk about her wages. She was already doing most of the editing work — did this mean they were planning to replace her? Or were they simply going to cut back her hours even more?

"He'll likely get paid a proper wage, too. That's why Bob claimed he couldn't *afford* my raise," Liz scoffed, slamming the laptop closed.

She looked around the desk at the work she brought home to do that evening. It needed to get done, but she had the urge to push everything off the desk – laptop and all. She gripped her hands on the armrests of the chair, the plastic creaking as it strained under her fingers. Her pulse rose as heat filled her cheeks.

"So, Bob feels the need to bring in someone else. Right when I need to start cutting back my office hours. This is such bullshit."

Liz stood up, suppressing the urge to trash the office, only because she would be the one who would have to clean it up. She stormed out of the office and went straight to the refrigerator in the kitchen, grabbing the cold bottle of white wine from the door before turning to find a wine glass. She needed a drink.

***

"Hey, Lizzie! I hope you guys are still hungry!"

Sarah walked into the house like she owned the place, toting large tubs of vanilla ice cream and bags of M&M's. Liz was already onto her second glass of wine, ignoring the pile of work in the office down the hall. She knew she would likely regret ignoring it at some point, as she still needed Bob to see her as an asset, but she didn't care right now. She smiled at Sarah from where she sat in the kitchen as Sarah plopped the goodies onto the counter.

"I figured we missed supper time, thanks to Lexi's swim practice. So, we brought dessert instead!"

Liz watched as Sarah moved around the kitchen, grabbing bowls and spoons before placing them near the ice cream tubs. Then Sarah disappeared into the pantry briefly, emerging with more toppings, including chocolate sauce, chocolate chips, mini marshmallows, and a small jar of rainbow sprinkles. She dropped everything near the ice cream before moving to stand beside Liz.

"What, we need to develop diabetes tonight?" Liz asked, looking through the pile of sugary goods lying across her countertop. The boys were already moving into the kitchen, lining up at the island, grins on all their faces. "Not too much, boys. I don't need you up all night buzzing on sugar."

"Oh, let them have their sundaes, Liz. It won't hurt them this once. It's not often they get to do this."

Sarah winked at Liz, licking chocolate sauce from her finger. She walked around the island to the cupboard to grab herself a wine glass before picking up the half-empty bottle still sitting in front of Liz. She poured herself a glass as they watched the kids in silence.

Once the kids cleared out of the kitchen, their piled-up sundaes in hand, Sarah smirked at Liz. "So, tell me what's going on. How's work and everything going?"

Liz slid off the chair at the island and moved to sit at the kitchen table behind her, grabbing the wine bottle back from Sarah. "Oh, fucking fantastic."

Sarah moved to drop into a chair across from her, as Liz poured more wine in her glass. "Uh oh, what happened now? Is Stan okay?"

"Oh, it's nothing to do with Stan," Liz sighed. "Although, I miss him so much. Especially today, after the news I got this afternoon. Life feels so much harder without him here."

"Liz, you'll get through this. Stan will get through this. He's improving every week, right? He just needs time to heal, and then he will be back, driving you crazy with his smelly habits in no time."

Liz laughed, "Yeah, he did drive me crazy sometimes. I would do anything to feel that way again."

"Now, tell me, what's going on with work?"

Liz explained the email she received from her assistant and about Bob's outrageous decision to consider a random person from Seattle for a job that should belong to Liz. She also explained the discussion she had to have with Bob about her wage.

"It's typical," Sarah said. "A woman pulls back from her career even slightly to take on more duties as a mother, and suddenly a man needs to be called in to replace her. I bet he'll get paid more, too!"

Liz laughed. She could always count on Sarah to act as the outraged feminist in her life.

"Well, hopefully that won't be the case. Maybe I'm over-reacting. We've always talked about expanding the newspaper to take on more serious stories, and maybe even a paid subscription. Plus, with the extra help, maybe I'll actually get to write again. Writing is what I took the job for in the first place. I wanted to be able to see a piece by me on the front page."

"Sure, you keep telling yourself that, Liz. I'll be here to watch your back, just in case."

They continued chatting until Lexi walked into the room carrying her empty ice cream bowl. "Mom, can we go home soon? I have homework tonight and swim practice in the morning."

"Oh, that's right," Sarah replied after popping a mini marsh-mallow into her mouth. "We should be going. Liz, call me if you have any trouble with anything, okay? I can be over here quickly no matter what time it is. I can come watch the boys anytime you want to go visit Stan alone, too."

Sarah stood up from the table, walking to the kitchen island. Liz quickly stood to follow her as Sarah began picking up the near-empty bags of sugary ice cream toppings. The ice cream had melted into a gooey, oozing mess. Liz pulled the bags from Sarah's hands, placing them back into a pile on the island counter.

"Don't worry about the mess, Sarah, I've got it," Liz said as she gently pushed Sarah towards the entryway. "I likely should get some more work done anyway. I have a pile of articles to finish proofing and a layout to plan. I don't want to give Bob ammunition for getting rid of me."

"Are you sure? I can stick around and clean up while you work."

"I'm positive. Besides, I can always get the boys to help me."

Liz pulled Sarah's jacket from where it was draped over the bench in the entryway and handed it to her.

"Okay," Sarah conceded, grabbing her jacket from Liz's hands. Lexi was a few feet away grabbing her own jacket out of the closet. "Make sure they actually help though. I don't want you left with a mess that wasn't even your idea. As for work, maybe you'll make more interesting articles after drinking over half a bottle of wine." Sarah laughed as she pulled on her jacket and then grabbed her dark brown, Ugg-style boots from the shoe rack. Right before walking out the door behind Lexi, she turned to embrace Liz for a moment. Then Sarah pulled back from the hug but held Liz's arms in her hands. "Call me if you need anything, even if it's just to talk."

Liz nodded her head in agreement before Sarah turned to leave. "Bye, boys! Be good to your Mom and help her out with the cleanup!" she called over her shoulder as she stepped out onto the front step. "Bye, Lizzie."

"Bye, Sarah. Thanks again for stopping by."

Liz closed the door and locked both the deadbolt and handle, feeling the need to ensure that no one else would be able to walk into the home on their own tonight. She returned to the kitchen to find Alex already there, putting the bowls and spoons into the dishwasher and snacking on a few stray M&Ms and marshmallows. Liz smiled and walked over to drape her arm over his shoulders, giving him a quick squeeze before quietly grabbing the dishcloth to wipe up the sticky mess left on all the surfaces in the kitchen. They worked in silence until the kitchen was mostly back to normal. Alex threw the last of the empty packages into the garbage on his way to the hallway.

"Thanks for the help, kiddo," Liz said before he could disappear down the hall. "Have a good sleep."

Alex briefly looked back at her, smiling, "Yep, night Mom."

"Carson... Jack... I want you two to get ready for bed now," she called into the living room.

A groan from one of them could be heard through the wall as they turned off the television. Liz could hear the two boys shuffling together into the hallway from the living room before they came into view at the entryway of the kitchen. Carson led Jack by only a few feet.

"Night boys. Come get me in the office if you need anything."

"Okay. Goodnight, Mom," Carson replied, not slowing down from his shuffle toward their bedrooms at the end of the hall.

Jack ran into the kitchen to wrap his arms around Liz's waist in a hug. "Night, Mom. I love you."

Liz smiled, leaning over her youngest to hug him back and kissed him on the top of his head.

"Night, Jack. I love you, too. Have a good sleep tonight."

"Okay," he said, letting her go and running back to the hallway to catch up with his brothers.

Liz turned back to the kitchen to fill the kettle with water. After turning it on, she opened a nearby cupboard for her favourite tea mug – a navy blue mug with small penguins skiing across the bottom. She then grabbed a chamomile teabag from the pantry as the mechanical sound of the kettle warming up filled the quiet kitchen. Liz pulled her phone from her pocket, looking through social media images while she waited for the kettle to click off. With the seeping tea in her hand, Liz moved around the house, turning off the lights that the boys left on and arming the alarm system by the front door. Once finished, she walked quietly from the dark rooms back to the bright office. The bathroom light at the end of the hall was on and she could hear the light banter of the boys as they got ready for bed. She smiled at the sound as she turned into the office and sat down behind the desk again, carefully placing her tea onto a black plastic coaster before pulling her work back in front of her. As she moved the chair closer to the desk, her head felt wobbly, as if she were a bobble head and the movement made her head bounce. She closed her eyes, pulling her hand up to cover her eyes until the feeling passed.

Maybe the wine was a bad idea ...

She carefully took a sip of the hot tea, trying not to burn her tongue, until the dizzy feeling passed. She would not let the buzz from the wine slow down her ability to focus on her work. The editing process had become second nature, allowing her to ease into it any time of day, no matter where she was. She could almost do this job in her sleep, which is likely why she didn't notice how fast the time passed as she worked.

At first, Liz was faintly aware of the familiar noises of the boys brushing their teeth. The odd laugh or word travelled down the hallway as they got ready for bed. Then, even those noises stopped, but Liz continued to work. When she finally looked up, she realized her tea mug was near-empty and cold to the touch. An ache had formed in her lower back from crouching over the desk. She raised her hands above her head and stretched before picking up her phone to check the time. It was after one o'clock in the morning. The house was quiet, the air around her heavy with the stillness as she looked up from her phone.

"Damn, I better get to bed. It's way past my bedtime," she whispered to herself, feeling the need to break the silence.

Liz stood up, stretching one more time, before moving the papers into a neat pile near the edge of the desk. She closed her laptop and grabbed her phone. She clicked on her Clock app and changed her alarm to wake her up a little later than usual, absent-mindedly leaving the office, turning off the lights as she went, and crossing the hallway into the bedroom without looking up, closing the bedroom door behind her. Liz crossed the room and plugged her phone into the charge cord on her bedside table before turning on the lamp. A soft glow took over as Liz moved to her bathroom.

After washing her face and brushing her teeth, she headed into the walk-in closet. The room was colder than usual, so Liz pulled out a pair of purple, plaid, flannel pyjamas from a drawer in the dresser against the back wall of the closet. As she changed, goosebumps raised all over her skin. The light in the closet flickered overhead, making Liz pause with her hands almost finished buttoning up her flannel top. She looked up at the light.

What is with the lights lately? Is there some sort of solar flare going on?

She quickly finished buttoning up the shirt before moving to turn the flickering light off. As she walked from the open closet to her bed, a chill passed over her neck, raising the small hairs in alert. She froze, trying to determine what could have caused the feeling.

Please ... no weird shadows tonight ... I thought maybe I had gotten over that momentary lapse ...

Liz stood still, holding her breath as she listened. The silence and stillness felt heavy. The only sound was the furnace turning on to warm up the house on the cool December night. Liz walked to the bedroom door, opening it an inch to listen to the hallway, wondering if one of the boys had gotten out of bed. The hallway was quiet.

Finally, she turned back to the bed, leaving the door open a crack so she could hear movement if someone was awake. She pulled off the extra pillows from the bed, dropping them on the floor behind her instead of stacking them neatly on the chair in the corner of the room like Stan usually would do. She didn't care if the room was neat tonight, she just wanted to crawl into the safety of her blankets. Pulling back the large duvet, Liz sat on the bed, her lower back pushing against her pillow as she lifted her feet to slide them under the blankets. She pulled the duvet back up against her bed to warm up.

The lamp flickered beside her.

Electricity seemed to flow through her body as she stared at the lamp as if it might explode. It flickered once more and then stopped, beaming brightly at her as if everything was normal. She quickly jolted and shifted her gaze to watch the open closet door. She thought she saw a shadow move in her peripheral vision from that direction. Feeling like she was five again, afraid of the boogeyman in her closet, she grabbed her phone, accidentally pulling it off the charger as she pulled it into the bed under the blankets with her. She sunk into the covers further, her eyes never leaving the closet. Her hands were gripping the phone hard, the duvet pulled up to her chin, waiting to see if something would emerge from the closet opening. Sitting perfectly still, she listened intently for any sign of movement. After a few minutes of nothing happening, she began to feel ridiculous.

"Okay, Liz," she whispered to herself. "No more late nights drinking wine when Stan isn't here to check for boogeymen. God, I need to get some sleep. I must be losing my mind."

She slid further into the blankets, resting her head back on her pillow. As she turned to switch the bedside lamp off, she paused as her fingers closed on the lamp's switch.

Would it be so bad to sleep with a light on? No one will ever know ... Just this once.

She pulled her hand back under the blankets, away from the light switch, and closed her eyes. It took longer than usual for her to fall asleep. Any time a creak or shift in the house caused a sound, her eyes would pop open to check the closet opening, just in case. Her hand remained gripped on her cell phone, ready to flick on the screen and dial 9-1-1 at any sign of trouble. She finally fell asleep as it neared three o'clock in the morning.

Chapter 33

- Serafine -

Serafine adjusted her scrubs and white, knit sweater as she walked down the hospital hall. They felt tighter than usual, not fitting quite right. Looking around, the hospital didn't look quite right either. The overhead lights had a bluish tone, instead of their usual cool white. They weren't as bright, allowing black shadows to creep along the edges of the floor. The shadows were thick, reminding her of black puddles of hot tar.

Did the power go out? Maybe we're running on generators.

Not wanting to be late for her shift, she shrugged and walked quickly toward the nurse's station. The hall seemed to go on endlessly, stretching out before her with doors lining each side, never-ending as far as she could see. It didn't intersect with other halls, and there were no doorways leading outside. She paused, looking to her right at one of the many hospital doors. Although it looked just like her hospital wing, the numbers on the side of the door were illegible. Their shapes were odd, as if using an unknown numerical system.

Wait ... What?

Serafine reached out to try the door handle, curious where the door would lead, but it was locked. Turning, she looked back down the hall from where she came. A black wall blocked the path only four doors behind her. She turned back to look ahead. It was the same as before – doors lining both sides as far as she could see, getting smaller in the distance. A breeze behind her made the hairs on the back of her neck rise in warning, making her spin around again.

The black wall was now only three doors away.

She stepped back. The dark void inched slowly along the edges of the hall. It wasn't soft at the corners like a normal shadow, but a sharp edge of pitch black. It was getting closer with every second. Her skin crawled as panic coursed through her. Something in her gut told her that substance could swallow her whole with a single touch.

This can't be real. I must be dreaming.

The thought didn't reduce the sense of urgency she felt. She turned back to jog away from the darkness. The doors continued to stretch in front of her, the end of the hall never getting closer. After a few minutes of jogging, her breath jagged and strained, Serafine saw an opening a few doors down on the left of the hall. A yellow glow cast into the blue-lit hall. She sped up, hoping to reach the door before the black wall behind her came too close. As she reached it, a woman stood in the doorway, her back facing Serafine. The woman had long, curly red hair that was standing up in multiple directions, as if the woman had just woken from a fitful sleep. She wore a long, white nightgown that was dirty and torn.

"Excuse me, miss?" Serafine said, coming to stand behind the woman. "Miss? Can you please let me in? I don't know where we are, but we need to get out of this hallway, quickly."

The woman didn't respond or move. It seemed she couldn't hear Serafine.

Maybe she's deaf.

"Miss?" Serafine said again, reaching out to touch the woman's shoulder gently.

Serafine looked behind to the black wall. It was encroaching on the final door that separated them from its shadow. When she looked back to the woman, thinking of pushing past her into the room, a small scream escaped her lips.

The woman had turned to face her, one eye dangling from her eye socket and her mouth gaped open. The woman's hand reached out as Serafine stepped back in horror. Skin hung from the woman's fingers, exposing sinew and bone along some of the joints. The woman's tongue was flailing in her mouth. It flapped around, as if the woman was trying to talk, but couldn't make the words. Instead, only a gurgling sound escaped her mouth, with no semblance of pronunciation.

Serafine backed away even further until the feeling of the door handle on the opposite side of the hall dug into the small of her back. With wide eyes, she risked looking away from the woman to her left, where the black wall was now only a few feet away. It would soon be upon them. Serafine started to shuffle sideways, looking back at the red-haired woman who hadn't left the threshold of the room. The woman's one good eye widened as she saw Serafine moving away. Her hands clawed at the door frame as if trying to dig her way out of the room.

Why isn't she running? Is she trapped there?

As the woman dug at the wood frame around the doorway, her skin and nails peeled off further. They stuck into the grain of the wood until she had nothing but sinew and bone for fingers. The gurgling sound from her throat became louder and more urgent the further Serafine moved down the hall. Serafine paused, her back still pushed against the wall on the opposite side.

Wait. She's in trouble. I should help her. No matter how horrifying she looks.

But it was too late. The consuming black barrier creeping along the hall was already too close. It seeped into the room behind the woman digging at the door frame. The woman looked over her shoulder to where Serafine's gaze fell. As the darkness swept into the room, she backed out of Serafine's view. The blanket of shadows swept across the threshold, with half the door now seemingly fallen into nothingness. The gurgling sound grew more urgent from somewhere outside of Serafine's view and then morphed into a stifled scream followed by horrifying silence.

Serafine turned back to the open hallway in front of her and ran as hard as she could. With adrenaline coursing through her, she no longer felt the exhaustion she had when she first approached the red-haired woman. She passed the first few doors without pausing, hoping to get distance from the darkness behind her. Then she moved back and forth, trying doors at random, checking to see if any would open. If she could find a room to hide in, with the door locked behind her, maybe the blackness would pass her by. Perhaps it wouldn't be able to follow her.

As she continued running, a door on the right up ahead looked familiar. It was only two doors down. A small sign on the wall beside it had a real number on it that she could read.

Finally, something familiar in this strange dream.

She stopped trying the doors on either side, instead running straight for the familiar one. Her heart was beating hard in her chest and her breath was shallow, but she couldn't stop now. She had to reach the door before her legs gave out from under her. She looked over her shoulder as she neared it. The black wall was still only a few doors behind her, appearing to have matched her running speed as she went. She needed to get into the room fast and lock the door behind her. Perhaps there would be a window she could crawl out of to get out of the nightmare hospital altogether. As she reached out to the door handle, her gaze briefly moved to the sign beside the door.

Room 136.

Stan's room.

It can't be.

She paused, her hand over the handle, wondering how much safer it would be in this room compared to the other doorways down the hall. She looked back over her shoulder again, realizing she had a choice.

Do I continue running down the hallway and hope for another door like this one? Or take the risk of walking into Stan's room, hoping the black wall doesn't follow?

She needed to figure out her next move to escape this nightmare. Taking a deep breath, she turned the door handle. Pushing on the door with everything she had, she fell into the room as it suddenly swung open with ease. Standing up quickly off the floor without paying attention to where she landed, she slammed the door behind her and locked it. Quickly turning, she scanned the opposite wall for a window, but it was like the real hospital room. White walls squared her in.

Serafine turned to watch the door, waiting. She raised a hand to her chest, her breathing rapid from the physical exertion. Her eyes stayed on the crease at the bottom of the door, watching the pale blue light that still glowed underneath.

Wait, I should cover it! Maybe that will help.

She looked around the room, but there were no extra blankets or pillows. Only those on the hospital bed.

My sweater!

Quickly pulling the fabric off her shoulders, she pushed it against the crack of the door the best she could. Then she stepped back and watched. Serafine held her breath, frozen in fear. Her eyes searched the edges of the door. The blackness was not seeping into the room. It was being held back.

Thanks be to all that is mighty.

The tension in her shoulders relaxed, and her breathing returned to normal. Then she heard breathing behind her that was not her own. Slowly, she turned to face the hospital bed that was to her right. Stan lay unconscious in the bed. He looked peaceful, breathing quietly. She inched closer to him, looking around the edges of the bed frame, searching for shadows that may be hiding below. The lighting in the room still had a blue tinge to it, but it was darker than the hallway, causing the shadows around the edges of the room to stretch out towards her. It was as if a pale blue spotlight had been focused on Stan's bed from above.

Serafine moved up the side of the bed to get a better look at him. Black cords came out from his body in various directions. The cords weren't for medical equipment – there were none in the room. The thick black cords were attached to his head, shoulders, back, and arms. They stretched up to something above the spotlight. She followed the cords with her eyes, but the overhead light was too bright. The cords disappeared in their glare.

She looked back down to Stan. His eyes were open again, staring up at the ceiling, just like she had seen a few times in the real hospital. Serafine paused about a foot away from the bedside near his shoulder. A smile slowly stretched across his face, until his cheeks looked painfully tight and his eyes became crazed. She gasped, taking a step back from the bed again. Then the cord connected to his head pulled tight from above, forcing his head to lift and turn toward her. The grin didn't change, but his eyes shifted in their sockets to focus on her face.

"Stan? Is that you?"

More cords pulled tight from above, forcing him to sit up in his bed. His head fell to the side at first, as if he was a marionette and the strings were no longer pulled tight enough on his heavy head to keep it up. Slowly, with the grin still stretched across his face, Stan's head lifted. His eyes found Serafine again, not leaving her while he shifted back to face her.

What are those cords for? Why are they attached to him?

Serafine stepped further back, her gaze following the cords up into the ceiling. Lifting her hand above her head, she tried to shade the glare to let her see past it. Stan's awkward body remained sitting up on the bed like a puppet waiting for its next command.

There was no ceiling above them. The cords went up high above the room, a black wall covering only a portion of the opening. Serafine strained her eyes to see past the black wall, but it was too dark. As she moved further back from the light's glare, near the edges of the room, she realized it was not a shadow or a wall blocking her view. It was a giant, black body hovering over them. The black creature was not like the others she had seen in her previous dream. This one had smooth, black skin without the tar-like substance dripping from it. The smoothness made it difficult to discern any details. The creature's hand came into view. Its massive, long fingers with pointed, sharp claws were attached to the cords controlling Stan.

Serafine glanced back at Stan. He swayed slightly in the bed, his head bobbing as its weight shifted from side to side. His eyes were still large and staring directly at her, the smile still ghastly and wide. When she looked back up, she saw the creature's other hand, except it had no cords attached to its fingers. It was empty and reaching down towards the opening of the room. Serafine stepped back as far as she could, her back pressed up against the corner of the room. The hand slowly entered the space, taking up a large portion of what would have been the ceiling. It wasn't interested in Stan: it was reaching for her. She screamed as she sat on the floor, pressing harder into the corner of the room to keep out of its reach. Its sharp nails continued to move closer, grasping at the air as the creature searched for her blindly. She covered her face with her arm and closed her eyes.

Serafine screamed as something wrapped around her body, squeezing her, making it hard to move. The binding was soft and hot, but not painful, so she opened her eyes. She was in her bed, soaked in sweat and wrapped up in her sheets like a cocoon. She pulled off the tight blanket and turned on the lamp nearby. The room lit up, revealing that it was empty with nothing out of place. No shadow figures lurked in the corners. The door to the living room was open and she could see nothing out of the ordinary through to the living room.

Remembering what she had found earlier that day, she turned and frantically felt under the pillow. At first, she only felt cool sheets around her hand, sending her into more of a panic, but then something grazed her palm. Relief washed over her as she gripped the small, bundled cloth. She pulled it out, turning the black pouch over in her hands. After spending hours reading through her mother's handwriting in the notebooks from the box, she found a note about this pouch.

It was the *gris-gris* her mother had said to find. Serafine read that the pouch was filled with items that would ward off evil spirits and protect whoever held it. Thankfully, all three were in the box, so she could spare one to help Stan and his family. All she had to do was get it to the hospital and find a way to keep it on Stan's body where no one else would be able to find it. She had already called her sons to make sure they were not having nightmares and were not in any trouble. They were safe. It seemed the creatures didn't know about them yet.

She had to keep it that way.

Going through the list of fellow society members' names from her mother's journal, Serafine made a plan. She would book a flight down to New Orleans as soon as she could get it. Then she would find someone who had known her Mother.

Maybe they can help me.

Serafine closed her hand over the pouch and held it to her chest, closing her eyes. The image of the creature looming over the hospital room and Stan's body strung up like a marionette were behind her eyelids, waiting for her. She quickly opened her eyes again and turned to look at the clock on the night-stand. It was nearly five in the morning. She sighed, realizing she wouldn't be getting back to sleep. Pulling the blankets off, she swung her legs out of the bed to put her feet down on the cold, carpeted floor. At least she had a plan.

Hopefully, it works.

Chapter 34

- Stan -

Stan wandered the hospital halls. The haunting image of the red-haired woman falling into the hole with the black creature riding her back wouldn't leave his mind. Carefully looking around corners before turning down new hallways, he worried the creatures would return for him. He avoided the shadows and dark rooms. The invisible tether with his physical body grew tighter as the hours ticked by, as if his time was running out. He hoped Liz would return to the hospital soon. Perhaps she could save him from the fate that had befallen the red-haired woman. The darkness outside the windows of the hospital meant it was nighttime outside. It could be hours before she returned. He searched the walls for a clock, but the same blank, white walls met him at every turn.

Voices drifted from around the corner. He moved towards them, hoping to find a nurse's station. There would be a clock at the desk. As he rounded the corner, he nearly ran into an old man standing in the middle of the hallway. The man had white hair neatly flattened against his scalp. He wore all white – pants and a long sleeve shirt – and his skin was transparent, even more faded than Stan's.

"Sir! Hello!" called Stan.

The man continued to stare ahead as if looking right through Stan. Stan waved his hands in front of the man's face.

"Sir? Can you hear me?" Stan tried again.

The older man didn't even flinch. He continued to stare at the wall as if frozen in time. Stan carefully walked around him, pausing behind him to see what the old man would do. The man remained still, like a statue.

Voices from behind made Stan turn and look down the hall. Two nurses were quietly talking to each other in front of a small desk at the corner where two hallways met. Stan turned back to look at the old man one last time, but he was gone, as if never there at all. Stan sighed, walking to the desk, and moved to stand behind it. The nurses were unaware of his presence. The clock behind the desk said it was a quarter past three. The tether around his waist felt tight.

Perhaps I should get closer to my wing at least.

He wondered if he could teleport there instead of searching the halls for the right direction. He had walked a long time, so he couldn't remember where he had started. Practicing teleportation might also help him get better at it. It would come in handy if the creatures ever did come back for him.

I'm sure they will eventually.

Stan didn't have anything better to do while waiting for Liz to return. He closed his eyes, visualizing the hall just on the other side of the nurses whispering in front of the desk. A slight breeze passed over him as a tingling sensation passed through his body. When he opened his eyes again, he was right behind the shorter nurse, her black hair inches from his face. He stepped back in surprise, not wanting to accidentally touch her.

"It worked!" he said with a smile.

He looked down to the end of the hall from the direction he had come and closed his eyes again. The same breeze and tingling sensation washed over him. When he opened his eyes, he was in the middle of the hall that intersected the one with the nurses. He turned to look at them, but they continued to whisper to each other, oblivious to his movement.

"Yes! I can do this!"

"I can do this. I can do this," a female's voice mimicked behind him.

He spun around. An elderly woman was walking slowly toward him from down the hall on the right. She was wearing a long white dress that reminded him of a nightgown. It covered everything except her hands and face. Her hair was white and curled up in a tight perm on top of her head.

"I can do this. I can do this," she repeated.

"Miss?" asked Stan.

She didn't look up, simply continued repeating "I can do this," as she shuffled closer. Stan sighed. It was going to be difficult to find another exactly like him – a spirit with their mind still intact. He turned back to the hall towards his wing and decided to try a larger jump. Closing his eyes and ignoring the woman muttering behind him, he slowed his breath. He imagined the hallway outside his hospital room with the hidden nurse's desk down the hall. He envisioned himself standing outside his door, looking down the hall towards the desk, unable to fully see its hidden entrance.

This time, the tether pulled strong as a blast of wind passed over him. When the loud sound of rushing air around him stopped, he carefully opened one eye. He was back in his hallway, although he was very close to his door, with his left shoulder touching it. He jumped, afraid the creature might reach through and grab him.

The hallway was quiet.

Shit, that was a little too close.

He walked toward the nurse's desk, hopeful to see someone he recognized. The nurse behind the desk, however, was new, at least to him. She had blonde hair, tan skin, and purple scrubs. She was reading a novel with a large knife on the front.

Probably a thriller or true crime.

The nurse looked bored with her chin resting in one hand while her eyes scanned the pages. She had a purple beaded bracelet on her left wrist.

Suddenly, the nurse looked up at Stan, as if feeling his eyes staring at her. He raised his hand in a wave, just in case, but she sighed and returned her gaze to the book. He dropped his hands to his sides in defeat.

She can't see me.

Stan turned back to his door, his eyes watching the base of the door frame as he moved closer. The gap along the bottom edge was dark. The lights were still off in his room. He didn't want to go back in there, especially in the dark. Placing his hands against the door, Stan leaned in, resting his right ear against it, and listened intently. The familiar sounds of the machines connected to his physical body hummed and beeped through the door. He pulled his head back to check the floor at his feet again, making sure nothing was reaching out from under it. The bright white linoleum glared back at him.

A soft thump came from inside the room. He pressed his right ear back up against the surface between his hands, closing his eyes. A soft murmuring came from somewhere in the room. Pressing his ear harder into the door, he tried to make out what the murmuring sound was, but it stopped. Now, he could hear heavy breathing.

Is my body trying to talk?

Something on the other side of the door exhaled heavily, wheezing slightly. It sounded much closer to the door than his physical body could be. It sounded like it was directly on the other side of where his ear was pressed. A massive force banged on the door, causing vibrations against his head and hands. Stan jumped back in surprise, his eyes dropping to the door handle. The long silver handle flicked once, then twice. He backed up against the wall on the other side of the hall and braced himself, ready to start running in case the creature came through the door.

Movement to his right made him jump to face it. He raised his hands to fight the creature. Only, it wasn't a creature, it was the night nurse. Her tall, thin body was walking down the hall towards him, her clipboard swinging at her hip. As she walked, she opened each door a crack, peeking into each room before closing it and continuing to the next. She had a confused look on her face as she moved down the hallway.

She heard the bang.

She was going to open his door. She was going to let the creature out.

"No, please don't open the door!" Stan yelled at her as she checked the last door before his room. "No, no, no. Please don't."

He tried to grab at her shirt as she reached his door, but she just smoothed her shirt down as if it was just a minor annoyance causing her shirt to bunch slightly.

I need to get out of here.

As the nurse grabbed the handle, Stan closed his eyes. He visualized a visitors' lounge he had passed earlier in the night. The door creaked as the nurse opened it, but he tried to concentrate on the lounge. The familiar wind passed over him and it went quiet again. Stan carefully opened his eyes. Couches and chairs surrounded him and a large window behind him showed the dark sky beyond the brightly lit parking lot in front of the hospital. No one else was in the room.

Oh, thank God. I'm getting better at this.

He moved to sit in one of the chairs, squatting down into the seat. The pull of the tether at his waist suddenly strengthened significantly and yanked him back. He fell to the floor. He was back in his hospital room, near the chair in the back corner. The lights were glaring overhead, and the night nurse was standing by the bed, poking at his physical body.

He craned his neck to look around the base of the bed. Only white, shiny linoleum reflected under it. The hole was gone. Relieved, Stan stood up and walked to stand beside the nurse. She had placed her clipboard on the bed while she worked. Written beside *'Name'* was *'Stanley Jason Stevens'* followed by his gender and next of kin. He skimmed down the page, looking for information about his condition. He managed to see the words "brain injury" and "comatose" before the nurse picked up the clipboard, covering the paper with her hand as she made notes. He shifted to stand at the foot of the bed, looking down at his body. The scratching of her pen on the paper was louder than the electrical sounds of the machinery connected to his body and the ticking of the clock behind them.

"So, I have a brain injury that landed me in a coma, eh?"

For the first time since entering this room, he noticed lines on his physical face that he didn't recognize. They were wounds slowly turning into scars. He moved out of the way as the nurse moved around the bed, laying her clipboard down to pull the blankets off his left leg. She pulled out a hard, white cast.

I broke my leg, too?

He looked down at the transparent leg connected to his current form. He pulled up the tan pant leg to see if there were markings from whatever required a cast. Instead, he saw three long, black scratches across his lower leg. It was from the creature when it tried to pull him under the bed into the gaping hole. He looked back up at his body's leg on the bed. The cast covering his entire leg made it impossible to know if the same three black gashes were present on his physical body, or if it was only on his ethereal form. He sighed, dropping his pant leg to cover up the marks, and moved to sit in the chair closest to the door. The nurse continued to write on her clipboard while he watched.

Why can't I remember what happened?

He tried to think back to before he was in the hospital room, before the shadow realm. He could recall many things now, including memories of him and Liz and how happy they were. He could also bring up multiple memories of the boys. Playing at the park, skiing, swimming at a lake, and even taking them to see the ocean for the first time. Why couldn't he remember the accident that landed him here in the first place?

Seeming satisfied, the nurse put the clipboard down again to push Stan's physical leg back under the blankets, tucking them tightly under the bed. Then she passed in front of Stan and walked towards the door. Stan jumped up to follow her out of the room, not wanting to be alone in the room again. As she swung the door open and passed through, he paused. She had left the overhead lights on, leaving the room bright. Stan looked back at his physical body lying peacefully on the bed. While the door slowly swung shut in front of him, the nurse no longer in view, Stan pondered what he should do.

Maybe I should stay here.

He looked up at the clock on the wall. It was nearing four o'clock. Morning would be coming soon.

Maybe those things can't come back during the day. And what if Liz comes soon? I don't want to miss seeing her.

He paced back and forth along the foot of the bed, the ticking of the clock on the wall indicating the passing of time. After a few minutes, the overhead lights still glaring, Stan moved to stand against the wall beside the door. He slid his back against it as he lowered into a cross-legged position on the floor. He leaned his head back, looking up at the light switch above him, daring it to flick off.

Chapter 35

- Serafine -

Serafine didn't want to go back into that room. Sitting at the nurse's station that morning, she tried to focus on a crossword puzzle in the newspaper. She ignored the itch to look towards Stan's door. She had already checked on every other patient so far but couldn't bring herself to enter his room. Every time she walked by the door, she physically cringed away from it. Guilt pulled at her thoughts, but she did her best to focus on the crossword for now. Even with one of the *gris-gris* in her pocket, she didn't feel comfortable. She brought the pouch to test in his room, to see if anything changed, before she committed to bringing a second one to give to him.

"Good morning, Nurse Bodette."

She started. She hadn't heard Dr. Bractor approaching the desk. Serafine folded the newspaper and placed it under her clipboard, folding her hands over both. Dr. Bractor was busy looking down at her own clipboard, unaware of Serafine's discomfort.

"Do you have anything to report to me this morning before I make my rounds?" the doctor asked, still not looking up from her clipboard.

"Hello, Dr. Bractor. It's a typical Monday morning, I s'pose. Fairly quiet."

"Fine," Dr. Bractor exhaled, turning away.

"I haven't been in to see Stanley Stevens yet," Serafine blurted. "The night nurse had checked on him right before my shift, so I left him for last today."

Dr. Bractor turned back, finally raising her eyes to regard Serafine. She pursed her lips slightly, showing her annoyance with the inconvenience.

"Well, then, come on. I don't have all day."

Without waiting for a response, she turned, walking straight towards Stan's room.

"Nurse?" Dr. Bractor impatiently inquired from somewhere out of Serafine's view.

"Right, sorry," Serafine apologized, putting a hand on the arm of the chair to push out of it.

Serafine grimaced at the ache in her lower back. Keeping her clipboard close to her chest, she shuffled her way around the desk into the hallway. As she emerged, Dr. Bractor stood a few feet away glaring at her, with one hand in the pocket of her white jacket. Serafine paused as she neared Dr. Bractor, hoping the doctor would turn and lead the way. Dr. Bractor wasn't having it though, giving Serafine an exasperated look while motioning for her to go first. Sighing, Serafine moved around Dr. Bractor and shuffled in the direction of Stan's door. Her stomach twisted as they approached, the tea from that morning threatening to rise. Her entire body was fighting her feet as they inched closer. When she reached the room, she placed her hand on the door handle and paused. Letting her senses drift into the room, she listened for movement on the other side of the door.

"Is there a reason we're just standing here?" The annoyance oozed out of Dr. Bractor.

Serafine closed her eyes and pushed the door open to walk into the room. She went as far as she could without letting go of the handle until her arm pulled back into a painful, awkward angle behind her. She paused, acting as if she was simply holding the door open. After Dr. Bractor passed, Serafine cautiously looked around the room. The overhead lights were bright, removing most shadows in the space. The room itself no longer held a sinister aura. It felt calm.

Dr. Bractor cleared her throat from Stan's bedside, so Serafine quickly moved to stand near his feet. Dr. Bractor didn't hesitate, barking details to her before Serafine came to a full stop at the bed. Quickly flipping open the clipboard, Serafine pulled the pen from its holder and started to write. When Dr. Bractor paused long enough, she wrote down Stan's name and room number at the top.

"Okay, let's check his reflexes," the doctor said.

Dr. Bractor pulled at the blankets along the bed, revealing Stan's right, bare thigh. She pulled a sterile package from her pocket and proceeded to pull a needle out of it. Serafine raised her hand to protest, but Dr. Bractor raised her free hand in irritation as she poked Stan's right thigh with the needle. Stan's leg twitched as soon as the needle entered his skin. A shadow flashed by Serafine's peripheral vision on the right. She quickly turned her face, but no one was there. The linoleum floor along the right side of the bed was empty.

"Good," Dr. Bractor said, ignoring Serafine and moving the needle to Stan's hand.

She pushed the needle into the fingertip. The entire finger recoiled in response.

The chair behind Serafine crashed into the wall causing a loud bang to reverberate through the room.

Both women jumped in surprise, looking at the back wall. Serafine quickly turned to look back at Dr. Bractor, only to see two eyes glaring at her.

"Nurse, can you please be more careful? I could have scarred him permanently. Focus."

"But I didn't—" Serafine began to protest, a tingling sensation crawling down her arms.

"Quiet, please. One more test then we're done."

This time, Dr. Bractor didn't push the needle into Stan's skin. Instead, she let it drag along the back of his hand. Stan's hand twitched again, this time less aggressively.

"Excellent. He's progressing well. Note he's more responsive than the last time I tested him."

Clearly feeling that she had accomplished a major, medical advance, Dr. Bractor pulled her shoulders back, standing up straight with a wide smile on her face. She dropped the needle into the bright yellow sharps container by the door before leaving the room. Serafine stood at the foot of the bed, her mouth gaped open, uncertain of what to do. Fear was telling her to get out as fast as possible. Her heart thumped loudly in her chest. She was not alone in the room for the chair to hit the wall like that. Yet when she looked down at Stan's bare leg, still uncovered, guilt washed over her. Her patient needed to come first, no matter how she felt. His care needed to come before any supernatural whims.

Serafine closed her eyes and scolded herself, "Take a breath, Serafine. Just focus on Stan."

Reaching into her pocket, she gripped the *gris-gris*. It gave her a brief sense of relief. Nothing could happen to her as long as she held it. Doing her best not to pay too much attention to anything but the task at hand, she put her clipboard down on the end of the bed and moved to tuck his leg back in, leaving the pouch in her pocket. A small droplet of blood had formed on his leg where Dr. Bractor had pierced it, so she pulled open the nearby drawer and grabbed a small bandage. Once the bandage was in place, she pulled the blankets over his leg and tucked them under the mattress.

The sink behind her turned on full blast.

She spun around to look at the sink. Her hands shook as she walked the two-foot gap and reached out. The water was hot, causing steam to rise from the cool ceramic sink, fogging the mirror slightly around the bottom. She turned the hot water tap until it shut off, watching the water drain completely from the sink.

"Okay, maybe that's good enough for today."

As she turned to grab her clipboard, something in the mirror caught her eye. She paused, looking more intently at her reflection. Black hair frayed loose around her head in the mirrored image, but she could feel her own hair neatly pulled back into a bun at the nape of her neck. She raised her hand to touch the side of her head. The hair wasn't hers. It belonged to someone behind her. At that moment, a woman stepped out from behind her. It was her mother, smiling at her in the reflection. Except her eyes weren't dark brown like she remembered – they were bright yellow. They even glowed slightly. Her mother's smile was also unnatural, curling up higher on her face than Serafine had ever seen. A droplet of green oozed out of her mother's mouth. Serafine turned away from the reflection quickly to face the being behind her, bringing her hands up to her chest as she gasped.

There was no one there. No one in the room, except for Stan laying on the bed. Serafine looked quickly back at the mirror, but the reflection showed only herself now. The thing wearing her mother's face was gone.

Deep breaths, Serafine. That wasn't really her. Now let's go.

She turned back to the bed to pick up her clipboard, giving Stan one last look. He looked like he was sleeping peacefully.

"I'm sorry, Mr. Stevens. I wasn't sure the pouch would help, but it seems to be keeping them at bay. I'll bring something to help you soon."

As she moved to the door, she did her best to keep her gaze on the floor in front of her, not looking around the corners of the room or back into the mirror. As soon as she was in the hallway, she pulled the door shut behind her, fighting against the electronic hinge to make it move faster. Her body melted against the door as soon as she heard the click of the latch into the catch on the doorframe. With her hand still on the handle and the clipboard in the crook of her left arm, Serafine closed her eyes to take a few deep breaths. The sound of another door closing nearby startled her. Dr. Bractor was a few doors down, looking at Serafine with disgust. Dr. Bractor shook her head and turned to move to the next room.

Serafine stood up tall, angry at herself for letting someone treat her so poorly, and also for behaving so irrationally. Even if the figure in the room had been real, there was no reason to let someone like Dr. Bractor talk down to her and treat her that badly. She turned her back to the direction that Dr. Bractor went and stalked back to the nurse's desk. After squeezing into the small space, she dropped her clipboard on the desk near the computer's keyboard. She reached into her pocket and pulled out the *gris-gris*, gripping it in her palm. Her mind drifted to her Mother and their old house in New Orleans. One of her favourite memories flooded her. It was when they would dance in the kitchen, arms swinging above them. Serafine smiled. Then her mother in her memory suddenly stopped, turning to face Serafine as her younger self. Her mother's face went still, then slowly contorted to reveal the same grin from the reflection in Stan's room.

"Mother," Serafine whispered, rubbing at the pouch in her hand, "if you're really still around, please watch over me now. I need your strength more than ever."

The phone started to ring, snapping Serafine back to the present. She cleared her throat, put on her friendliest voice, and picked up the receiver as she slid the pouch back into her pocket.

"Hello, Nurse Serafine speaking."

Chapter 36

- Stan -

Stan was stuck in the room. Serafine had closed the door quickly as she left, making it difficult for him to follow her out. He was amazed at the number of emotions he had felt in such a short period. First, shock when the chair hit the wall. He had kicked it in anger over the doctor poking him, but when he actually connected with it, he was just as much surprised as everyone else. Then guilt washed over him when Serafine took the blame, but also excitement that he had finally made something move in the physical world. It felt good to connect with something in a real way. Unfortunately, that excitement didn't last long.

When the water turned on by itself, he knew the creatures were coming. He could feel their pulsing energy, but it seemed like they were held back by something. Like they couldn't fully enter the room. He didn't realize they could manipulate physical objects. When the legless creature had been inching down the hall, the hospital staff took no notice. The creature's noise and destruction appeared to only be visible in his realm. Serafine had been terrified of something in the mirror, too. When Stan tried to peer over her shoulder, he saw nothing but her reflection. Not even his own was reflected in the glass.

Something was trying to scare her out of the room, that was all he knew for sure.

He turned his gaze from the door back to the sink. It was off, but water dripped rhythmically from the faucet.

What has the power to do that?

A whining started in the back corner of the room as a gust blew across him. It felt like it came from the door and into the back corner of the room behind the bed. The whining reminded him of listening to heavy gusts of wind passing over a corrugated metal roof. Turning, he searched along the edges of the room for the cracks forming along the floor. The lights were still on, so the floors shone white. For a moment, the sound died down, returning the room to silence, but he wasn't fooled. He was on alert, unsure of what creature he would be meeting next – the black ones from the hall or whatever had the power to influence the physical world.

When the sound started up again, however, it changed. It was heavier as if the wind had become sticky and thick, like a snail slowly climbing out of its shell. Bracing himself for the worst, he couldn't help but move to the other side of the bed to check for the hole. The floor was still empty. The creatures weren't here yet, but they were coming. Whatever had held them back while Serafine was in the room seemed to have left with her. The lights flicked off, changing the atmosphere of the room back to that sinister orange glow.

Shit.

A movement in the mirror over the sink caught his eye. A woman was standing in the reflection. She had wild, dark hair with tight curls. A thick purple cloth was wrapped around her head, trying to hold her hair away from her face. She wore a long black dress with a gold scarf wrapped around her waist. Her eyes glowed yellow as she smiled at him through the glass. Stan couldn't move. Her eyes were mesmerizing, holding him in place.

"Who are you?" he finally stammered.

The woman grinned wider, revealing black, pointy teeth. Her lips curled back as the smile grew too wide for her to be human. A droplet of green oozed through her teeth, dripping down her chin. Stan shuddered, involuntarily closing his eyes. As soon as his gaze broke away from hers, he could feel control over his limbs return.

Mind control? What are these things?

Determined to keep his eyes off the new creature in the mirror, he immediately turned his head down to the floor before opening his eyes again. While squinting at the floor, he put his arms out in front of him and shuffled towards the door.

I need to get out of here.

As he moved, he could feel the eyes of the woman in the mirror on him. The urge to look at her was strong, but he forced his gaze to stay low. It was difficult. His head wanted to lift. Feeling like he was going to lose the fight, he put his hand over his eyes and moved faster as the sound in the room grew louder. The wind moving through the door grew stronger, pushing against him. He leaned into it, trying to keep moving, but his feet were slipping. He was being pushed towards the back of the room.

A loud crack sounded behind him. Without thinking, he spun around, the wind pushing him down to his knees. Creaking started in the back corner behind the bed, like an old, rusty cupboard door opening up. His clothing whipped painfully at his arms in the wind as he watched. The creaking grew louder and the air around him shifted. He didn't dare wait to see what could be causing the suction behind the bed. He looked back to the door, accidentally glancing towards the mirror. The woman had her body pushed up against the glass now. The hideous grin was still on her face, her chin shining with green drool, but the skin of her human mask couldn't take it. Her cheeks cracked along the edges of her mouth and chin. She reached up with her hand, which had long, black, dagger-like fingernails. As soon as she touched the cracking skin, it began to shed, revealing scaly black skin underneath.

Stan dropped his gaze to the ground instantly, afraid of his mind being controlled again. Crawling now, fighting against the suction from the opposite direction, he moved to the door. The wind was the strongest at the door, pulling his skin, along with his clothing and hair. He reached up to the door handle, gripping it tightly so he could stand. Once standing, he gripped the door handle with both hands, trying not to be pulled away. He closed his eyes, focusing his thoughts on the hallway. The familiar wind didn't wash over him. He opened his eyes. The door still blocked his path. He hadn't been transported out of the room. Something was keeping him inside. He kicked at the door in a panic, but it felt hard and firm as if it were a steel wall in front of him.

"No, no, no, no. Let me out, let me out!" he yelled at the door.

He looked over his shoulder at the sink, worried the woman from the mirror had made it out and was coming towards him. The room was still empty. A red glow was creeping up the walls from the other side of the bed, slowly shifting the glow in the room from orange to deep red.

He was running out of time.

Squeezing his eyes shut tightly, he visualized the visitor's lounge this time. He thought about the faux brown leather chairs, and the light coming through the tinted windows during the day. He tried to feel the white, linoleum floor under his feet.

A scratching sound came from behind him. He closed his eyes tighter, trying to keep the image in his mind. A loud bang from his right shook the mirror on the wall, the metal frame shook violently. Something scratched along the linoleum behind him, bringing back the sound of the nails on a chalkboard.

It was getting closer.

Focus, Stan, focus! Think about the comfy chairs. Think about the lounge.

A weight lifted, like the air around him became lighter. A different kind of wind washed over him. The temperature became noticeably warmer, and the strong wind stopped pushing at his body. Stan opened his eyes. The familiar brown chairs lined the wall in front of him.

"I did it!" he exclaimed, punching the air in excitement.

The movement instantly drained him of all the energy he had left. He dropped his arms to his sides and fell back into one of the chairs. Someone sat in the chair at the end of the room, their face hidden by their hands as they leaned over their knees. Stan smiled, grateful to be back with the living. He closed his eyes and crossed his hands over his chest, leaning his head to rest on the wall behind, his elbows on the arms of the chair.

I need to figure out a way to get away from those creatures. I need to get back into my body, so they leave me alone.

He stayed there, his eyes still closed, thinking about the hospital. About all the places he had visited when wandering the halls. He knew, ultimately, he would need to return to his body. That was likely the only way to get rid of the creatures for good, but he didn't know how, and they weren't giving him the space and time to figure it out. They were getting too close. He needed time to think. If only there was somewhere safe and quiet that he could go. Somewhere that would give him the time he needed to figure out how to connect back into his body so that he could wake up from this hell. Stan's eyes popped open, and he sat up in the chair when an idea hit him.

I can go home!

Home with Liz would be safe. Perhaps she was the key to getting back into his body and waking from the coma. She had been the key to everything else he had accomplished so far.

He sat forward in the chair, resting his elbows on his knees, as he contemplated how to get to the house. He tried to think about what the house looked like, about how he and Liz used to move from room to room, but the memories blurred around the edges. He couldn't get a clear picture. It was too far to teleport.

I'll wait for her to come back. I'll teleport into the vehicle when she goes home. I won't let myself get pulled back. She'll save me. She'll set me free.

Chapter 37

- Liz -

The day had been hell for Liz. When she brought up the editor coming from Seattle, Bob had told her not to worry about it. He refused to go into details about what the interview was for, or where the money was coming from to potentially hire someone new. When she mentioned that she would have applied if she'd known a position was open, Bob had brushed her off saying that it wasn't an official opening, just something he was considering.

It didn't help that shortly after that argument, she had screamed in the middle of the lunchroom. She could have sworn someone following her to the bathroom. She had heard footsteps behind her through the hall all the way from her office. Every time she turned to look back, there was no one near her. The other staff continued working at their desks as if nothing was unusual. The lights had flickered as she neared the bathroom door, so she turned back to cut across the lunchroom. A thump behind her made her jump to reach for the drawer with cutlery. She spun around wielding a spoon, the first thing she could get her hands on, and screamed, "Stop!"

Except, it was her assistant Jane standing on the other side of the lunchroom. Entering from a different direction, not following Liz. Jane screamed and ran from the room, terrified of Liz holding up the spoon between them. The next minute, Bob was there.

"What the hell is going on?" he'd yelled. When his eyes had reached hers, he seemed to deflate, as if he was dealing with an irrational, unruly child, not his top writer and acting editor.

Liz had cowered to her office, refusing to even open the door the rest of the day. She was sure they all thought she was incapable of continuing her position. It was only a matter of time before they would escort her from the building, forcefully taking away her laptop and dignity.

She slunk into her house later that afternoon just in time for the boys to walk in after her. She was grateful for their smiling faces.

At least they didn't see my irrational outburst. They still think I'm normal.

She dumped her extra work for that evening into the office before returning to the kitchen to start supper, relieved to be in the sanctuary of her home. She poured a large glass of wine, and they all ate and cleaned up. Then the four of them watched television in the living room until nine o'clock when Liz announced it was time for bed. She was back to feeling like herself, the episode at the office almost completely forgotten. The boys groaned in unison as they slowly peeled themselves off the living room furniture.

"Come on, boys. You've all got school tomorrow. I should really get some work done tonight, too."

"Okay, Mom," Carson sighed, shuffling to follow his brothers down the hall.

Liz moved through the other exit from the living room into the kitchen. She placed cups and popcorn bowls in the sink. Jack ran into the kitchen behind her, wrapping his arms around her waist.

"Night, Mom. I love you."

She smiled, putting an arm around his shoulders, and squeezed him back. Leaning over, she kissed the top of his head.

"Night, Jack. I love you, too. Have a good sleep."

He released her to run down the hall towards their bedrooms.

She turned back to the counter and pulled the kettle from its base to fill it with water. After making herself tea, she went about the familiar movements around the house, turning lights off as she went. Then she got back to work, half listening to the boys getting ready for bed. The repetitive evenings were almost calming. At one point, while reading a story planned for the third page of Wednesday's paper, she took a moment to rest her head on her arms on the desktop. Her eyes ached from staring at the bright screen, so she closed them to give them a break. After a few minutes, she looked back up at the screen, but her eyes began to water from the strain.

"Maybe I should just get some sleep," she muttered to the empty room.

Standing up, she stretched her arms above her head and then turned off the lights as she moved out into the hallway. Everything was dark in the house now, with no lights on in any direction. The hallway was so black, she couldn't even see her bedroom door across the hall. She stepped into the hall, putting her hands out in front of her, searching for the familiar feel of the door frame. When her hands touched the opposite side, all she could feel was a bare, cold wall. The office door slammed behind her. She spun around to look at it, but it was too dark. She stepped back until her back pressed up against the wall. She reached out on either side, searching for the doorknob to her room, but could only feel a flat, hard wall behind her.

What the hell? Where's my bedroom door?

A light glow from the direction of the kitchen caught her attention. She turned to face it, but it seemed too far away to be a glare from the kitchen windows. She moved towards it, keeping her right hand on the wall as she walked. She felt for a light switch or door frame. The hallway grew brighter, but she never reached the kitchen. The hall seemed to stretch out endlessly in front of her. She turned to look back toward the office, but the hall behind her had changed as well. Doors lined both sides, stretching out far into the distance. She looked over her shoulder, but the dim kitchen light was also gone. The hall now stretched out in both directions; doors lined both sides evenly as far as she could see. She walked to the nearest one on her right, trying to open it. It was locked. She walked across the hall to the opposite door, but it wouldn't budge.

How did I get here? Where am I?

A scratching sound came from behind her, like an animal frantically pawing at one of the doors. As the scratching grew more fervent, a door on her right began to rattle. Liz walked over to it, opening it with ease. As she stepped into the room, her reflection stared back at her. Mirrors lined every wall. She held the door open, looking around the room for the source of the scratching, but the room appeared empty. Only her reflection stared back at her from each direction.

A small dark spot formed in the corner of the room. She squinted her eyes, trying to make out the shape that was forming. As the black spot grew larger, spreading across the corner of the mirrors opposite her, a long black hand came out. Dripping with a tar-like substance, skinny claws scratched at the floor in front of it. The mirrors shattered as a black head came through the dark opening with yellow eyes focused on her. As the shards of glass flew towards her, she covered her face with her hands and stepped back into the hall, pulling the door closed in front of her. Her feet crunched on something, and pain shot up through her ankle. Shards of glass surrounded her, lining the floors of the hallway in both directions, as if hundreds of mirrors had shattered along the walls. She lifted her heavily bleeding foot, dripping blood onto the clean shards of glass littering the floor.

"Son of a bitch!" she yelled, trying not to move her other foot amongst the glass.

The sound of dragging along the floor made her look up. A few feet behind her were three more black creatures inching toward her. They were slowly crawling closer as if the shattered glass wasn't scraping along their bellies. Two more creatures appeared on the ceiling above, matching the speed of the other three. Liz looked down at her feet again, trying to find a place to step that wasn't covered in glass. Her legs were bare. She was no longer wearing sweatpants and a white t-shirt. She was now wearing a small, white teddy nightgown. The same teddy that she pulled out on her and Stan's wedding anniversary every year.

What the...? How could that be? I must be dreaming...

Liz looked up to yell at the creatures, hoping to scare them off, but nothing came out. She gripped her neck, trying to clear her throat, but her voice was gone. The creatures on the floor were getting closer; she was running out of time. The one nearest her opened its mouth, revealing long, dark fangs. Green drool oozed and dripped out of its mouth. Looking down the hall in the other direction, the shattered glass glittered in the strange light illuminating the hall, which slowly shifted from white to blue. With one final look at her bare feet, she took a deep breath and took a step. Shards of glass broke into the skin of her other foot, pain radiating up her leg. She picked her foot back up and saw another bloody footprint left behind amongst the glass. She looked back over her shoulder. The creatures were inching closer, the details of their scaly, black skin now clearer.

I don't really have a choice. And if this is a dream anyway ...

She took a deep breath and started to run along the edge of the hall, trying to ignore the pain in her feet as the glass tore at them. She tried every door handle she passed.

I need to get out here.

She looked back over her shoulder while she ran, limping heavily now from her torn-up feet. The creatures matched her speed, and they were all grinning widely. She tried to scream again, but no sound came out. As she turned back to face the direction she was running, she lost her balance and fell onto the shards of glass. She reached her hands out to break her fall. Glass crunched against her palms. The pain was unbearable, so she tried to lift her hands, but that made her fall onto her knees. Pain now radiated all over her body as the glass tore into the flesh of her legs. She shifted her weight, trying to balance on the edges of her knees and feet, and picked up her hands. Blood ran down her forearms and tears fell from her face.

I can't. I just can't.

She couldn't keep running; the pain was too much. She turned back to the hall behind her in time to see a creature had reached her. It raised its arm above its head as it opened its mouth. Liz tried to cover her face with her bloody arms to lessen the blow as its claws came down towards her face.

Liz woke with a start, nearly falling out of the chair. She was back in the office, wearing her sweats and t-shirt. The laptop screen had gone black while she slept on the desk. Her lower back ached from crouching over. She rubbed her hands on her face, trying to wipe away the terror from the dream. Her face was wet with tears that had fallen while she slept.

"Damn nightmares. I need a better sleep," she muttered, feeling the need to break the silence in the room.

She picked up her phone to check the time. It was after three o'clock in the morning. The house was silent, the air heavy and cool around her. She stood up from the desk, stretching one more time before closing her laptop and picking up her phone.

Her fingers hesitated on the light switch for the office – her nightmare making her fear the dark.

It was just a dream ... Nothing more.

She flicked the switch off. The hall wasn't as dark as her dream, a light glow coming from the kitchen because of the open windows. As she stepped into the hall into the darkness, her foot crunched down on something sharp, causing pain to shoot up her leg.

"What the fuck?" she said as fear ripped through her.

She hopped on one foot to flick on the nearby light switch. The hall flooded with a yellow glow. She looked at the floor in front of the open office door. The picture frame that had held a photo of her and Stan was on the floor, its glass shattered around it. She sighed and looked up to where the picture frame should be hanging. Its empty spot was a slightly different colour, showing where the paint was faded and dusty. She looked down at her foot. Small red droplets had formed a trail on the floor between her and the office.

Great. The boys must have knocked it down. I'm surprised I didn't hear it. Although, maybe I did subconsciously, and that's where that awful dream came from.

Liz contemplated this while looking down at the broken frame. Her and Stan's smiling faces looked back up at her through the shattered glass, their faces distorted. She turned and hopped toward her bedroom to search for a bandage to stop the bleeding before returning to clean up the hall.

So much for a good sleep tonight.

Chapter 38

- Serafine -

Serafine couldn't wait to get to New Orleans. Her flight was booked for later that evening, so she was in her bedroom, packing things into a large suitcase in preparation for her departure. She needed to get away from Stan Stevens. She needed to get away from Vancouver altogether. She didn't know what she saw in the mirror yesterday. Although it looked a lot like her mother, she knew it wasn't really her. At least she hoped the creatures weren't really the cause of her mother's death. It wouldn't be fair. After all the ways her mother had helped people, for her to end up in these creatures' grips for all eternity wouldn't be right.

Not to mention, I need to know that I won't end up in the same place.

Hopefully, the creatures wouldn't be able to follow her to New Orleans. At least not right away. She assumed their world didn't work like the physical realm, with the need for airplane travel, but she still needed a break from them to find one of her Mother's old friends. One of them would know how to help Serafine.

They must know how to get these things off my scent.

Serafine paused in her efforts to pack her suitcase to close her eyes. She inhaled deeply to calm her nerves. The memory of her mother's face in the mirror, with its yellow eyes and grotesque grin, flooded back. She opened her eyes quickly and exhaled forcefully.

I won't let them win.

Knowing that her sons were safe, she had called in sick to the hospital early that morning. She told them she would need the rest of the week off to recuperate. Although she was flying to New Orleans tonight, she wasn't sure if she would be back by Monday. She wasn't sure how long it would take her to find someone from her Mother's old secret society.

What if they're all dead?

The thought had come up a few times already, but she kept pushing it back down. Surely at least one would still be alive. Or maybe, like her, they would have a child or heir who would be able to point her in the direction of someone who could help. Someone who would be equipped like her Mother had been. Serafine wished she had taken her Mother more seriously while she was alive. Maybe she would have been able to handle the creatures herself today if only she had.

Or maybe they would have found me and the boys sooner.

She couldn't think about that now. The path that led her here was a thing of the past. There was no point worrying about her choices. All she could do was move forward. That meant getting on a plane and finding help.

But first, I need to sneak into the hospital.

She didn't want the nurse covering her shift to see her, so she would need to come up with a sneaky way to get in and out of Stan's room without being noticed. Given it was a Tuesday, that wouldn't be easy. The hospital would be fully staffed during the day, making it even harder to remain unseen. Since her test run with the *gris-gris* at the hospital the day before went well and her boys were still safe, not plagued with nightmares, she would happily give a *gris-gris* to Stan. Thinking of him, she walked over to her dresser where she had placed the two extra *gris-gris* pouches from her mother. Picking one up, she looked at it on her palm.

She planned to go in during the lunch hour. Typically, most nurses would go down to the cafeteria to pick up their lunch. Then immediately following, they sometimes would do the rounds, checking in on each of the patients. Serafine hoped to sneak by when the nurse left for the cafeteria, or right after she checked Stan's room on her rounds. That should give Serafine time to get into the room, plant the *gris-gris* somewhere hidden, and get back out.

A loud bang from the kitchen made her nearly drop the *gris-gris*, but instead, she managed to grip it in her fist. Walking to the open bedroom door, she peered out to search for the source of the noise. All the cupboards and drawers were open. As she watched, one of them slammed shut, startling her. She gripped the *gris-gris* tighter. Then all the cupboard doors and drawers started to slam violently.

"Get out! You're not welcome here! Get out!"

She stretched her hand with the *gris-gris* out in front of her and walked across the threshold out of the bedroom. As soon as she entered the small kitchen space, all went quiet. One cupboard door sat partially open, having bounced back after being slammed shut. A drawer was also still half open, showing her tea collection.

"Maybe I'll take an extra one of these with me to New Orleans, just in case," she said, putting the one in her hand down on the kitchen counter. "It might come in handy."

Picking up the salt container from her kitchen table, she shook it around the room before turning back to her bedroom, her mind returned to focusing on packing her things. She needed to get to the hospital soon. It was nearly eleven-thirty already. Once the *gris-gris* was in place for Stan, she would come pick up her things and get a taxi to the airport. She needed a drink, and the airport lounge felt like the best place for it.

Surely these things won't bother me there.

Chapter 39

- Stan -

Stan was bored. He managed to stay out of his room all night, and the creatures hadn't found him. It was surprising that they only seemed to attack him when he was near his body, but the joy of not fearing for his life was too enticing. Something nagged at him the longer he stayed away, though. The tether to his physical body was no longer as tight as it used to be. It seemed to loosen its grip the longer he stayed out of his hospital room. The change was beginning to worry him. Could the creatures affect the connection between him and his physical body somehow? Was staying away from that room, and away from those creatures, the right thing to do?

Is it possible they're keeping me from my body on purpose?

He stopped in the middle of the hall, pondering what that could mean. He had to go back and figure it out.

When he finally found his way back to the nurse's station in his wing, he was surprised to see a nurse he didn't recognize sitting at the desk, picking at chipped pink nail polish. As if aware she was being watched, she sighed and picked up her clipboard before moving into the hallway. Her long, black hair was tied up into a high ponytail, and it swished back and forth as she walked. As she passed by him to go into one of the rooms, Stan pressed himself against the wall to avoid being touched.

As soon as the nurse disappeared, another woman peeked her head around the corner at the end of the hall. Although he couldn't see her face clearly, he could tell she was searching for others in the hall. He turned to look in the same direction. It was empty except for him, so he turned back to face her, confused about what she was looking for.

A few moments passed, and then the woman quickly shuffled fully into view, as if satisfied that the coast was clear. She hunched over and wore a large, puffy, purple jacket pulled up to cover part of her face. She wore a black hat pulled down over sunglasses covering her eyes. Her face darted back and forth as she slowly moved closer. She clutched at something in her hand and ducked down as low as she could as she passed by the nurse's station. Something about her was familiar, but Stan couldn't place who she was or why she would be walking down the hall in such an unusual manner.

As she passed by him, he felt compelled to follow her. He had to know what she was up to. She obviously didn't want to be seen, and he wanted to know why. Staying a few feet behind her, he stopped as she came to stand in front of his door. As her hand reached out and gripped the door handle, she paused to look up and down the hallway again. Unconsciously, Stan did the same. The hall was still empty. When he turned back to the woman, she had already turned the handle and was quickly moving into the room, not letting the door fully open. Stan teleported himself to stand at the foot of the bed, his curiosity growing over what the woman could be up to. He watched as she turned to look at Stan's physical body.

"Good morning, Mr. Stevens." Stan recognized Serafine's New Orleans accent instantly. "I hope you don't mind me popping in on you like this. It will have to be a short visit. I don't want the other nurse working my shift to know I stopped by."

She pulled the sunglasses and hat off, dropping them on the foot of the bed. She looked down at the thing she had been clutching in her hand. Stan couldn't see what it was, but it emitted a soft white glow through her fingers. A calm feeling washed over him as he stepped closer, trying to see what it was.

"I found this for you. My mother had made it ... back when she was still alive. I guess you could say she dabbled in magic. I didn't think I did, but after the events of the last few days, I now believe in all the warnings she used to give me. And you, Mr. Stevens ... you're in grave danger."

Serafine looked about the room, worry creasing her forehead. She stepped up to the side of the bed, near Stan's right arm. Neither of them noticed the mirror behind them blurring around the edges.

"You need to get yourself back into this body of yours, Mr. Stevens," she continued, a motherly tone taking over her voice. "You're likely moving around the hospital, thinking you're pretty smart pretending to be a ghost and all. But I need you to understand. Those creatures – and I know you know which ones I'm talking about – have a plan for you. Or at least for your body, although I'm not entirely sure what that plan is. You can't let them win. You need to get back into your body, soon. They can't have control of it."

So that's why they only attack me in here. They don't want me to wake up.

The mirror rattled lightly behind them, making Serafine go still. Stan looked back over his shoulder. The mirror was changing, no longer reflecting the hospital room. Instead, it was grey with a cloud of black fog coming up from the bottom of the reflection and filling up the space. Stan looked back to Serafine, who had closed her eyes. Her fingers were tight around the small object in her hands. Finally, she took a deep breath but didn't look behind her.

She opened her hands in front of her and revealed a small pouch before continuing. "I'll leave this object here to help you. It's called a *gris-gris*. My mother made it when I was young. It should help keep those creatures at bay and out of this room. Now, this doesn't mean you can avoid the hard work ahead of you. This pouch might not be able to keep them away forever. It's old, you see, and I don't know how much power it has left. You need to use the time this grants you wisely ... before it's too late."

Serafine lifted his body's right arm and tugged at the blankets, pulling them down to reveal his body lying underneath. Stan looked back to the mirror behind them. Whatever was trying to form in the mirror was having difficulty. He could see a woman's body, but it was blurry around the edges, as if the fog couldn't hold the form. He looked back to the pouch in Serafine's hand. The bright glow from it intensified, pulsating.

"Now, I need to hide this somewhere on you. Somewhere the other nurses won't find it. They won't understand what it's for and would likely throw it away."

A loud bang hit the mirror, reverberating across the small room. Serafine jumped and dropped the pouch on the bed. Closing her eyes, she remained facing forward. Stan was sure she could sense what was trying to break through the mirror behind her, but she didn't look. With shaking hands, she picked the object back up and continued to pull at the blankets until both of his legs were uncovered. Serafine tucked the pouch into the top of the cast covering Stan's left leg, pushing it down with her fingers up to her knuckles before pulling the blankets back up.

The bang on the mirror was louder and more violent this time.

Stan quickly shifted his gaze to check for the woman that was in the mirror the last time, but the black fog was still shivering and unable to hold its form. A crack slowly crept down the center of the mirror, inching out from the middle of the fog. Serafine paused for only a few seconds and then continued to tuck in the blankets on the bed.

"Remember, Mr. Stevens... Stan," she said, turning to look directly at where his ethereal form stood at the foot of the bed.

Wait, can she see me?

"You need to hurry up and stop your gallivanting around," she continued. It felt like she was staring directly into his eyes. "It's time for you to return to your body now before those creatures can force you out forever."

His jaw dropped open. If she couldn't see him standing in front of her, she obviously could sense him. Her eyes on his sent electricity down his spine.

She sighed, turning back to her hat and sunglasses on the bed. "I've already gotten myself involved too much. Those creatures are starting to take notice of me. They don't want me to help you, and I can't risk them going after my own. I hope you understand that."

She carefully placed the hat and sunglasses back on, covering as much of her skin as possible. She moved over to the door and grasped the handle. Pausing there, she looked over her shoulder at the foot of the bed, directly at where Stan stood.

"These creatures, they seem strong. They have a plan for you and your body, Mr. Stevens, and they don't want you catching on. I don't know how long it will take them, but they may try to side-track you from what needs to be done here. You gotta ignore them. Get back in that body and lay your claim. Before it's too late."

She sighed, looking over at Stan's body on the bed. Pressing her lips together in worry, she turned and opened the door. First peeking up and down the hall to check that it was empty, she stepped out of the room and disappeared out of view. He quickly looked back to the mirror. A small crack about three inches long was in the middle of it, but the reflection was back to the hospital. The black fog was gone. The pouch that Serafine gave him appeared to be doing something, although Stan still didn't know exactly what it all meant.

Leaning over the foot of the bed, his hands gripped the railing as he contemplated her warning. He didn't like spending any more time than he had to in this room. His body's chest rose and fell with each breath, the smile not returning. The room was quiet, and a sense of calm filled the air. He wondered if this meant that the creatures were unable to come back as long as the pouch was in it. He walked over to the side of the bed near his left leg where the pouch was hidden. A faint white glow could be seen through the stitching of the blanket. He sat down on the edge of the bed near the pouch, debating how much of Serafine's warning he should believe.

"How the hell am I supposed to get back into my body anyways?" he snapped. "It's not like there's a manual for what I'm going through."

He stood back up, throwing his hands up in the air. Pacing back and forth, he wondered how long this break from the creatures would last. He didn't know if he could even trust Serafine and her little pouch.

He turned to the door, where Serafine last stood, and shouted, "What if your little glowing object doesn't work? Do I risk letting my guard down?"

He knew Serafine couldn't hear him, so his question sat in the air, unanswered. Moving to the corner of the room, he dropped into the chair. He put his head in his hands, thinking through what she had said between the distraction of the fog in the reflection trying to scare her.

What if she is right?

He had already noticed that the tether was growing weaker. Maybe the creatures weren't after him his ethereal form like they had been with the redhead. Maybe they just wanted him out of this room and away from his body. Maybe he had been going about this all wrong this entire time. He needed to find a way back into his body.

He could only hope it wasn't too late.

Chapter 40

- Liz -

While Stan spent the day trying to mend the tether with his body, Liz finally enjoyed a positive day at work. It started not so great: an unknown vehicle occupied her parking spot when she arrived at work, forcing her to use Visitors' Parking. Slightly annoyed, she walked into the office, but the front desks were empty. A male voice boomed from somewhere in the back. She didn't recognize the voice but assumed it was the man from Seattle. She dropped off her things in her office before following the sound of the voice, realizing it was coming from the back boardroom. As she neared the door, the words became clear enough to understand.

"That's why I think this little newspaper could be a competitor of the majors one day. We have a fantastic staff here, with some great journalists. Although, I'm still surprised that one of your best writers is stuck behind a desk doing layouts and proofreading."

Liz paused a few feet from the door. The comment about her current position made her ears perk up and her back go straight.

"With a little rearranging of assignments and a major push in marketing," the voice continued, "we can easily increase the reach of this newspaper. Then we'll be on the search for a larger office space to accommodate the increase in our egos."

Laughter filled the room. Liz rolled her eyes and moved to stand in the doorway. People stood along the wall near the door; there were no seats available. The laughter went silent as everyone turned to look at her.

"Liz!" Bob exclaimed from the head of the room behind a man in a shiny blue suit. "I'm glad you were able to make it. This is Zane Griffin. He's the editor from Seattle I was telling you about."

"Yes, I remember. Hello, Mr. Griffin. It's nice to meet you."

"The legendary Elizabeth Stevens!" Zane boomed as he moved to shake Liz's hand. "You have no idea how excited I am to finally meet you. It was some of your pieces that drew me to this little newspaper to begin with."

Liz narrowed her eyes, contemplating Zane.

"Thank you."

"I was just telling everyone how it's a shame you aren't writing full-time. I think, given the right topics, you could easily increase the demand for this little paper!"

Liz held back the urge to roll her eyes again.

"Well ... I would agree we have a few great writers in this very room that can contribute to the success of the paper. Not just me."

"Don't sell yourself short, Liz. Everyone in this room agrees you should be the lead writer of this place."

"Well," Bob spoke up, "I think we should move to my office to talk logistics. Perhaps everyone else should return to work. Zane, Liz, let's retreat to my office."

Instantly, the room buzzed with people moving and chattering excitedly with each other. Liz stood by Zane and Bob as the three of them waited for the boardroom to empty.

"There we go, now that everyone is out of the way, let's go to my office where we won't be interrupted."

Liz followed immediately behind Bob, not letting Zane get in front of her. It may have seemed like a childish move, but she wanted to emphasize that she was a leader around here, not a follower. Once they all passed through the door of Bob's office, Bob closed it behind them and moved to sit behind his desk. Zane motioned for Liz to take a seat first, so she sat directly across from Bob, leaving the seat to the side for Zane. Bob moved the monitor blocking his view of Zane before folding his hands on his desk.

"Right, okay, Liz. To catch you up to speed, we are currently negotiating the terms of the contract with Zane here. However, he felt it was important you be in the room for the discussion since it would influence your position to some degree."

Liz stammered, "Well, sure. I would be happy to be involved, just like I am with everything else."

"See, that right there ... that's what I am talking about," Zane interrupted. "I think you're forced to wear too many hats in this office, Liz. Of course, my main concern is that my terms are met in this contract, but I also feel you need to be involved in deciding how things change around here. Starting with you telling us what you want your position to be."

"I don't mind helping with the organizational stuff. Especially if it will help the team."

"Liz, I'm not saying you aren't doing it well. But you don't have to be the warrior woman here. I'm hoping to come on and take on some of the more mundane tasks from your plate so that you can focus on what drives you. You're a fantastic journalist. Don't waste your talent on something like proofreading and layouts. I'm surprised to find someone like you here instead of in the major Vancouver papers downtown."

Liz felt her body tense, "I don't need a skyscraper newspaper office to be fulfilled. I'm happy with my team here."

Zane laughed, "I don't mean to strike a nerve, Liz. I'm trying to say I admire you."

Liz didn't know how to respond. She wasn't expecting a compliment from the man she thought was trying to steal her job.

"If you don't mind," Bob interrupted. "I'd like to interject." He'd been watching the discussion unfold between Zane and Liz, his eyes darting back and forth. Liz and Zane both turned to face him. Liz had completely forgotten he was even there.

"Of course, Bob, let's get down to business," Zane said.

As the meeting went on, Liz was surprised to learn that Zane didn't want to push her out. He wanted her to become the lead writer while he tackled editing and layouts. She was still free to voice her input, but she could ultimately hand those duties over in whatever capacity she chose.

"This would also help you in your current predicament, Liz," Bob explained. "With you needing more time working from home, you could use that time to focus on writing. Zane doesn't have kids, so he's more flexible to shift his hours around the teams' needs."

Not to mention, my recent outbursts make you uncomfortable. Liz couldn't stop the thought. She was glad she at least had the control to not say it out loud.

The rest of the day went by quickly. She kept waving back and forth between joy about the ability to focus on writing and worry that her unusual experiences at work and home would lead them to force her out entirely.

Will agreeing to the changes and signing a new contract be a mistake?

She nibbled on her fingernails nervously the entire drive home. The house seemed to greet her with silence and heaviness, as if it had been waiting for her to return to swallow her whole. The boys wouldn't be home from school for another thirty minutes or so. It would be empty when she entered. She wanted her husband, to hear his voice and feel his arms around her. To hear his opinion on her looming career changes.

Deflated, she dropped her bags and files from work to the floor as soon as she entered. Paper scattered around her feet, but she didn't notice at first. Her mind was busy with the realization that the house was sucking the happiness from her. Anger rose inside of her. Her husband was in the hospital, unconscious and unaware of what was happening at home. It had only been a month, but it looked like he was going to be missing Christmas now, too. Liz couldn't imagine putting up the tree and celebrating Christmas without Stan. It was all so unfair. Sighing, she looked down at her feet. Water from her boots seeped onto the floor, forming a puddle that slowly reached out to the papers scattered around the entryway. At least the dreary, cold, and grey December weather matched her mood today.

She sighed and stepped back from the papers. The silence in the house was deafening. She carefully pulled off her boots and jacket, wincing at the pain as the boot rubbed against the bandage on her foot. Putting her wet clothing away first, she then knelt on the floor to pick up the papers and laptop bag. As she moved to the home office, she found herself humming, trying to fill the silent hall. After placing the papers in a pile on the desk and pulling her laptop out of the bag to put down beside them, she contemplated the room.

I need a glass of wine, she thought, defeated.

Turning from the desk, she walked back into the hall toward the kitchen. As she passed her bedroom door, the shadow of a person walking by her open bedroom window made her pause, quickly turning her head to look into the room. Her heartbeat sped up a little.

Is there someone in the house?

Slowly, she stepped across the threshold, searching the corners of the bedroom with her eyes. The bed was half-made, and clothes were scattered on the floor, but that's how she had left it that morning.

"Hello? Is someone there?"

She paused for a moment to listen. The house was silent and still, the room empty. Her eyes fell on the door across the room that led to the master bathroom. It was closed.

Did I close that this morning? Or was it open when I left for work?

She couldn't remember. She had been in a hurry after the boys left for school. Liz let out a breath, realizing she had been holding it. Scanning around the room, she didn't see anyone lurking in the corners. She got down on her knees, confirming there was no one hiding under the bed.

She stood and looked around the room, trying to find something she could use as a weapon in case she found someone hiding in the bathroom. Nothing seemed worthy. She tiptoed out of the bedroom, her eyes never leaving the bathroom door, and continued across the hall. Stan had an old hockey stick in the closet of his office.

That will work.

After quietly opening the closet door and pulling out the hockey stick, she returned to the bedroom. Holding the stick out in front of her, she moved to stand before the closed bathroom door.

"Is anyone in there? I'm warning you, I've got a weapon, so don't come near me!"

She let go of the stick with one hand to turn the handle, nearly dropping it in the process. As soon as the door clicked open an inch, she stepped back, replacing her double-handed grip on the stick.

"I'm coming in!" she called before kicking the door open.

It slammed against the back wall, revealing a dark, empty bathroom. Liz stepped closer, waving the stick back and forth in front of her, just in case. As far as she could tell, the room was empty. Then a shadow in the corner shower caught her eye.

"Who are you?" she yelled, quickly flicking on the light, trying to raise the hockey stick with her other hand.

As the room brightened, she realized she had been yelling at a dark blue towel hanging on the shower door.

I've officially lost my mind. Now I really need that glass of wine to calm my nerves.

A crash of glass exploded from somewhere else in the house. Liz's heart jumped into her throat, blood pumping loudly in her ears, as she spun around to raise the hockey stick back up but got it caught behind the bathroom door, nearly causing the door to slam against her face.

"Fuck, get out of my way," she yelled at the door.

Dropping the stick long enough to get it out of the bathroom, she slowly moved to the hall, peering around the corner of the doorframe toward the kitchen. The silence had returned to the house, as if it had never been broken.

Could they have snuck past me while I grabbed the hockey stick?

She didn't think she had taken her eyes off the bedroom long enough for someone to do that, but maybe she had taken longer than she thought.

Or maybe they're just that *fast.*

Slowly, Liz tiptoed down the hall, thankful for the carpet to mute her steps as she crept toward the intruder. She paused before the opening to the room, listening for movement. The only thing she could hear was the sound of her own breathing and the ticking of the clock in the living room. Liz closed her eyes, trying to decide if she should make a run for the front door and leave the house instead of facing whoever caused the crash in the kitchen.

Maybe the crash is completely innocent. It just had really convenient timing.

Gathering the courage to face a potential criminal, Liz quickly turned the corner to face the kitchen. The room was empty. The blinds along the covered porch were pulled wide open, letting in the grey, dull light from outside.

Who opened the blinds?

The thought only lasted a second, as Liz remembered she was potentially dealing with a person hiding in her house. She slowly walked into the room, searching for the glass that had crashed. Pieces of glass were scattered on the floor that led behind the kitchen island. Liz looked up and saw that a cupboard on that side was open. The very one that she was about to go to – the shelf with the wine glasses. She counted the glasses sitting in the open cupboard. There were only three when usually there were six.

"What the hell?" she yelled at the silent house. "Why is everything in my house falling apart around me?"

Turning back away from the kitchen, she walked down to the hall closet to pull out the broom, leaving Stan's hockey stick leaning in its place. She returned to the kitchen and carefully swept in front of her as she made her way to the cupboard. When she reached the corner of the island, she peeked around it and saw three wine glasses shattered across the floor. Angry, she kneeled to pick up the larger pieces. A loud bang from behind startled her, making her spin on her knees to look. Pain shot up her right knee as a shard of glass she had missed ground into it.

"Fuck!" she screamed as she fell back into a seated position.

Pain radiated through her leg as blood started to rush out of the wound, dripping down her shin. The red against the white linoleum floors was bright. Even in the dull light from the windows, the blood glistened. Liz sat in disbelief, looking around the empty kitchen, as the pain in her knee throbbed. She couldn't tell what the source of the bang could be, but the house was silent again, so she turned her attention to her knee. A curved piece of wine glass stuck out of the wound.

Her mind reeled as she tried to reason how three glasses could have smashed at the same time.

Did one of the boys leave the cupboard open and I didn't notice? And how did such a large piece end up so far around the island?

Even as she tried to come up with a logical explanation, she was grasping at straws.

If it were only one glass falling from the cupboard, it would be believable, but three?

Doing her best to shift her weight off her injured foot from the picture frame, she stood up. Her knee throbbed and blood continued to drip down her shin as she hopped away from where the broom had dropped when she fell back. She leaned around the refrigerator, watching where she placed her feet more closely this time to avoid any more broken glass. As she ripped a piece of paper towel off, her phone rang from where she left it on the desk in the office. Carefully placing the paper towel on her wound, she looked for the piece of glass amid the pooling blood. She gripped the edge of it with her finger-tips and pulled it out, opening the wound fully. After dropping the bloody piece of glass into the broom tray, she pushed the paper towel onto the wound and hopped toward the main bathroom near the boys' bedrooms.

Deciding not to turn on the light and get blood all over the wall, she sat on the edge of the tub and lifted her foot onto the toilet seat across from her. Keeping pressure on the hole in her knee, she pulled open the drawer nearest her and found the largest bandages she could. She ripped the paper off and stacked them back and forth over her knee.

It will probably bleed through quickly, but it will have to do for now.

She leaned over to pick up the stray papers from the ban-dages that had fallen all over the floor. When she looked up to put them in the garbage, movement in the corner of her eye made her gaze shift to the mirror above the sink. It looked like a black fog rolling across the bottom of the reflection.

What the hell is that?

The fog collected at the centre of the reflection, growing in size, until it formed shoulders, a neck, and lastly, a head.

"What the fuck?"

Liz jumped up, slamming her hand onto the light switch on the wall. The bulbs above the sink flickered on, bathing the small room in its yellow glare. Liz stared at the reflection of her own face in the mirror.

The fog was gone.

"What is wrong with me lately?" she scolded her reflection. "Why am I seeing things now? This day has got to end!"

Turning to the light switch, she contemplated the smeared blood on the wall. Exactly what she had wanted to avoid.

"For fuck's sake..." she cursed, searching under the sink for something to clean the blood with. "What's going on in this house?"

Chapter 41

- Stan -

Stan paced back and forth at the end of the hospital bed, staring down at his physical body. Since Serafine had left, he had been trying to figure out ways to reconnect with his body. Touching its hand, climbing onto the bed with it, closing his eyes and feeling for the tether ... Hours had gone by, but nothing worked. His frustration grew. Placing both hands on the bottom railing of the bed frame, he leaned forward and let out a long exhale.

At least the room has been quiet. The pouch Serafine gave me is obviously helping.

The silver handle of the hospital door turned with a loud click, making him spin around as it pushed open.

"Hey, my love. I needed to see you today."

"Liz," he breathed with relief.

She pulled a chair up to the bedside and dropped her purse on the floor beside her. As she pulled off her jacket and draped it behind her, she continued. "You wouldn't believe the week I've been having. It's like I've become unbalanced or something. I can't seem to stop hurting myself."

She pulled a small paper bag onto her lap that Stan hadn't noticed her carrying in. He tilted his head as she unrolled it, waiting for her to continue telling him what was going on, but her focus was on the contents of the bag. Grease spotted it, and it had a familiar label. She placed a white cup with a plastic lid and straw on the small hospital table beside her before pulling out a little bundle of white, waxy paper. Next, she pulled out a red box of fries, grabbing a few with her fingers before setting them on the table. While putting the fries in her mouth, she looked back at Stan's body on the bed, leaning back in her chair.

Chewing on the fries, she sighed. "I realize you can't really talk to me, but I needed to see you. It's so much harder without you and Jules. I miss having her around. Losing you and her in the same month ... it's been difficult."

"Jules is gone?" Stan asked, moving to lean on the bed near her. His eyes watched her closely, wishing he could comfort his wife while she vented.

Liz paused to lift the waxy paper bundle and unwrap a cheeseburger, oblivious to his movement. She took a big bite, grease dripping down her fingers. Dropping the burger back on the waxy paper, she looked inside the paper bag.

"Shit," she said, obviously disappointed. She dropped the bag back onto the table and stood up from her chair, looking around the room.

"What do you need?" Stan asked aloud, instinctively moving to stand beside her.

She went to the paper towel dispenser near the sink. She paused, then turned on the faucet and rinsed her hands. Then she reached up and pulled down on the lever of the paper towel dispenser. Nothing came out. She pulled it down repeatedly, getting harder and louder each time before giving up.

"Great. That about sums up my luck this week."

She looked down at her wet hands before shrugging and wiping them on the bottom of her pants. Then she turned back to the chair and plopped down. She looked over at her meal on the table. A look of disgust passed over her face.

"Oh well, I came here to see you anyways, right?" she said, looking back towards Stan's body on the bed.

Stan moved around to the other side of the room, smiling down at her. Her hair was tucked tightly back into a bun, but a few stray strands had fallen around her face. He couldn't believe how beautiful she was. Suddenly she jumped up out of her chair. The chair screeched across the linoleum, nearly crashing into the sink. He stepped back in surprise.

"Stan?"

Resting her hands on the side of the bed, she leaned over his body, looking down into his face. Stan followed her gaze. His eyes were open, staring up at the ceiling again. She searched his face with wide, hopeful eyes.

Wait, did I do that?

No longer paying attention to Liz as she plopped back into her chair, he leaned over and looked down into his face on the pillow. He waved a hand in front of the face, but nothing registered in the gaze.

"I sure hope one of these days, the opening of your eyes will mean something," Liz sighed. "I swear, I thought I saw your mouth twitch, too. I thought maybe you were trying to smile. I guess I must have imagined it, though."

He looked back up at her in surprise. "My mouth twitched?"

Looking back down to his physical body, its eyes still staring up at the ceiling, he wondered how he had made it move.

Could she be the key again? After all, she helped me get through to this world. Maybe she's the one that can get me back into my body!

She reached out, rubbing his physical arm. Stan could feel tingling along his ethereal arm as he watched. He looked down at his physical hand below her arm, holding onto the feeling of her touch in his mind.

Maybe I can connect with it through her…

His finger on his physical hand twitched. Liz jumped up on the other side of the bed, making Stan lose concentration.

"Stan! Your hand moved! Are you here? Can you hear me?"

"Yes!" he replied, joy filling his body. "It worked. I'm starting to reconnect. Liz, you're the one that can save me!"

The mirror rattled violently against the wall, causing them both to startle. Stan's face dropped, joy turning instantly to fear as he searched the reflection for the fog. Liz gasped in surprise from her chair as she turned quickly to look behind her. The reverse of the hospital room reflected in the mirror. No fog or creatures were there. Stan moved around the bed to stand closer to it, putting himself between the mirror and Liz.

"Why do things get banged around so much in this hospital?" Liz asked the air. "You'd think they regularly demolish rooms in here with all the banging."

Obviously deciding that what she had witnessed was not important, Liz returned her attention to Stan's physical body on the bed. Stan, however, wasn't convinced this was a bang from the staff in the hospital. He brought his face close to the mirror, inspecting the reflection that he could see in it. Nothing changed.

A scratching noise came from the hospital door, like something was dragging nails slowly from the top to the bottom of the frame on the other side.

"Who the hell is scratching on the door?" Liz asked, standing up to open it.

"Liz, wait," Stan said, putting a hand up in hopes to stop her, but she passed right through it.

The electricity that went through his hand seemed to affect her as well, as she paused to rub at her arm where they had connected. She looked directly at where Stan stood. He watched her face, wondering what she could be thinking.

Did you feel me? Can you sense that I'm here?

Something slammed heavily against the door, making them both jump back to attention. The lights switched off, plunging them into darkness. Even the light above the bed was off. Only the screens of the heart monitor emitted a soft glow.

"Why does this keep fucking happening to me?" Liz yelled, reaching her hands out in front of her to feel for the wall.

Stan scanned the room, but there was nothing inside with them. The creatures were still being held off by the pouch in his cast. They were safe in here.

But obviously, those things have figured out that I'm gaining control over my body again. And they aren't happy about it.

Using her hands to inch along until she found the light switch, Liz clicked it up and down. Nothing happened.

"Is there a power outage?" she said as she reached for the door, opening it an inch.

Light flooded in from the hallway.

"Okay, not a power outage. Only this room is off."

"Liz," Stan said, calmly. "You need to go back to the bed. You need to help me finish reconnecting. They're trying to distract you."

He reached his hands out to her, hoping he could influence her emotions to calm her down. If she left now, his progress would stop. He was sure of it. She was the secret to him pulling through. He needed her to help him before the creatures separated them.

Liz opened the door the rest of the way, looking up and down the hall.

"Liz!" he said, urgently. "Please don't leave! You're my only hope."

She flinched in surprise, spinning around to look directly at him.

"Wait, did you hear me?" he asked, surprised by the way she seemed to be looking directly at his face.

"Miss?" a female voice came from the hallway. "Have you checked in?"

Stan turned back to the hall. Liz braced herself in the door frame while keeping the door pushed fully open. Her eyes were wide as she stared into the room, as if contemplating what she should do.

"Miss?" the voice came again, getting closer.

The lights in the room flickered on as if the light switch finally connected. Stan turned to look back at his physical body. His eyes were closed and the connection he had felt briefly was already faint.

"Miss!"

The voice was closer, and it sounded annoyed. Liz turned to face the person who was coming, still propping the door open.

It was a nurse. She had short, straight hair. It was so blonde against her sienna skin that it almost looked white. She was a foot shorter than Liz, but looked tough, even in her light blue scrubs. She looked at Liz as if she were dealing with a small child scared over something insignificant.

"I'm sorry," Liz murmured. "I just came in to see my husband. There was no one at the desk when I walked by, so I planned to let you know I was here after I finished eating."

Liz motioned to the food sitting on the table beside the hospital bed.

"Okay, I suppose that's fine, but we're getting close to the end of visiting hours. I'll need you to clean up before you leave."

"That's okay," Liz replied, obviously rattled by the events of the short time she had spent in the room. "I seem to have lost my appetite anyway. And I should be getting back home."

Quickly walking around the room, Liz gathered her jacket off the back of the chair and slipped her arms into it. Then she leaned down to pick up her purse before throwing her half-eaten meal into the paper bag at the edge of the small table.

Grabbing it, she threw it all into the garbage under the sink before turning to walk past the nurse into the hall.

"Shit, Liz, no!" Stan exclaimed, moving to follow her. "Stay here! I can do this, I know that now, but I need you!"

He made it past the nurse just in time, as she moved to let go of the door. Liz raised a hand in a final goodbye without looking back or saying another word.

She's leaving. The creatures got what they wanted.

He looked back at Liz as she continued down the hall. Then he looked back at his hospital door.

Well, I'm not going to be able to get anywhere in there tonight anyway. I might as well see if I can go home with her to see the house.

He shrugged his shoulders, ignoring the nurse walking past to return to the nurse's station. He ran after Liz down the hallway. Liz was walking fast, making it difficult for him to keep up. She obviously wanted out of the hospital. He wished he could explain to her what was happening. He was sure she would stay and help him if she only knew.

Once they reached the parking garage, he followed her to the SUV and teleported into the passenger seat. He sat quietly as Liz crawled into the vehicle beside him. She put on her seatbelt and turned on the engine, then sat still for a moment as the heaters forcefully blew air into their faces.

"What the hell happened in there?" she muttered. "Am I going crazy now too?"

Stan looked over at her, longing to comfort her. He reached out a hand to touch her shoulder but pulled it back when he remembered what had happened last time. Instead, he sat quietly, unsure of how to comfort her, as she put the vehicle into reverse and started the journey home.

***

As Liz pulled into the driveway, Stan saw lights on in most of the windows. They glowed against the dark, cloudy sky above them. While Liz put the SUV into park and turned off the engine, Stan had already transported himself onto the sidewalk. He couldn't wait to see the boys. He walked to the front of the house, his hand reaching out and touching the door. Closing his eyes, memories flooded through him of the many times he passed through that threshold. All the emotions he had felt in the past rushed through him. Every emotion, from exhaustion after a long day to excitement to surprise his family with a present he had picked up in the city. The memories flooded through him within the seconds it took for Liz to gather her things from the vehicle and walk up behind him.

As she approached the door, Stan backed away slightly, careful not to let them touch. He didn't want to get pulled back to the hospital when he had made it this far. Liz unlocked the front door and swung it open. He ran through the opening behind her before she could close it. Standing to the side near the entryway table, he looked around the small room in awe as more memories flooded him. Familiar voices floated from down the hall. His boys were arguing over something in the living room. He left Liz in the entryway as she took off her jacket and shoes, the voices of his children drawing him in. He walked through the kitchen in a daze, a large smile on his face. As he walked by the counters, he reached out and touched the familiar surfaces, happy to be back home.

At the opening on the other side of the kitchen, Stan peeked into the small living room. Alex and Jack were on the couch, while Carson was spread out on the floor with one leg propped up against the armchair on the side of the room. A girl that Stan couldn't remember was sitting in the chair. Her face was familiar, her blonde hair tied up into a tight bun on her head. She was around Alex's age. Stan could faintly recall seeing her, but he couldn't remember who she was. Then he noticed the woman standing on the other side of the room near the opening of the hallway. It was Sarah, Liz's best friend. The girl was her daughter, Lexi. The memories of all the time they spent in their lives flooded back in.

I wonder how many other people I still don't remember. How long will it take for all those memories to come back? Could some be lost forever?

The doctor and nurse had said something about brain damage, so he wondered how much of it would be permanent. Sarah turned to leave the room down the hall, likely to greet Liz. He watched his three boys as they watched the television. It felt so good to be back home with them, even if they were unaware of his presence. Voices behind him finally pulled him away. He turned back to the kitchen, where Liz was pulling down a wine glass from the cupboard before turning to the fridge.

"So, how was your visit tonight? Anything new with Stan?"

"Well ... actually, a few new things did happen."

Liz pulled a bottle of white wine from the fridge and poured a heavy glass.

"Oh? Good things, I hope."

"Well, some of them were fantastic," Liz sighed. "Stan's hand moved while I was rubbing his arm. I don't know if it was an involuntary twitch or something, but he moved."

"What? That's awesome! Did you ask the nurse what it could mean?"

"No, after everything else that happened, I just wanted to get the hell out of there."

Sarah paused, her face showing her confusion. "What do you mean? What else happened?"

"I don't even know how to explain it, Sarah. The vibe in that room has changed. Fuck, the vibe around me has changed. I'm worried I'm starting to lose my mind."

Liz leaned over the kitchen island, staring down into her wine glass. Worry covered her face as she paused. Stan moved to lean over the kitchen island on the other side of the room, watching her closely.

"Okay," Sarah said, pulling the chair out from under the island counter and sitting down on the edge. "Now I really want to know what's going on."

"It was all so strange. I was sitting and talking to Stan, letting him know about my day. You know, just the normal stuff."

"Right."

"Well, Stan opened his eyes again. It was just like the last time. He just stared up at the ceiling. I waved my hand in front of his face, and there was no recognition. So, nothing really new. I swear I thought his lips twitched, like he was trying to smile. This all happened before his finger twitched."

"It's good he's responding to you, even if it's involuntary, right?"

"Of course! I'm glad he's responding in any way. It's just what happened next."

Liz looked up from her wine glass to Sarah. Stan could see her eyes were partly glazed over as her mind walked through the memories in the hospital room.

"And that was?"

"I felt like something was trying to get me out of that room. First, the mirror started vibrating against the wall, like something had hit it. Then, something scratched the outside of the door."

"Could someone be doing stuff out in the hall to make those sounds?"

"That's what I thought. So, I got up to check, but something banged on the door, hard, before I could get there. Then all the lights in the room went off. It happened so fast."

"Jesus," Sarah said, leaning in closer. "Did the hospital lose power or something?"

"Again, I thought the same thing, but they have backup generators, right? Plus, the monitors hooked up to Stan were still working. When I checked the hall, the lights were on everywhere else. Only Stan's room was dark."

"Okay, yeah, that would have been creepy," Sarah interrupted, forcing Liz to focus on her. "But were the lights on a timer or something? Maybe there was a motion sensor, and you just didn't trip it?"

"That's just it. I flipped the switch on and off multiple times. The lights wouldn't come back on. So, I opened the door to go ask the nurse. That's when, I swear, I heard someone behind me say my name. It scared the shit out of me."

"Seriously? Holy shit. I would have run out of there so fast. Who was it?"

Sarah leaned in so far over the kitchen island that the chair teetered on two legs underneath, threatening to tip over. Liz looked back down at the wine glass in her hands and took a large gulp of it before continuing.

"I don't know. No one was in the room with me when I turned back to look. The light from the hallway lit up the room enough that I could tell the room was empty except for Stan, but he couldn't have said it. And that isn't even the creepiest part of the night! When the nurse showed up, likely from all the noise, the lights in the room suddenly switched back on. No one was near the light switch; they just came on as if on their own."

"Geez, Liz. It sounds like something straight out of a horror movie. What did the nurse say? Did she have control of the lights at her desk maybe?"

"I didn't ask. I didn't even stay to find out if everything that happened had a logical explanation, or if I imagined it all. I don't understand what the hell is going on with me lately."

Liz looked up into Sarah's face, her eyes wide with worry. Stan instinctively moved to stand beside her, wanting to comfort her. Without thinking, he reached over to rub Liz's back. He wanted her to know that he was there for her. That she wasn't alone. The electric jolt through his arm startled him, making him realize his mistake, but it was too late. He saw her jump and look over her shoulder to where he was standing as the tether pulled at his torso. With the blink of his eyes, he was back standing at the foot of the bed in the hospital room, his hand still reaching out as if Liz was still standing beside him.

"Shit!"

He turned to face his body in the bed. It lay there peacefully, as before, and the lights in the room were off. The light above the bed emitted its usual orange glow across the small space. Stan's gaze fell on the mirror across from him.

Although it was faint, he could see the outline of the woman standing in the reflection. Slowly, her eyes opened, revealing two glowing, yellow slits staring back at him.

Chapter 42

- Liz -

An electric shock hit Liz's shoulder. She looked back quickly to see what had caused it, but nothing was there. It felt like a hand had touched her back.

Again?

"Lizzie, are you okay?"

Rubbing her shoulder, she turned her gaze back to Sarah, whose face looked painted with concern.

"Sorry, I just got a shock from something. It's been happening more than usual lately."

"Maybe it's from the weird weather we're having."

"Yeah, maybe. It's been a long day. I think I'll go to bed early tonight."

Sarah got up out of her chair and placed a hand on Liz's shoulder.

"Do you want me to stay here tonight? Lexi and I can share the bed in the spare room downstairs. Maybe you would get a better sleep."

Liz shrugged Sarah's hand off her shoulder, taking a large sip from her wine glass. She smiled.

"Don't be silly. I'm fine. I just haven't been sleeping well. Plus, the stress of handling the boys on my own is still new. It's likely all just catching up with me."

"Okay, but you can call me, you know. Anytime. Even if it's in the middle of the night."

"Honestly, Sarah, I'll be okay. And I have three big boys in the house with me. I appreciate the offer, though."

Sarah gave Liz one more concerned look before turning away to walk into the living room.

"Lexi, it's time to go. Grab your stuff and say goodbye. Boys, be good and listen to your Mom."

Liz smiled again before drinking the last of her wine and placing the empty glass down on the counter. As Sarah walked back through the kitchen towards the dining table, Liz moved to join her. Sarah paused at the last chair at the table, pulling her purse from the seat and shrugging it onto her shoulder.

Sarah turned to Liz one more time. "Lizzie, are you sure you don't want me to stay? I can get that ex-partner of mine to pick Lexi up. We could have a girls' night."

Liz laughed, putting her arm around her friend's back, and giving her a gentle nudge towards the door.

"Sarah, seriously. No offence but get out. No girls' night tonight. Maybe this weekend, but tonight I need to go to bed. Alone."

Lexi came into view, walking down the hallway from the living room, her backpack slung over her shoulder. She looked up from her phone in her hand when she realized Liz and Sarah were watching her.

"Alright kid," Sarah said. "It looks like we aren't welcome here anymore. Let's go."

Lexi rolled her eyes and turned towards the entryway, saying over her shoulder, "G'night, Aunt Liz."

"Night, Lexi. Thanks for coming to watch over the crazy boys for me. Hopefully, they weren't too much trouble for you."

Lexi smiled up at Liz while bending over to slip on her beige winter boots.

"Nah, they're okay. See you later."

Lexi pulled her jacket from the nearby closet and walked out the front door, her jacket dangling from her finger while her eyes returned to her phone.

"Sure," Sarah called after her. "Why put your jacket on? It's only December!" Sarah rolled her eyes and looked at Liz. "I'll never understand preteens. Can you believe we'll have teenagers soon?"

As Sarah pulled on her shoes and jacket, Liz responded, "Ugh, don't remind me. I'm not ready to be the mother of one teenage boy, let alone three."

Liz leaned against the wall by the hallway closet. Fully dressed in her outdoor clothing, Sarah turned back and wrapped her arms around Liz.

"Lizzie, please remember you don't have to be brave for me. I'm always here for you. Reach out if you need me, okay?"

"Thanks. I really appreciate it. I'll call you if I feel like I'm in over my head. I promise."

Sarah pulled back from the embrace and opened the front door to step out. A cold blast of air hit Liz, causing goosebumps to climb up her arms.

"Okay, have a good night, Lizzie. Get some sleep," Sarah called over her shoulder before going out of Liz's view.

Liz closed the door and locked the deadbolt. She turned to look around the empty entryway, rubbing her arms to warm back up. Her mind returned to Stan's hospital room.

It must have been my imagination. What else could explain everything that happened?

Laughter from the boys in the living room snapped her back to the present. She turned and double-checked the deadbolt lock on the front door one more time before moving into the living room to sit down in an empty chair. She allowed her mind to focus on the movie they were finishing, briefly forgetting about the fear the hospital room had caused.

***

After the credits of the movie started to roll on the screen, Liz turned off the television. She motioned for the boys to get up.

"Come on, boys. You have school tomorrow, time to get ready for bed. It's getting late."

The boys slowly rolled out of their positions draped across the couch and floor. Jack was the first towards Liz, wrapping his arms around her waist.

"Goodnight, Mom."

She smiled down at her youngest and squeezed him back.

"Goodnight, Jack. Have a good sleep. I love you."

The other two boys started pushing each other as they passed Liz to walk down the hallway.

"Night, Mom," they each called back at Liz, before pushing each other again.

Liz shook her head before turning back to the coffee table. Empty cups and snack wrappers were strewn about. Stacking the cups, she picked everything up and moved into the kitchen, turning off the lamps as she went. After placing the cups into the sink, she threw the wrappers in the garbage. She pulled her phone out of her pocket to check for messages as she turned to walk towards the hall. She noticed her empty wine glass still sitting on the kitchen island. As she walked over to pick it up, a shadow moved in the corner of her eye. She snapped her head towards the door to the covered porch.

What was that?

She placed her hands on the kitchen counter, putting her phone down in front of her, as she looked over at the glass door. Picking up the wine glass, she placed it in the sink and then moved to look through the glass. The porch was empty, and the furniture looked like it always did. Liz shrugged, turning the deadbolt on the door to lock it before closing its blinds.

Rubbing her forehead, she turned away from the porch. Continuing to turn off lights as she walked, she started down the hallway toward her bedroom. The boys were at the end of the hall, talking as they got ready for bed. She smiled at them as she neared her door. Her phone rang. She reached into her back pocket before realizing she had left it on the counter in the kitchen.

"Of course."

Liz turned back down the dark hall. Dull light from the night sky and neighbourhood lights lit up the kitchen just enough to see where she was going. The phone sat face up on the kitchen island, its blue light glaring in the dark room. Liz walked over and looked down at the screen before picking it up. The caller ID flashed Karen's name.

"Ugh, Stan," she groaned, "what could your Mother possibly want now?"

Hesitating at first, Liz debated letting it go to voicemail. Slumping her shoulders in defeat, she pushed the 'answer' button on the screen and put the phone to her ear.

"Hello?"

"Elizabeth! Finally! I haven't been able to get through to you for a few days. How is Stan?"

"I'm sorry, Karen. It's been a busy week. Stan is coming along. He's starting to respond to more things almost every day."

Another shadow passed in the corner of her eye, making her turn to face the porch again. The blinds on the porch door were wide open, swinging lightly and tapping against the window. Liz just about dropped the phone in surprise.

"What the..."

"What? Liz?" Karen's annoyed voice was shrill through the phone. "Are you listening to me?"

"Sorry, Karen. I'm going to need to call you back."

Liz ended the call without waiting for Karen's snarky response. She gripped her phone in her hand, contemplating the blinds. Their swaying slowed down, no longer tapping on the window. A sense of foreboding made the skin of her arms crawl.

"But I closed those."

Liz watched the door, waiting to see if anything moved outside the window or behind the dining table on the other side of the dark kitchen. Her blood ran cold. Looking down at the phone in her hands, she unlocked the screen and dialled the number 9-1-1. With her finger hovering over the 'call' button, she peeled herself away from the counter and slowly walked to the porch door. The inside of the porch was the same as before. Although it was dark in the room, nothing had changed. The outer door was still closed. She could see the deadbolt was locked through the glass. Turning to the right, she moved to the other side of the kitchen table, but the area was empty. She walked over to the doorway to the basement. The stairs were empty and the door at the bottom was closed.

I'm sure I closed the blinds. How are they open again?

Her heart pumped hard in her chest as she checked to make sure her screen didn't go to sleep. With her thumb still hovering over the 'call' button, she moved to the living room. Her eyes passed around the small space, but the room was empty. She turned on the nearby light switch and the room flooded with warm, yellow light. There was no one there.

"Okay, I'm hallucinating *doing* things now. I need to go to bed."

Liz turned the living room light back off and quickly moved to the hallway. The light was still on, but the end of the hall was now quiet. The boys had each moved into their rooms for the night. Wary of going into her quiet, empty bedroom just yet, Liz passed her door and opened the door to the bedroom that Alex and Carson shared. They were each lying in their own level of the bunkbed that took up over half the room. Alex had his phone held up close to his face as he leaned back on his pillow. Carson was tossing a softball against the bottom of Alex's top bunk.

"Boys, not too much longer, please. It's getting late."

"Okay, Mom," they replied in unison.

Liz closed the bedroom door and turned to the other side of the hall to Jack's room. His square, red Minecraft nightlight cast an eerie red glow on everything. Jack already had his green blanket pulled up under his arms. His eyes were open, and he turned his gaze to Liz as she walked in.

"Hi, Mom."

"Hey Jack," she replied softly as she sat on the edge of his bed near his hip.

"Do you think Dad will be home for Christmas?"

"Maybe. We'll have to wait and see. You get to sleep now, okay?"

"Okay. Goodnight, Mom."

Liz smiled. "Goodnight, Jack."

She leaned over to kiss Jack on the forehead before leaving the room. She closed the door behind her and walked towards her bedroom. She reached into her room and flipped on the light before turning off the hall light. She looked over her shoulder down the hall. The living room at the end was too dark, making it impossible to see any details. Goosebumps crawled up her arms and neck, making her move faster into her bedroom. Her skin tingled with an eerie certainty that someone, or something, was watching her, so she closed the bedroom door behind her, blocking the view of the dark hall. Still holding the door handle, she leaned her other hand on the door and took a deep breath.

"There is no such thing as ghosts. The cord of the blinds probably just got stuck on something when I walked away, and it pulled them back up without me realizing. Or maybe the boys did it without my knowing. There must be a logical explanation."

She felt on edge. Something didn't feel right. She wondered if she should gather up the boys and go stay at Sarah's house after all. She shook her head at the thought of trying to explain why she was there, after spending all that time insisting that she could handle things herself.

"Don't be silly. I have an overactive imagination right now because of my stress levels and lack of sleep. That's all."

Then she remembered the house alarm. She forgot to arm the panel by the front door. Opening the bedroom door again, she peeked around the edge of the wall, looking down the dark hallway. It seemed blacker than the last time she looked.

"You know what? This is why there's an app. I can arm it from right here."

Liz pulled her phone from her back pocket and opened the alarm app. Once active, she closed the bedroom door and moved to her nightstand to turn on the lamp. She grabbed the charge cord for her phone and plugged it in before going into the master bathroom. She needed a hot shower before bed, something to calm her nerves. Dropping her clothes into the hamper against the wall just outside the door, she turned on the water and waited for it to heat up. As soon as she stepped into the steaming water, the tension in her body melted away. She put a shower cap on before stepping fully under the water, letting it run down her neck and shoulders. After a few minutes, Liz started to feel more like herself and less like the nervous wreck she had been before entering. The muscles in her shoulders slowly relaxed; the knots that had formed under her shoulder blades still ached. Her skin turned red from the hot water, so she turned off the shower and reached for a towel. The room was full of steam. She didn't remember closing the bathroom door all the way. She paused briefly in the middle of removing her shower cap, contemplating the closed door. Shrugging, she assumed she did it out of habit and put the shower cap on a nearby hook. She then stepped out of the shower to dry off with the oversized bath towel.

Once she was mostly dry, Liz wrapped the towel around her chest and walked over to the sink. She picked up her face lotion and gently massaged it into her skin. As she did, she looked up at the mirror. Three lines streaked across the steam on the mirror. She tilted her head to the side, trying to think what could have caused the steam to have a pattern like that.

"Weird."

She grabbed a facecloth from the nearby drawer and rubbed the steam off the mirror. Once the marks were gone, she picked up her toothbrush. Once finished, she opened the bathroom door and walked out of the room, pausing as she reached up to turn off the light behind her. She looked back over her shoulder at the bathroom, the white surfaces reflecting the bright overhead bathroom lights. She closed her eyes.

Can stress bring back childhood fears, like being afraid of the dark? Am I regressing?

She turned off the light switch but leaned into the bathroom to grab hold of the door handle to close it behind her. She moved into her closet where she hung the towel up on a wall hook before pulling on her warm, flannel pyjamas. It was cool in the room again. She assumed it was from the December weather. As she did with the bathroom, she turned off the light in the closet and then pulled the sliding door shut behind her. Satisfied with no doors open to show the dark spaces beyond, she walked over to the bedroom door and turned off the overhead light. The soft glow from the lamp lit up the room, but shadows gathered in the corners.

Liz quickly moved across the room and crawled under the heavy duvet on the bed. Lying back against the plush pillows, her head and upper back resting on the headboard, she closed her eyes. The cool heaviness of the blanket after the hot shower felt good. She took deep breaths, counting each one until she reached ten in her head. Feeling calmer about being alone in the room without Stan, she reached for her phone on the charger. She felt guilty for hanging up on Karen in the kitchen. Her hand touched the nightstand where she had put her phone before entering the bathroom, but it wasn't there. Surprised, she turned her head to look. The charge cord sat alone by the lamp. She looked over the side of the bed, thinking it had fallen off, but the floor was empty.

Where did it go?

Her thoughts turned to the boys, wondering if one of them had come in while she was in the shower, but that didn't seem right. The thought of placing her feet on the carpet beside the bed to go ask them sent fear coursing through her. Something in her gut told her not to move. The bed started to vibrate slightly beneath her. She sat up on her knees, her heart beating faster in her chest.

Someone is under the bed.

Someone had taken her phone and was waiting for her to reach under to grab it.

That was the only explanation she could think of. The vibration of the bed grew in intensity. She couldn't decide what to do. Reach under the bed to grab her phone and call 9-1-1 or run from the room screaming for the boys to get out of the house.

But I don't know where to reach ...

The phone started ringing, the shrill ringtone coming from under the bed. The bed went still. Liz leaned over, placing her hands on the edge of the mattress to support herself as she peeked towards the sound. The light from her phone screen reflected just out of view, but not so far underneath that she couldn't grab it easily. Goosebumps formed on her arms. The temperature of the room felt like it was getting lower with every passing second. The sound of heavy breathing came from under the bed, just beyond the phone.

Seriously though. I need to think. I need a plan. I need to get myself and the boys out of this, fast.

She sucked in a breath and held it, trying to remain still and silent as she listened. Then she remembered Alex's phone in his hand on the top bunk. Looking up at the door from where she crouched on her bed, she wondered how hard it would be to get to the other side of the room and into the hall.

If someone tries to stop me, I'll hold the door closed and yell for the boys to run to the neighbours to call the police.

With a plan in mind, she quietly pulled her legs out from under the blankets, trying to move slowly so as not to alert whoever was under the bed. She propped herself up onto her feet, ignoring the phone ringing loudly, and she looked over at the door to the hallway. She jumped from her crouched position, but her feet weren't ready for the landing. Hitting the floor hard, she lost her balance and fell into the wall under the light switch. Something in her wrist cracked and pain shot up her arm. The fear and adrenaline of the potential intruder outweighed the pain, so she jumped up quickly and turned on the bedroom light, spinning to face the bed. The phone had stopped ringing; silence filled the now bright room.

Nothing moved. Everything was still.

As she lowered herself onto her knees to peek under the bed, the door to the bedroom flew open.

"Mom? What are you doing?"

Liz fell to the side, cradling her wrist into her body. Alex was looking down at her, his eyes wide as he took in the sight of her crouched on the floor. He looked from her to the bed and back again.

"You know your phone has been ringing, right?" he said, annoyed.

He walked over to the bed, leaning down to reach under.

"Alex, no!"

She stood up, trying to grab at the back of his shirt before he could be pulled under, but nothing happened. He stood up with her phone in hand, turning to hold it out to her.

"Why was it under the bed?"

She took the phone from his hands and quickly turned on the flashlight app, pain shooting up her arm while trying to use her wrist. Grimacing, she knelt and pointed the light under the bed.

There was no one there. The space was empty except for some dust bunnies that had gathered along the furthest edge.

Liz closed her eyes, leaning her forehead onto the floor. She took a deep breath, her heart slowed, as a new feeling passed over her. Embarrassment. She sat up, leaning back on her feet, and looked up at Alex.

"I'm sorry, honey. I don't know what came over me. I thought someone was hiding under my bed."

Carson came into the room, rubbing his eyes.

"What are you guys doing?"

"Nothing," Alex grumbled as he turned to walk back into the hall past Carson. "Mom thought a monster was under her bed."

"Okay ..." Carson paused, confused. "Mom, are you okay?"

She stood up, careful of her now throbbing wrist.

"Yeah, sorry for waking you, bud. I'm okay. Just fell and thought I saw something, but everything's okay. Go back to bed."

"Okay. Night, Mom."

Carson turned and left the room, leaving the door open behind him. Liz walked over and closed the door most of the way, leaving it partially ajar this time. She turned off the over-head light again. Looking down at her phone, she realized it had been Karen calling moments before.

"I just can't deal with you right now, Karen. You'll have to wait until tomorrow."

She looked at the battery level on her phone. It was over sixty percent.

"Good enough."

Crawling back into bed, she curled her hand around the phone, gripping it tightly. She wasn't going to leave it on the nightstand again tonight. Just in case. She leaned over to turn the lamp off, but the pain in her wrist grew when she reached for the switch with her fingertips.

"What's another night of sleeping with the light on?" she shrugged, dropping her injured wrist back onto her lap. "Your kids already think you're irrational."

Liz crawled under the covers, getting fully into the comfort of the bed while gripping her phone in her uninjured hand. She eventually fell asleep.

Chapter 43

- Stan -

Stan spent the night trying to get back into his body, but it seemed impossible without Liz present. She needed to come back. Pacing along the foot of the bed, he finally threw his hands up in frustration.

"This is ridiculous. I need a break. Maybe I'll go check on Liz ... see when she plans on coming back to the hospital."

His gaze fell on the mirror above the sink where the faded shadow had been lurking when he had first returned to the room. It had disappeared within a few minutes after making it obvious it was pleased Stan failed to stay with Liz. Since then, the reflection mirrored only the hospital room he stood in.

I can't let them win.

There had to be a way to end this nightmare.

Liz is the answer. She can end this.

Standing still at the foot of the bed, he looked down at his unconscious body. His thoughts turned to Liz. He closed his eyes and thought back to the kitchen, where he was standing with her the night before when he accidentally touched her shoulder. Before the tether forced him back. He felt the familiar rush of wind pass over him before everything went still. When he opened his eyes again, he was standing in the middle of their kitchen, but it was empty. Sunlight poured in the open windows, casting shadows across their small backyard and the covered porch. The ticking clock on the wall was the only sound in the house.

They aren't here. It must be a weekday.

Stan didn't know Liz's office well enough to teleport there. The only other place he could go now was back to the hospital.

I might as well look around while I'm here. It beats wandering the hospital halls again.

Turning, he walked to look out into the covered porch. The blinds on the door were open fully, allowing him to peer into the small space.

Liz forgot her blanket out there again, I see. Some things don't change.

He smiled. It was comforting to see that his family was able to continue living their lives, even if it was without him. Although the thought caused his stomach to sink, Liz was a strong, independent woman – one thing he loved about her. She was capable of handling anything.

Stan slowly meandered into the living room. It was darker than the kitchen, the curtains on the windows were mostly closed. He moved to sit on the couch, breathing in the space that his kids frequented the most.

A small thump from somewhere on the other side of the house caught his attention. He paused, the familiar sound should be comforting, yet unease crept into him.

Is someone home?

He recalled his home office down the hall, across from their master bedroom.

Could Liz be working from home? She did say that Jules is gone. Maybe she transitioned to working remotely.

Standing up quickly, the unease now forgotten in the excitement to see Liz, Stan left the living room and went down the hall. As he neared the office door, the silence returned to the house. Peering around the corner of the door frame into the small space, the desk was empty.

She's not here ... but then what made that noise?

A cold pocket of air bubbled out of the bedroom door across the hall, sending shivers down his back. The air seemed heavier, a chill seeping into his body. He turned to face the room.

Did she leave a window open? It's December, Liz!

He poked his head inside, looking around. The drop in temperature was noticeable, even to him. He stepped across the threshold and waited, holding his breath out of habit as he waited for the cool breeze to wash over him again. It never came. Walking over to the window, he peered through the opening of the curtains. The window was closed.

Hmmm ... so it wasn't the window. Maybe the breeze came from a different room.

Stan moved to walk back out to the hall to check his sons' bedrooms, but something caught his eye. Movement in his peripheral vision from beyond the open bathroom door made his gaze shift. The room was dark, the lights off, but he couldn't shake the feeling that he needed a closer look. He moved to stand in the entryway, passing his eyes over the small space.

A shadow figure was standing on the other side of the bathroom, watching him.

"What the fuck ... Who are you and what are you doing here?" Stan demanded of the shadow, but it dissipated as he stepped into the bathroom.

They can't be here ...

He scanned the bedroom behind him, searching for anything out of place. The bed was partially made, and clothing was scattered throughout the room. As he continued to turn in place, an oily sensation crawled down his neck across his shoulders. He was being watched. From where he couldn't tell. He shuddered, sensing something was waiting for him to turn his back.

The sliding door to the closet was partially open, so Stan moved to peer into it. It was too dark to see clearly, but he sensed a presence inside. The air grew dense and colder standing in the doorway of the closet. Stan reached out to push the closet door the rest of the way open, but it wouldn't budge. He waited, his face inches from the opening. After a few seconds passed, he stepped through, searching the dark space beyond. His gaze panned to Liz's clothes hanging on the right and then along the back wall where the dresser stood. As his gaze reached the far left side of the room, where his clothes hung, he noticed two small yellow, glowing slits. Eyes gazed back at him from amongst the clothes. He went still, his eyes opening wide as he waited to see if the creature would attack. Then a second set of eyes appeared above the hanging clothes, as if the creature perched on the shelf above.

No, it can't be!

Stan backed up as panic set in. A third set of eyes caught his attention. They were floating in the top corner of the open bathroom door. The creature hung upside down from the ceiling inside. Stan continued to back up, moving toward the door to the hall. As he passed through the doorway, a fourth set of eyes opened, glowing, from underneath the bed.

"Shit," he whispered. "They're everywhere!"

Once in the hallway, Stan paused to see if the creatures would follow. If they did, maybe he could get them out of the house and away from his family. None of them approached the bedroom door. They weren't moving. He took a deep breath and looked down the hall towards the boys' rooms. He hurried sideways toward them, looking over his shoulder to watch if the creatures came out of the bedroom as he went. When he reached the boys' rooms, he walked into each, scanning the closets and under the beds for more creatures. The rooms were empty of creatures. Stan felt his shoulders relax slightly in relief.

"They're focusing on Liz," he pondered as he emerged from Jack's bedroom. "But why?"

Returning to the doorway to his and Liz's bedroom, he peered in. He could no longer see eyes watching him, but he could still feel their presence.

"Why are you still hiding? I know you're there. Come and get me. It's me you want! What are you waiting for?"

He paused for a response, readying himself to turn and run if they came out of the shadows. He needed to get the creatures away from his family, so he could return to the hospital and finish what he started.

They must have figured out she is the key. She's the one who will be able to help me stop their plan – the one to pull me back into my body.

That's why they were crawling around their family home and focusing their attention on Liz. They wanted to stop her from helping him take back control of his body.

I have to get them away from her. I can't leave her unprotected.

Thinking quickly, he tried to come up with a plan.

"Wait, you think I need her to stop you?" he laughed, hoping he was convincing. "You don't know I've been able to grow stronger while you've been trapped out of my room! You can't stop me now. I don't need her to beat you."

The glowing eyes under the bed opened back up. A low growl came from somewhere in the room.

"Ah, I struck a nerve, have I?"

The creature under the bed stretched out one of its hands. Claws uncurled as it dug into the carpet to pull itself out. The thumping and dragging that usually accompanied its movement was muffled by the carpet, but Stan was sure it was coming for him now.

It's working. They believe me.

Slowly, the creature, its body still half covered by the bed, reached its arms out to drag itself closer.

"I'm not scared of you anymore. I can go back into my body anytime I want now. It's just a matter of time. Your plan has failed."

The creature's glowing yellow eyes became slits, and its mouth opened, revealing its large, dagger-like teeth, green drool dripping out. Instinctively, Stan took a step back.

I need them to follow me. They need to come back to the hospital and leave Liz alone.

The dampened thumping and dragging drew closer. A claw stretched into view of the hall as the creature drew closer to the threshold. The growling from the creature reminded Stan of rabid dogs in the movies. He took another step back, feeling the edge of the doorway into the office bump into his shoulder.

"Yeah, come after me, you assholes! You're weak. I'm too strong now. I'll go back to the hospital and prove it! You've been banished from there, and there's nothing you can do to stop me."

The creature on the floor was only a few feet away, but a second was hanging its head into the opening upside-down from its position on the ceiling. They would reach him in seconds if he didn't act fast.

I need to move. I hope this works and they follow me back to the hospital.

Fear crept into the sides of his mind. He didn't like the idea of leaving Liz unprotected, leaving their home, but he needed to act confident. The creatures needed to think he was serious.

"Kiss my ass," he snarled to the creature closest to him.

He closed his eyes and felt the rush of air pass over him as he allowed the tether around his waist to pull him back. When he opened his eyes, he was in the hospital room. He looked down at his body thinking back to the creatures in his home.

Hopefully, I'm doing this right.

His gaze moved over to look in the reflection. The fog was thicker, nearly forming the woman with the curly, erratic black hair. Stan could still see the reflection of the hospital room through her. The creatures weren't at full strength yet, but they were getting stronger. The power from the *gris-gris* wouldn't hold them off for much longer. The yellow glowing slits and snarling mouth returned to the shadow creature's face.

Good, it's angry. That means I have a chance of keeping Liz safe.

Stan smiled back, assuring himself he'd made the right choice.

Chapter 44

- Liz -

Liz's wrist ached while she typed on her laptop at the office. After jumping across her room in the middle of the night, she'd barely slept. Between her aching wrist and the embarrassment of imagining an intruder was hiding under her bed, she tossed and turned for the remaining hours before her alarm went off. After she managed to get the boys up and off to school, she went straight to the walk-in clinic near her office. She had to wait for three hours in the small waiting room amongst people coughing and sneezing before a doctor finally told her that had a sprained wrist.

It was the middle of the lunch hour when she finally was able to get into the office. Thankfully, her boss was willing to overlook her time away, again. Liz hated that the people at her office still felt pity when they saw her. It made it easier to miss work, but she didn't like the idea of anyone thinking she was anything less. She was still capable of accomplishing everything she needed to at work, with or without Stan at home.

Pain pulsed behind her eye, causing her to pause and rub at her forehead.

I should have had some coffee before I went to the walk-in clinic. Maybe it would have prevented this headache.

The morning had been too rushed, and her wrist hurt too much. Her first cup of coffee didn't happen until nearly one o'clock in the afternoon, adding caffeine withdrawal symptoms to her day.

"Ugh, why can't I concentrate?" she muttered to herself, closing her eyes behind her hands.

Maybe I need to move around a bit.

She stood up and decided to go to the women's washroom. She hoped the movement around the office would help her feel better. Passing by various colleagues who were busy working on the upcoming Friday edition, she smiled and muttered niceties as she went. Internally, she hoped that no one would stop her to make small talk. She especially didn't want to talk about Zane. She didn't think she could stomach even thinking about him at that moment. She pushed the small bathroom door, looking over her shoulder to make sure no one followed her in.

I just need some space to myself.

"Woah, Liz," a voice startled.

Liz turned to realize she had nearly walked into her assistant, Jane, who was washing her hands at the sink, water dripping on the floor in front of Liz's feet.

"Oh, sorry, Jane. I didn't mean to barge in here like that."

"No problem. I know you've got a lot on your plate right now," Jane said with a smile.

Liz could feel the pity radiating from Jane. "Right," she replied, pinching her lips together in a straight line.

Without saying another word, Liz moved around her assistant and walked into the last stall against the wall. It felt good to put a barrier between them. She stood with her hands against the metal stall door, listening for Jane to leave the bathroom. She could imagine her assistant primping herself in the mirror. Finally, footsteps moved away to leave the room. The familiar squeal of the hinges echoed across the small space as Liz imagined Jane walking out.

Liz didn't exhale until the click of the closing door sounded. Then she turned, putting the seat down onto the toilet, and collapsed onto it. Dropping her face in her hands, she took a deep breath.

I just need to get through this afternoon. The day is almost over.

The overhead lights flicked off, plunging Liz into complete darkness.

"Wait, I'm still in here!" she called out to whoever turned the light off.

I didn't hear someone come back in.

She was sure Jane didn't turn off the light; it would have clicked off before the door closed if she had.

Unless Jane didn't leave?

She imagined her assistant standing in front of the door. It didn't make any sense, but it was the only explanation she had.

"Jane? Are you there?"

No response.

Heavy breathing came from somewhere outside her bathroom stall. There was definitely someone in the room with her.

"This isn't funny," she said, anger suddenly rising in her chest. She stood up quickly and opened the bathroom stall, eager to face the jokester.

Stepping into the main area, she found it empty. The only light came from the small nightlight above the sink, its yellow bulb casting an eerie glow on the tile that lined the floor and walls.

"This is ridiculous," Liz said, annoyed. She moved along the other two stalls, checking each one.

They were empty. She was alone.

But then who turned off the light?

A tapping on the mirror drew her gaze. Her reflection was surrounded by a fog, making her look as if she were enveloped in hazy smoke. It spread, covering the reflection of the room behind where Liz stood. Only her face and body remained in focus.

What can be doing that?

Then, in the reflection, a woman stepped out from behind her. Her dark hair was held back by a scarf, and her eyes glowed yellow as she stared at Liz.

Liz spun around, spitting out, "Who the fuck are you?"

The woman wasn't standing in the actual bathroom, only in the reflection.

Did I imagine it?

Slowly, Liz turned back to the mirror. The woman in the reflection smiled, revealing black, sharp teeth that didn't suit her face.

Liz screamed and ran out of the bathroom as quickly as she could. As soon as she entered the common lounge, she yelled, "There's something in the bathroom mirror! We need to get out of here!"

Surprised glances stared back at her. Jane paused in the middle of stirring her coffee cup on the other side of the room. Her boss must have just walked in, as he paused in the entryway. A few other staff sat on a nearby couch, presumably mid-conversation. They now stared at Liz, their mouths hanging open and eyes wide.

"Liz?" Bob said, calmly. "What do you mean, you saw something in the bathroom mirror? Are you okay?"

Liz's gaze fell onto his face. Regret instantly washed over her. Everyone thought she had lost her mind. She would too if she was on the other side of this.

They think I've finally snapped.

Her mind raced to think of what to say next. There had to be something she could say to make this go away. Maybe she could pass it off as a bad joke.

"Um ... uh ... I thought I saw someone," was all that she could manage.

"Here, why don't I go take a look," Bob said, calmly walking past Liz to the woman's bathroom door. He knocked on it first, announcing, "It's Bob! I'm coming in. Be warned!"

Liz watched, partially terrified that the woman in the reflection would hurt Bob, but also partially hoping he would see her. Liz couldn't stand what it would mean if the woman wasn't actually there. Except the lights were on in the bathroom again. Liz could see the bright walls of the bathroom as Bob walked in before the door shut behind him.

Looking around at the other people in the common lounge, they all busied themselves, avoiding making eye contact with her.

They don't believe me. Hell, I don't know that I believe me either. Could I really have imagined it all?

The bathroom door opened behind Liz, making her spin around again to face Bob. His face told her everything: he didn't believe her. The woman in the reflection wasn't there. Liz had imagined it. She felt her body deflate as Bob came to stand in front of her.

"Liz," he whispered, "there's no one in the bathroom." He paused, looking down at her wrist. She hadn't even realized she had been rubbing at the tensor bandage wrapped snugly around her sprain. "I'm worried that maybe you came back to work too soon. Perhaps you need a little more time."

"No," she started, "I'm fine. Really ... I don't need more time. I just didn't get enough sleep last night. I must have an over-active imagination from exhaustion, that's all. Honest."

Bob eyed her, placing a hand on her shoulder. Liz could tell he wasn't convinced.

"Well, I still think maybe you should go home and rest. Take the rest of this week—"

"No, I don't need to," she interrupted. "I'm fine."

"Now, Liz," Bob continued, applying enough pressure on her shoulder to turn her to walk alongside him as they started back in the direction of her office. "I insist. Don't worry about us. Go home, and get some rest. Use the rest of this week to catch up on sleep if you think that's the issue. I'll call you on Monday … don't come in. We'll talk about maybe adjusting your schedule a little more until you are back on your feet. Zane will be starting soon, so he can pick up any slack."

A cold wave of panic washed over. The thought of losing her job to Zane, her only source of income keeping the family afloat, made her chest squeeze. She forced in an unsteady breath.

"Really, I'm fine," Liz tried again, but she could tell Bob's mind was made up. She slumped her shoulders, giving into his light push, and continued the walk to her office. She kept her eyes down, avoiding the gazes of her colleagues.

What is happening to me?

After packing up her things, Liz got out as quickly as she could. She avoided talking or looking at anyone. She jumped into her SUV, ready to get away as fast as possible. Once she was a few blocks away, she realized she had instinctually started driving to the hospital.

Stan. I need to go see Stan.

She pulled onto the ramp that would take her across the Lion's Gate Bridge toward downtown Vancouver. Her mind drifted to the bathroom in the office.

Did I really imagine her? I know I didn't get any sleep last night, but surely it wouldn't cause hallucinations so soon. And what about the intruder under the bed?

Her preoccupied thoughts made her unaware of the SUV's engine revving up at first. As the vehicle got onto the bridge that would take her across to the water to Stanley Park, it slowly picked up speed. It wasn't until she saw the bumper of the car ahead of her quickly getting closer that Liz realized she was going faster than the speed limit. She looked down and saw the speedometer at seventy-five kilometres per hour, fifteen over the speed limit.

"Woah, obviously I need to pay more attention."

Letting her foot off the gas pedal, she pushed lightly on the brake.

Nothing happened.

She looked down at the speedometer. It slowly crawled towards eighty.

My foot's not on the gas. Why am I speeding up?

She pushed harder on the brake pedal. The speedometer showed no signs of slowing.

"What the fuck?" she yelled at her SUV, swerving into the middle lane to miss the car's bumper in front of her. An '*X*' on the traffic light above her indicated that the middle lane was open for oncoming traffic, not for her.

"Shit," she exhaled, pulling back into the right-hand lane.

The speedometer read ninety. She was thirty over the speed limit now and her SUV didn't show any sign of slowing down. Panic set in, her hands slick with sweat and her eyes grew large. She was approaching another vehicle, a big truck this time, and fast. This time, traffic occupied the middle lane from the other direction. It wasn't an option anymore.

"Fuck, stop!" she screamed at her vehicle as she tried to slam her foot on the brake repeatedly, but the truck's bumper came up quickly.

Instinctually, she pulled back into the middle lane. This time, an oncoming car rushed towards her, so she swerved back to the right, nearly missing the front bumper of the truck she now passed. The driver of the truck blared its horn.

"Sorry!" she yelled back, although she knew no one could hear her.

What do I do, what do I do?

The speedometer was now one hundred and the bridge was starting to slope slightly down to the other side. If her brakes wouldn't work, she would pick up speed even faster.

Suddenly, an idea struck.

She slammed the SUV's gear into neutral. The clunk of the transmission was angry, but it worked. The engine was no longer engaged, the revving stopped. Now it was just the hum of the vehicle coasting on the concrete.

Okay, now what?

She was still driving too fast down a slope and there were more vehicles ahead of her that she was quickly approaching.

I'm glad it's not rush hour at least.

Although the thought wasn't helpful at the moment, Liz still felt her shoulders relax slightly. She was gaining control of the situation.

At least I'm not still speeding up.

Without thinking, she pushed down on the brake pedal again. Her SUV jerked as the brake pads finally engaged under her feet.

Yes!

Grateful, she pushed on the brakes further, slowing the vehicle down to sixty quickly. As the bridge touched the ground near Stanley Park, she pushed the brakes further. The SUV continued to slow. She saw an emergency stop zone on the right, so she quickly pulled in, slamming her brakes harder until she came to a stop. Putting the gear shift into park, she quickly turned the vehicle off and exhaled. She placed her shaking hands on the steering wheel.

A loud horn blared beside her, making her scream in surprise, as the truck she had nearly hit passed by.

"It's not my fault! I couldn't stop!" she yelled at him, but he was too far away already. She was alone on the side of the road. Tears swelled in her eyes as a sob escaped her throat.

Now what do I do?

Chapter 45

- Stan -

Pacing in the hospital room, a constant bombardment of scratching and banging noises on the walls and door surrounded Stan. The creatures were searching for a way into the room. He had no doubt they eventually would. The pouch Serafine left behind continued to hold them back, but he wasn't sure how much longer it would work. Time wasn't on his side; he needed to hurry. Soon the creatures would find a way past the invisible barrier and then it would be too late.

At least they're here. Hopefully, they're staying away from Liz now.

As each attempt to reconnect with his body failed, Stan grew more frustrated. The relentless ticking of the clock amplified his irritation. It was already the middle of the afternoon. Feeling defeated, he moved to sit in the chair in the corner. He closed his eyes and leaned back, trying to relax and think over everything he had tried so far. Each tick echoed above him, pressing down on him.

If only Liz was here. She could make it happen.

Physically touching his body wasn't helping. He even tried transporting himself into his body, as he had around the hospital and to Liz, but that only ended with him standing in the middle of the bed on top of it. The constant electrical jolts to his ethereal form drained his energy. He wasn't sure he would be able to transport now, even if he tried a small distance like the hallway.

Perhaps rest is a good idea. It just can't be for long, he thought as he let his body melt into the hard chair beneath him.

Eventually, the click of the door alerted him to a nurse arriving.

"Good morning, Mr. Stevens. You won't believe the nice day we're having. The clouds have finally parted, and we're getting to see the sun this morning."

Stan kept his eyes closed, ignoring her chatter to his physical body as she worked. A sharp pain pricked his arm. He looked at the nurse, rubbing the spot with his hand, unsure what had caused the sensation. She was drawing blood from his body with a needle. Her fingers brushed his skin as she wiped the spot and placed a bandage over it. He could feel it as if she were doing it directly to his ethereal form. Stan leaned forward, excited. The strength of these sensations had to be a positive sign. He was getting closer to reconnecting. He waited for the nurse to finish her checks and leave the room. As soon as the door clicked behind her, he stood and focused on his body. He wasn't sure what had brought on the progress, but he had to keep trying.

Growling came from above. He looked up, expecting to see a creature hanging over him, but the ceiling was empty. Whatever it was, it sounded big, angry. They knew he was getting closer. Stan walked over to stand beside the bed. There had to be something he hadn't tried yet. Silence filled the room, as if all sound had been sucked out of it. He could no longer hear even the ticking of the clock. A sense of foreboding filled him, the air thick and oppressive. Stan looked around in surprise.

Why can't I hear anything?

His gaze moved over to the mirror above the sink on the other side of the room. Although the reflection showed the hospital, he could see the familiar fog building along the bottom of the frame. The woman in the mirror was attempting to show herself and push past Serafine's protection.

How are you sucking the noise from the room? he wondered as he stared at the growing mass.

The hospital room door handle turned.

Stan jumped back, pressing his back against the wall.

It can't be. They can't come in.

"Stay out!" he yelled at the door. "You aren't welcome here!"

Slowly, the door creaked open, ignoring his demand.

Wait, I can hear again.

Relief washed over him as Liz walked into the room. She carried a large coffee cup with a small paper bag in her hand. Her hair was messily balled up into a bun on her head, and she looked like she hadn't had much sleep – dark circles apparent under her eyes. He didn't care how she looked. She was here.

"Oh, thank God. Liz, you're okay," he sighed, moving to stand at the end of the bed as she walked into the room. "If you're here, then everything must have gone okay last night at home."

"Good morning, Stan. You won't believe the day I'm having. Fuck, the week. I needed to come see you. Although, I swear, something tried to prevent me from getting here."

"What?" Stan paused as a chill passed down his spine. "They're still after you?"

Not hearing him, Liz pulled the tray table closer to the bed and set her coffee and paper bag down. He saw her wrist wrapped in a bandage as she reached over.

"What happened? What did they do to you?"

Walking past him, she moved to the chairs against the wall. She pulled her jacket off and dropped both it and her purse on his chair in the corner. She then grabbed the second chair and dragged it across the linoleum floor to sit by the bed. She flopped down into it, causing the metal legs to scrape against the linoleum. Stan flinched at the screech it made.

"Sorry, Stan, I didn't mean to startle you."

Stan looked at her in surprise, "Wait, how did you know I flinched?"

Liz jumped up.

"Hold on, you've never flinched like that. Stan? Can you hear me?"

She leaned over his body to study his face, placing both her hands around his right one. Stan moved closer to the bed to hover over his body, like her, on the opposite side. He was unsure of what she had seen. Looking from her face to his own and back, he watched as Liz leaned closer to his body's right ear.

"Stan, please. If you can hear me, please give me a sign. You have no idea how much I need some good news right now."

He could feel her breath on his ear.

She's here. I can do this now. It will work.

Stan looked down at the right arm of his ethereal body. He could feel her weight on his hand. He put all his concentration into trying to move it, unsure if what he was feeling was real or if his imagination playing tricks on him.

"Stan, did you just grip my hand?"

He looked back up at Liz. She was looking down at his right hand in disbelief. Her hands were still wrapped around his.

"Liz, it worked! Keep going, we can do this!"

Stan's gaze caught a glimpse of the mirror behind Liz. The fog was now covering the entire reflection. Two yellow slits were in the middle of it. The creature was angry, but it couldn't fully form.

"We don't have much time."

Stan closed his eyes, concentrating on the feeling of her fingers grasping his hand and ignored the woman forming in the mirror. A low growling started from above. He tried to block it out, keeping his concentration on the feeling of her grip.

"Stan? Maybe I should get a nurse."

He opened his eyes in a panic. She was standing up straight, looking over her shoulder at the door. Her two hands gripped his, but he could see the indecision written on her face.

"No!" he yelled.

A moan escaped from his body at the same time. Liz whipped back to face Stan's physical body on the bed. He watched as she leaned back over him, her breath shallow and eyes wide.

"Stan? Are you trying to talk?"

A scraping noise overhead drowned her out; the growling turned into a snarl. Stan looked up. In the corner of the ceiling behind him, one very long, black claw, at least one foot in length, had reached out of a small hole in the corner of the ceiling. Something was breaking through. He was running out of time.

The mirror rattled, forcing his gaze past Liz. The woman in the mirror was nearly materialized, her hands with long, black fingers pushed up against the glass. Stan could see her teeth solidifying as she snarled at him. Liz must have heard it as well, as her eyes widened while she turned to look at the mirror behind her.

"No, Liz, keep your focus on me!" Stan yelled, squeezing his eyes shut again to focus on her grip.

His physical body moaned again, making her turn back to him. She leaned over to lie across his chest, burrowing her face in his neck.

"Oh, Stan. Please tell me I'm not going crazy. Things keep happening around me, and I don't know what they mean."

The weight of her on his chest flooded him with warmth. His heart felt like it was growing with the love that he felt for her, and the love he could feel coming from her physical body connecting with his. His thoughts flooded with memories of curling up next to her in bed, the feeling of dancing with her in the kitchen. He focused on her hands wrapped around his, on the presence of her body's weight on him, and the loving energy she radiated.

The snarling above grew louder above him, vibrating in his skull. A loud cracking sound sent chills down his spine, but he closed his eyes tighter, refusing to lose his focus.

A breeze passed over his face. Stan's thoughts instantly went to the creature's breath on his skin.

The creatures are too close. They're going to get me. I can't let them take Liz, too.

He tried to yell, tried to duck down, but all that came out was a moan. The moan made his throat vibrate.

"Stan?"

Liz's voice was loud against his ear. It was excruciating, his head throbbing. A migraine spread across his forehead. He imagined the creature's grip on his skull as it tried to grab hold of him. He tried to open his eyes to look back up at the ceiling.

Did the creature get in? Are we too late?

His eyes wouldn't open. They felt sealed shut.

Panic rose in his chest as he squeezed his eyes as hard as he could, willing them to open. He tried to raise his hands above his head, but he couldn't control them either. Everything was dark, and he felt paralyzed. His muscles were no longer under his control. He took a deep breath and tried to yell for Liz, but even his mouth felt sealed shut. It too had betrayed him, remaining immobile to his commands.

Another moan escaped from his throat.

"Stan! Stan! I'll go get a nurse. Just hold on!"

He tried to grab at Liz to stop her, but he couldn't move. He couldn't see.

What's happening to me? What have they done?

The low growling was fainter, replaced by a loud whooshing sound in his ears. It was his heart. It was pounding, blood rushing through him. His panic grew. He needed to get out of this room. They needed to get away from the creatures before they could no longer escape.

A commotion came from somewhere in the room. Loud thumping moved quickly towards him. He tried to raise his arms to protect himself, but they were too heavy.

"Mr. Stevens!" a female voice yelled by his head. "Mr. Stevens! I need you to calm down."

"What's happening? Is something wrong? Please help him!" Liz's voice begged.

Stan tried to reach out to her, hoping she was okay, but his arms were like lead. Fingers brushed his face. His moaning became panicked as he tried to thrash his body away from them. A weight pushed down on his chest; the fingers grasped more forcefully at his eyes.

"Mr. Stevens, please. You're safe. You're in the hospital. I'm a nurse. You need to calm down!"

"What's going on?" a male voice boomed.

"Dr. Danton!" Liz cried out. "Thank God you're here! Please, help my husband."

The weight on Stan's chest doubled. A stronger hand gripped his face, forcing him to be still. Then a finger was on his eye. Stan recoiled in panic.

No, you can't take my eyes.

The finger was too strong, and it pried his eyelid open. The bright light pierced his vision, blinding him slightly. He pulled back, trying to lift his arms to protect himself, but the weight on his chest was too heavy. The bright light moved back and forth in front of his face.

Stan realized that his other eye was finally listening to him. It was open and under his control again. With both eyes open, he saw he was looking up at the white ceiling of the hospital room. The lights were blinding, but he could make out fuzzy shadows leaning over him. He could hear Liz crying somewhere in the background, but he couldn't make out her shape. He tried to move his gaze around the room, but the lights were too bright. The blurry shadows in front of him were not the black, tar-covered creatures. Different shades of colour were blotched within their frames.

As his eyes slowly adjusted, he realized he was lying on his back. Opening his eyes as wide as he could, he tried to talk, but his mouth was numb and clumsy. Instead, another moan escaped his throat.

"Mr. Stevens ... Stanley," the male voice said. "Welcome back. My name is Dr. Danton, but you can call me Sam. I was hoping you'd join us one day. Glad to see you could make it."

Stan stopped fighting as it dawned on him. He was back in his body. He had no idea how he did it, but he wasn't trapped or tied down. The heaviness was his muscles being stiff and weak from weeks of not moving.

He was awake. His body was his.

We did it. We beat them.

He let his body relax as relief washed over him. Liz's soft voice came from behind the nurse to his right. "He's awake? Are you saying he's awake?"

Something gripped his left leg. Two fuzzy people he assumed were the nurse and doctor slowly came into a bright focus, like an over-exposed photograph. He watched the doctor and nurse as they passed in and out of view. He could feel them moving his body around, as well as something cold being placed on various parts of his chest.

"Well Stan," Sam said. "It looks like you're coming along. Your heart rate is a little higher than I like, but I imagine waking up in a hospital room can be a bit of a shock. It may take you some time to regain motor function, so you need to stay patient with yourself. Your brain has undergone major trauma. We won't know for sure if you'll regain all function back, but hopefully over time, with lots of physical therapy, you'll be able to return to a somewhat normal life."

"Can I please see my husband now?" Liz's voice was soft and pleading. Stan longed to reach out to her. He felt tears falling down his cheeks. He hadn't realized he was crying.

"Yes, of course," the nurse replied. "Dr. Danton, can you please call Dr. Bractor to come now that we have done the initial assessment? I'm sure she'll want to take over now."

"Yeah, that's likely best. I need to get back to the ER. I'll leave him to you, Nicole. Welcome back to the real world, Mr. Stevens."

Seconds later, Liz's face came into view. Stan couldn't raise his hand but strained to turn his head toward her.

"Oh, Stan. You have no idea how happy I am to see you awake. *Finally.* Don't strain yourself. I can move closer to you, don't worry."

"Here," the nurse said from somewhere out of view. "I can raise the bed a little."

Stan felt his bed vibrating as his head slowly rose. He moved his eyes about the room, searching for the creatures, but there was nothing. The growling was gone. The only sounds were the moving bed and Liz happily sobbing beside him. He shifted his eyes back to her as his bed stopped, happy to finally see her face through his physical eyes again. She wiped at the tears on her cheeks as she thanked the nurse before turning back to Stan. She threw herself on him, wrapping her arms around his neck. Stan was elated to feel her embrace. He closed his eyes and inhaled her scent, happy that he finally made it back.

The creatures didn't win. He did it.

Chapter 46

The next two and a half weeks were draining for Stan. Numerous tests and hours of physical therapy filled his days at the hospital. He learned about Darrin and the accident. At first, he was angry at the man who had done this to him, but as Christmas approached, he began to feel sorry for him. Darrin would have to live with the decision that he made that night in early November for the rest of his life. Stan had a long process of healing ahead of him, but at least he was alive. He was back and he was able to spend time with his family again. That was all that mattered.

The creatures never came back. The exhaustion and stress that had radiated from Liz that day he woke in the hospital slowly disappeared completely. After a few days off work, she was back to her normal, cheerful self. She told him about her inability to sleep and outbursts at work that plagued her while he was in the coma, but they, too, had disappeared completely. It seemed they both improved, physically and mentally, after they were finally able to reconnect on his hospital bed. She was even looking forward to Zane, her new co-editor, starting in the new year.

Through Liz, Stan found out that Serafine was missing. Liz had helped create an article in the newspaper about her disappearance. Serafine's two adult children were asking for any information about her whereabouts, but Stan didn't think his dreams during a coma would be helpful, or even welcomed. Still, he hoped she was okay, wherever she was.

When they removed his cast, the pouch was gone. He didn't remember anyone removing it before that, but it made him wonder if it had all been a hallucination. An elaborate dream created by his brain damage and the medicine they injected him with while he was in a coma.

Surely it wasn't real. It didn't really happen.

Liz never brought up seeing the creatures, so Stan left it alone. He was determined to let it all go and concentrate on returning to his former self so that he could return to his family at home. Liz had gone through a lot, he could tell. She told him about her SUV acting up, so she sent it to the mechanics. Apparently, they couldn't find anything wrong with it, but that didn't mean the creatures had been real. Something logical had to explain what had happened to her that day on the bridge.

Although the doctors were reluctant at first, Liz convinced them to allow Stan to take a break from the hospital to spend Christmas Eve at home with his family. It required them to hire a nurse to help Liz take care of Stan for the forty-eight hours he would be spending at home. Stan was still in a wheelchair and his voice hadn't returned, so she would need the help.

Liz was able to find a nurse named Natalie, who was single and not travelling to see family for the holidays. Natalie stayed with them in their spare bedroom, but Liz and Stan didn't mind the extra company. All they wanted was to spend Christmas together as a family.

On Christmas morning, Stan and Liz woke early. She rolled over to smile at him as he opened his eyes. The house was quiet, the boys still asleep. He grimaced as he raised his arm above his head, letting Liz cuddle into him to rest her head on his chest.

"Now, don't hurt yourself," she whispered.

He gripped his arm around her back, rubbing her waist lightly. It felt great having her in his arms again, to be back in his own bed, even if it was only for two nights. He tried to make a happy moan, smiling down at her. She kissed his chest, and then his neck, before reaching his face and kissing him softly on the lips. They gazed into each other's eyes. He could tell Liz was hoping for something more. Then the stomping of feet down the hall interrupted the thought. She quickly shifted back down to his side before the door crashed open. Carson and Jack ran into the room, jumping onto the bed.

"It's Christmas!" Jack exclaimed. "Can we go see what Santa brought us yet?"

"Whoa, slow down. Be careful. Don't hurt your Dad."

Liz placed her arms above him, trying to shield his body from the flailing arms and legs of the excited boys.

"Is Alex even up yet?" she asked. "You know the rule. No opening presents until everyone is awake and ready."

"Mr. and Mrs. Stevens?" Natalie called from down the hall. "Are you up? I can come to help Stan if you like."

"Just one second, Natalie!" Liz replied.

She shifted carefully out from under Stan's arm, shooing the boys off the bed.

"Okay, boys, go get Alex up," she said as she grabbed her housecoat from the back of the door. "Come on in, Natalie!"

The boys tore out of the room excitedly. Stan laughed as he heard them crash into the room where Alex still slept. Alex's complaints drifted down the hall as Natalie appeared in the doorway, already dressed in her scrubs. They were red with little candy canes scattered across the fabric. Stan sat up in the bed, dragging his legs towards the side.

"Okay, Stan," Natalie said. "Let's try flexing your toes before you get up."

She moved his wheelchair near him as Stan did as she asked. Liz watched them from the doorway. As Natalie helped Stan into his wheelchair, Liz backed out of the room.

"I'm going to go make sure those boys aren't opening anything yet. And that coffee is on. Holler if you need me, Natalie."

Liz left the room and closed the door behind her, leaving Stan and Natalie alone. Stan didn't enjoy being helped to use the bathroom and get dressed, but he was grateful for Natalie. Without her, he wouldn't be spending Christmas at home. It was a lot better than being in the hospital. They worked through his morning routine quickly and silently, both aware that the children would be waiting impatiently for them.

After Stan was dressed, Natalie opened the door and wheeled him down the hall to the kitchen.

"How much longer, Mom? How about the stockings? Can we just open those?" Carson whined.

Natalie wheeled Stan into the kitchen, announcing, "Here he is! Ready to open some presents!"

The boys jumped up from where they sat at the kitchen island and ran into the living room without a word. Liz smiled at Stan from near the coffee pot. She picked up a travel mug from the kitchen island and moved to stand in front of him.

"Here, babe. I put your coffee in a travel mug. Hopefully, it will work better than a cup for now."

He reached out and gripped the handle of the mug. The weight of it surprised him. The mug dipped down before he could adjust, causing Liz to reach back out for it in surprise.

"See, I knew this would be better than a regular mug," she laughed.

Once Stan was able to get a good grip on the handle, Liz let go. He placed it between his thighs. Liz then took over wheeling him into the living room as Natalie poured herself a cup of coffee. The boys were each sitting around the floor near the Christmas tree, their full stockings in their laps.

"Okay boys, you can go ahead."

Stan laughed as each of the boys turned over their stockings, dumping the contents all over the ground. Liz locked Stan's wheels on his chair and sat on the edge of the couch nearest him. Stan smiled over at her as they watched their children open their presents, excited chatter filling the air. His mind briefly returned to the creatures he had dreamed about while he was in the coma. The fear and urgency that had swallowed him while his body was unable to wake.

How could my mind have dreamed up such a nightmare? Was it just my subconscious pushing me to come back to this?

Absent-mindedly, Stan reached over and gripped Liz's hand that was resting on his knee.

"Merry Christmas, my love," she said, pulling him out of his thoughts. "I'm so glad you could be here this morning."

He gripped her hand again, letting her know he agreed. Then he remembered the present he had for her in the bedroom. It wasn't easy, but with his friend Eric's help, he was able to get it paid for and dropped off at his hospital room a few days before. Then Natalie helped him get it into the house and hidden in a drawer in the closet without Liz noticing. With the boys busy opening their presents, he waved at Liz to take him back down the hallway.

"Did you forget something?" she asked, putting her coffee down on the table in front of them. "We'll be right back, boys."

Liz stood, unlocking Stan's wheels before turning to take him back through the kitchen. Natalie looked up from where she sat at the kitchen table, reading a book with a coffee in her hand.

"I've got him, Natalie. Sit and enjoy your coffee while it's hot."

Liz wheeled him down the hall, following his directions as he pointed to where he wanted to go. As they entered the bedroom, he pointed to the closet.

"What could you possibly need from in there?"

He motioned for her to keep going. When she got close enough to the dresser against the back wall near the mirror, he slid open the drawer where he had seen Natalie hide the gift. Reaching in, he dug around the clothing until his fingers found the small, wrapped box. He pulled it out and handed it to Liz, smiling.

"Stanley, how the heck did you manage to get me a present with everything going on?"

She turned her back to the mirror and began tearing open the paper giddily. Stan watched her, laughing softly.

Movement in the mirror made his gaze shift to regard his reflection. The woman with wild black hair stood in the closet doorway, watching them. Her glowing eyes shifted from Liz to look directly into his. Stan's heart dropped as fear gripped his chest.

Slowly, she started to smile, causing his own grin to fall from his face.

Liz was still trying to get into the small box, unaware of Stan's change in demeanour. Stan looked back at his reflection in the mirror. The face, his face, was still smiling in the reflection. His eyes opened wide as he watched the reflected smile slowly grow, stretching the skin of his cheeks into a ghastly grin, as the woman behind his reflection began to laugh.

--- *THE END* ---

Acknowledgements

First and foremost, I am grateful to my three boys. Although writing and publishing books has been a dream of mine for as long as I can remember, it took becoming a mom for the drive and determination to make it a reality to kick in. Now I can honestly say that dreams really do come true if you're willing to put in the effort.

Of course, getting this book published was not something I could accomplish on my own. I'm very blessed to have found partners in my editor, Robyn Dansereau, and my publisher, Annabel Townsend, at Pete's Press. This book wouldn't have happened without you both, and I am so grateful for your help. I am also very grateful to Jayla Jacobs for doing a sensitivity read through Serafine's chapters. Jayla's insight helped Serafine's character shine that much brighter.

I am amazed at the support that the Saskatchewan Writers' Guild provides their community. Without them, I would never have met the lovely ladies of the Queen's Crew: Yolanda, Marilyn, Beth, Paula, Shauna, and Heather. Our writing "support group" meetings and writing retreats, although irregular, helped me keep going through the obstacles of writing, editing, and finding a publisher.

Through the Saskatchewan Writers' Guild, I also had a fantastic manuscript evaluator, whom I don't know their name. I am so grateful for their kind words and suggestions on the manuscript. They helped pull everything together to create this final novel that you're holding in your hands.

The Horror Writers' Association is another fantastic organization that I don't think I would have been able to complete this novel without. Through their mentorship program, I was able to meet Robert and the crew of Weird Writers. They became my very first writing critique group, teaching me not only to improve my writing but how to critique! I'm grateful for their support and lessons in the writing craft.

Thanks to my parents, Brad and Lianne, who have been supporting me in all the crazy decisions I have made since I was born, not just the latest of publishing a book. Thanks for helping with the kids when I needed quiet to write, for endless pages of proofreading, and for cheerleading me on when it felt like it wasn't going to happen.

There are so many others to thank, that I'm sure I'll forget some. To my big bro, J.R., for being a beta reader of my early drafts (sorry...). To my sister-in-law, Colleen, mother-in-law, Gayle, and father-in-law, Wally – thank you for your words of encouragement and support. To all my family – nieces, nephew, aunts, uncles, cousins, and grandparents – and many friends: thank you for the likes, comments, and motivating words along this journey. You've all helped keep me going.

Of course, I had to save the biggest thanks for last. To my husband, Justin: thank you for being my rock when the dreams nearly swept me away. I know I can accomplish anything with you in my corner.

About The Author

K.D. Kulpa grew up in a haunted house in Nipawin, Saskatchewan, Canada, which sparked her interest in the horror genre and all things eerie and mysterious. She lives in Saskatchewan, with her husband, three boys, and a beagle. When not writing, she loves reading, painting, travelling, and touring haunted buildings. Her fascination with horror, mysteries, and the unknown has led her to also host ParaGhoul Paranormal, a Canadian paranormal radio show and podcast. Coma is her debut novel, although she also regularly releases short stories to her readers via her monthly newsletter.

Connect with K.D. Kulpa online:

kdkulpa.com

@kdkulpa on Instagram, Facebook, Youtube and Tiktok